# MOONLIGHT RISING

## The Lindisfarne Series
## Book Two

# BY THE SAME AUTHOR

# MOONLIGHT RISING

## THE LINDISFARNE SERIES
## BOOK TWO

# JOHANNA CRAVEN

ISBN: 978-0-6451069-6-1

HOLY ISLAND OF LINDISFARNE
ENGLAND

OCTOBER 1715

# CHAPTER ONE

It's a dream she has often, both asleep and awake. A dream of taking flight and finding a life beyond this. In sleep, it's a fractured, unfollowable dream, with indistinct colours like paint swirled on a canvas. When she is awake, it's a thing with edges; a tangible but distant hope of vanishing over the water like her sister has.

Harriet throws her pencil onto the blank page of her notebook and reaches for the whisky beside her, dark and oily in the bottom of the glass. Vivid and violent though these dreams of escape are, they are bringing her little in the way of inspiration. In the hours she has been tucked down here in her workroom, she has managed just a few sorry sketches— of the candleholder and the scattered pencils, and once, in desperation, her old house in London—each scribbled out with aggression, the page turned over quickly to hide her failures.

She empties the whisky glass, squinting in the muted light of late evening. The liquor makes her frustration soft around the edges—heightened by the thrill of having stolen it from her husband's liquor cabinet—but the taste is too familiar now for it to really make an impact. Perhaps that's the problem with this workroom too, with its worn armchair and bowed mantel and the table she has crammed half her notebook beneath to keep from wobbling: it has all become too familiar. Too uncomfortably comfortable. This room, this house, this island; it has all become so predictable she could scream.

Harriet reaches down for the whisky bottle she has hidden behind the table leg. She refills her glass to the top and carries it to the window. The sky is a rich cobalt blue, and in the last threads of daylight she can she see the inky outlines of a ship in the water beyond the house. Faint light blooms from the firebasket on the island of Longstone, where her sister Eva has made her escape. Building her unconstrained life.

Harriet closes her eyes. It's an ache inside her, that unreachable dream.

There is a knock at the door of her workroom. She hurriedly dumps her glass on the floor beside the whisky bottle.

Her husband Edwin does not wait to be invited inside. He steps through the door, eyes scanning the notebook and pencils strewn across the table. "Ah," he says, "you're working?"

Harriet presses her lips into a thin smile. She is fairly certain the blank pages of the notebook make it screamingly obvious she is not working, but so be it. "I am," she says tunefully. "Yes."

The thud of the door knocker echoes through the house. She hears footsteps, muffled voices in the entrance hall. Watches Edwin try to disguise his annoyance that she is downstairs to hear the knocking, rather than being tucked away in her bedchamber like an obedient wife.

"Please come in, gentlemen." Harriet hears her brother Nathan in the hallway, muttering greetings in his polite and stilted way. Welcoming men that are most unwelcome.

She knows who is at the door. She knows why they are here. And she takes some twisted pleasure in the fact that her husband and brother believe her ignorant to the whole damn thing.

No one had bothered to tell Harriet that Highfield House is being used by government spies in the fight against the Jacobites. Messengers come here regularly, posing as workmen in the manor's restoration. Tonight, she guesses, they are here for more than just an exchange of messages. Tonight, perhaps, the spies are meeting.

Had Nathan and Edwin assumed she would not notice that these so-called workmen appear and disappear without so much as picking up a hammer? Or did they just assume she would not care? She supposes that's a fair enough assumption—she has never had the slightest interest in politics. But disinterest is hard to maintain with spies creeping about their hallways.

Edwin spares a quick glimpse over his shoulder in the direction of the front door. "I assume you will be down here for another few hours?" he asks stiffly. He is uncomfortable at having the spies in the house, Harriet can tell. Possibly even more uncomfortable at the thought of his wife knowing anything about it.

She keeps her face deliberately empty. "I will, yes. I'm right in the middle of what I hope will be a very fine piece." Edwin glances back at the blank notebook, but her sarcasm remains unregistered. Or at least unacknowledged.

"All right." Another surreptitious glance in the direction of the hallway. "Good. Stay in here for a while, do you understand?"

She nods. Edwin comes towards her; leans in, in a rigid, practised motion. Harriet turns her head, offering him her cheek, but she knows it is not enough for him to miss the sear of whisky on her breath. His eyes narrow and he looks past her, collecting the bottle and half-drunk glass from the floor. He opens his mouth to scold her, then seems to remember he has more pressing concerns. Such as closing her away in her workroom and keeping her blind all that is going on in the house.

He is out the door without a word.

Harriet waits for his footsteps to fade. Then she opens the door a crack and listens. She can hear a dull murmur of voices coming from the parlour.

Harriet knows Nathan had agreed to the spies' use of the house to clear Eva's name over the death of Donald Macauley some weeks ago. She had overheard Edwin and Nathan speaking of it not long after Eva had absconded to Longstone. Low, secretive voices, of course. There's suspicion everywhere these days. Since the Jacobites took up arms last month, distrust and rumours fill every alleyway on Holy Island. There are spies on both sides of the conflict in the village, they say. And Harriet knows her family is at the top of the list of those who are suspected to be working for the government.

She cannot blame the villagers for their suspicions. For reasons she knows nothing of, her mother and siblings had fled Lindisfarne twenty years ago. And they had reappeared on Holy Island, so close to Scotland and the Jacobite heartland, just as the Rising was beginning. But her family are not working for the government; they are just sorry fools coerced into letting the spies gather between their walls. Though she is fairly certain that will provide them with little leniency if the Jacobites in town discover what is taking place at Highfield House.

Harriet slips out of her shoes and makes her way silently down the passage. Rusty lamplight dances over the faded seascapes and portraits hung on the walls of the entrance hall. The rich smell of pipe smoke drifts beneath the closed door of the parlour.

She waits, motionless, in case Nathan or Edwin show themselves. But beyond the hum of voices in the parlour, the ground floor of the house is quiet.

She presses an ear to the door.

*Cotesworth*, she hears. Yes, she knows this name. Knows this is the Newcastle merchant who has set these government spies into action. The man tasked with gathering the information that will quell the Rising in this part of the country. The man tasked with finding the leading Jacobites with warrants to their names—and making sure men like her friend Julia's wayward brothers are strung up by the neck to keep King George upon the throne.

Harriet knows this name because she listens. At the dinner table. At church. As she walks through the gossip-filled streets. Listens, with the practised art of a blank expression. A look of stark disinterest. Let them think her head is empty. Let them think her as blank and unintelligent as the unfilled pages of her notebook.

It is a powerful thing to be underestimated.

Meanwhile, she observes the world with the eye of an artist, trained to capture every nuance of the complicated life around her. *Listen*, she thinks. *Observe. Gather the pieces.*

Because she senses that each fragment, each word she collects might one day become useful. Perhaps they will come together to inspire a great piece of art. Or perhaps she will cobble together these fragments of knowledge and use them to build her own unconstrained life. Because knowledge, she knows, is power. Knowledge allows you to manipulate. Coerce. Build something from nothing.

There are more pieces: *Lesbury Common* and *an army gathering,* and *troops active.*

The stairs creak and she darts away from the door.

"Harriet?" Edwin's voice. She curses under her breath. "I told you to stay in your workroom," he says in a fierce whisper.

She is after a cup of water, she will tell him. Or an extra shawl against the evening chill.

And with her excuses forming on her lips, she hurries back towards her workroom, these new pieces of knowledge held close, like scraps that will keep her from starving.

# CHAPTER TWO

Eva pauses on the path leading to Highfield House, smoothing her skirts and tucking windblown hair beneath her bonnet. The manor looms over her, gloomy and grey, even now, with the sun at its highest.

She feels like a child on her way to face the headmaster's wrath. Nathan is just four years older than her; why does she feel so damn scared? She tells herself she is being foolish. Tells herself it does not matter what her brother thinks of her, or the choices she has made.

But she knows this is a lie. Knows it is precisely because Nathan's opinion matters so much to her that her stomach is rolling and her heart is fast. She does not want to lose him. And she knows she is on the verge of doing so.

This is just her second visit to Highfield House since escaping to Longstone last month. She had first had Finn take her back to see her family two days after she had left Holy Island. Enough time, she had hoped, for her brother's anger at her leaving to have settled somewhat. And for her former betrothed, Matthew Walton, to have skulked back to London without her.

Eva had planned a long, drawn-out apology to Nathan; for disappearing without explanation, for shunning the marriage he had cultivated for her, and for leaving Walton standing alone in the parlour of Highfield House.

Nathan had refused to see her.

Perhaps it was for the best. Because she does not regret leaving Matthew Walton, or choosing this life with Finn on Longstone. But she does regret hurting her brother. She knows how much Nathan had been relying on her marriage to Walton. Aligning their family with the wealthy Waltons would have done much to restore the good standing of the Blake name, after the collapse of Nathan's merchant business last year. But the pull of life on Longstone had been too strong to resist.

This time, she does not announce her arrival. When Mrs Brodie, the housekeeper, lets her inside, she follows the sound of hammering towards the staircase. She guesses her brother is up on the second storey, working on his perpetual restorations.

"Auntie Eva!" Nathan's seven-year-old daughter Theodora bursts from the parlour, throwing her arms around Eva's waist. Eva gives her niece a squeeze. Thea looks up at her, her blonde hair spidery around her face and a fat blob of porridge on the front of her smock. "Are you back for good? Papa and Uncle Edwin said it was only a matter of time."

Eva smiles wryly to herself. "Where's your father?" she asks, sidestepping the question. "And your Auntie Harriet?"

Theodora points up the staircase. "Papa is up there, working. And Auntie Harriet is... I don't know... Not here.

She went out."

"All right." She kisses Theodora on her forehead. "I missed you."

"Papa says we're not to disturb him when he's working," says Thea, fluttering up the stairs behind Eva, then pausing on the landing.

"I shall consider myself warned." Eva feels quite certain that, whether she interrupts Nathan's work or not, she will get the same brusque reaction.

She follows the sound of indistinct crashing to the room at the end of the hallway. The room beside Edwin and Harriet's that she thinks was once her mother's dressing room.

She knocks. But steps inside without being invited.

The room is chaos. The fireplace is in pieces, bricks strewn across the floor in a sea of dust and crumbled mortar. Several floorboards are missing, revealing the weighty beams beneath. A gaping hole in the wood panelling looks through to the worn stone of the outer wall of the house. Eva is not sure if Nathan is restoring the place or trying to destroy it.

Her brother has his back to her as he pries the last of the loose bricks from the fireplace and lets them thunder to the floor.

"Good afternoon, Nathan," she says.

He whirls around in surprise. His cheeks are pink with exertion, his sleeves rolled to his elbows and the brown waves of his hair tied at his neck. Patches of sweat darken the linen beneath his arms, his shirt discoloured with dust. A complicated look falls over his face at the sight of her. It's a look of irritation and profound anger, but there is something softer beneath. Something faint, that gives her the courage to get out what she has come here to say. He looks at her expectantly, the pry bar dangling from one hand and a hammer in the other.

Eva's mouth is suddenly dry. Whether from nerves or the dust-thick air, she cannot tell. "Thank you for not sending me away."

Nathan leans the tools up against the wall. "That would be rather petty, don't you think?"

*No more petty than refusing to see me*, she wants to say. But she bites her tongue. "What happened to the fireplace?" she asks instead. "Was it in such a state when you arrived back at the house?"

Her brother folds his arms, a hard look in his eyes telling her he does not appreciate the question.

"Mr Holland and the other government spies have been using the house?" Eva asks.

"Yes. They have." His voice is crisp and cold. Matter of fact.

"Has there been any suspicion from the villagers? From Martin Macauley and the other Jacobites?"

"Nothing more than usual. As far as I can tell, they are unaware of what the house is being used for."

Eva nods. Though it is hardly an assurance of her family's safety, it goes some way to allaying her concern for them. Not to mention her guilt. If it weren't for her, Nathan would never have had to agree to something so dangerous. And she has hardly gone out of her way to repay him. "I'm glad to hear it," she says.

"Is that why you came?" Nathan lops off the conversation before she can take it further. "To discuss the spies' use of the house?"

"No." Eva clears her throat. Inhales. "I came to tell you that Finn and I are to be married."

Nathan's lips twitch. "I see." He picks up the pry bar again and pretends to examine the broken fireplace.

"I know you're angry," says Eva. "And I know I've disappointed you. Let you down. And I'm sorry. Truly."

"But that does not change what you are about to do," Nathan finishes.

She swallows. "No. It doesn't."

Finally, he turns back to face her. Despite his attempt at nonchalance, Eva can tell her news has surprised him. He rubs his free hand across the back of his neck, as though trying to find the right words. Perhaps he really had expected her to return home any day, meek and full of apologies. "And Mr Murray," he says finally, tapping the pry bar mindlessly against his thigh, "he did not see fit to discuss this with me first? To seek my permission?"

"Would you have given it?"

Nathan doesn't reply. He clenches his jaw—a gesture Eva knows well. A gesture that tells her he is doing his best to keep his anger from escaping. Although for what purpose, she can hardly tell. She is already well aware of how he feels towards her.

This role of patriarch, this role Nathan had grown into after the death of their father and elder brother, is one that was never supposed to be his. He is not a natural leader: too compliant, too affable, too averse to any kind of conflict. And yet the task of finding his sisters a husband is one he had approached with the utmost gravity. Eva knows that, by flitting in here with her scandalous news, she has stomped all over his carefully laid plans.

She thinks of Finn, waiting for her on the beach in front of the house. He had been adamant that he come with her, let Nathan know of his intentions. But she does not want him stepping into these rooms. Does not want him drawn back into the memories they will no doubt unearth, the shadows they will cast. This bleak weight that is always there; that she has come, perhaps too easily, to ignore. The night when Finn had come to Highfield House with Henry Ward, the privateer he had sailed with as a cabin boy. Tucked away in a bedroom upstairs, Finn had fought with Eva's eldest brother, resulting in Oliver's death.

She and Finn never speak of it—what is there to say? It had been a terrible accident that he has carried on his shoulders for the past twenty years. Eva knows stepping into Highfield House will paint those memories in fresh colours again. She cannot bear to put him through such a thing. Nor can she stand the thought of her family ever finding out the truth. Harriet and Nathan would never forgive her if they knew she was to marry the man who had killed their brother.

"Finn did wish to speak with you," Eva tells Nathan. "Very much."

He shifts the pry bar to his other hand.

"Will you put that damn thing down?" Eva reaches out and snatches it. "I told him I needed to speak with you first," she says. "To explain myself. And to apologise. I know I've treated you terribly. And I'm sorry."

Nathan tilts his head, studying her, as though trying to determine if her apology is genuine. His critical eye stings, though she knows she can expect little else. However close she and Nathan had once been, she had destroyed that the day she had run away to Longstone without a word of explanation. He is looking at her as though she is a stranger, and she supposes she cannot blame him.

"Well," he says finally, arms folded across his chest, "if nothing else, I'm glad you'll not be living in sin any longer."

Eva grits her teeth. "Finn has been a perfect gentleman," she says stiffly.

"I should hope so."

She sighs. She had hoped for more than brusque, obligatory conversation. Forgiveness, perhaps, had always been a step too far, but she had hoped for the chance to explain herself properly. But at least, she supposes, she was able to get a word out this time. She misses her warm and gentle brother. But perhaps it is too late for that. Too late to fix things. She sets the pry bar down with the rest of Nathan's tools and turns for the door.

"When?" he says suddenly. "And where?"

The words catch her off guard. "You wish to attend?"

"I'm your brother," he says, without warmth. "Of course I wish to attend."

Eva hesitates. She had not expected this. Had assumed she would marry Finn Murray away from the eyes of her family. And while there is a big part of her that is happy at the thought of her siblings attending, there is also a faint pull of dread. Because Nathan, at eight years old, had watched through the keyhole as Finn had struck the blow that had ended Oliver's life. And though twenty years have passed, there is still a part of her that is terrified of her brother recognising the man she is to marry. There would be no worse place for him to do so than while they stand at the altar.

Still, keeping secrets is a price she is willing to pay to become Finn Murray's wife. And she knows forbidding her family to attend her wedding will put an end to any hope she might have had of reconciling with Nathan.

"St Aiden's Church in Bamburgh," she says. "Next Thursday at four."

"St Aiden's," says Nathan. "Where Father is buried."

"Yes." Half of her had chosen the church for that reason. The other half had wanted to stay as far away as possible from the gossip on Lindisfarne. Eva knows that if there's one thing the villagers love to prattle about more than the Blakes' fictitious ties to the government, it's her tryst with the Longstone lightkeeper.

Then, of course, there is the reason she is trying hard not to acknowledge: that marriage at St Aiden's will also keep them away from the grave of her eldest brother, who lies in the churchyard on Lindisfarne.

Nathan picks up his tools and returns to attacking the fireplace. "We shall be there," he says, somehow managing to sound both scathing and completely disinterested. Eva supposes that takes a special kind of talent.

# CHAPTER THREE

This business with her brother has Eva distracted, Finn can tell. As they had sailed up to Highfield House, they had come within two hundred yards of the barque lying at anchor beyond Emmanuel Head. With her eyes fixed on the manor, Eva had not even noticed it.

Finn had not said a word to her about it. The last thing she needed before she faced her brother was to see Henry Ward's ship in the sea beyond her family home.

Five weeks ago, Finn's former privateering captain had taken him aboard his ship, seeking to punish him for the death of Oliver Blake. He and Eva had managed to escape, but both knew they had only done so because Ward had allowed it. The weeks since have been a waiting game, in which Finn's heart jumps at every light on the sea, expecting Ward to return for him. Ward and the *Eagle* have been on the edge of his consciousness for twenty years, but never more acutely than in the past five weeks.

Each time he sails to the mainland, to earn a little coin with days of farm work, he finds himself restlessly combing the sea. Out on Longstone, they spend days and nights with their eyes on the ocean, waiting for the masts of Ward's barque to cut through the cloud. But it's no surprise they have not seen him if Ward has been hiding away on the north side of Holy Island, Finn thinks. He and Eva have had little cause to come out here of late.

There is something painfully familiar about the sight of the *Eagle* in the sea beyond Highfield House, dark and skeletal and faintly threatening. It's a scene from Finn's childhood; a scene from haunted memories he can't push away. And a scene he is about to tie himself to forever, by making Eva Blake his wife.

Finn digs his hands into the pockets of his greatcoat and stares up at the ship, colourless and still in the afternoon haze. The furled sails tell him Ward has no plans to leave any time soon.

Eva's footsteps crunch across the embankment, pulling Finn's thoughts away from Henry Ward. Her face is hard to read beneath the shadow of her bonnet, but there is no anger there, or tears, so he dares to hope things have gone better than they did the last time she tried to explain herself to her brother.

"All right?" he asks, reaching for her hand. He turns her slightly, so her back is to the sea, Ward's ship hidden from her view. She will see it soon enough, of course. But one problem at a time.

She slides her arms around his waist. Rests her head against his chest at the place his heart is beating. "Well. He allowed me through the door this time. So I believe we're making progress."

"And? What'd he think of your news?"

Finn regrets leaving it to her to tell her family of their betrothal. As little as he knows about social decency, he is well aware he ought to have gone to her brother first, or at least been the one to tell him of their plans to marry. Still, Eva had been adamant that she go alone—and Finn has come to recognise that steely look in her eyes that tells him there is no room for argument. In any case, Nathan Blake's anger at his failure to follow convention is the least of his problems.

She looks up at him, catches his eye with a faint smile. "He's a stubborn bastard. But he will come around. I'm sure of it." She takes a step back, looks down at their interlaced fingers. "He wishes to attend the wedding."

"And you're not pleased by that?"

She hesitates a moment too long. "Of course I am." He can see behind her eyes. Can read the unease hiding there. A fear of what her brother might see when he looks at the man she is to marry. Finn doesn't blame her. It's a fear he has too.

Though he had not said a word of it to Eva, he is relieved that he had not had to step inside that house today. The memories the place conjures up are already vivid enough. Even now, he can feel his glance being pulled back to the ivy-covered walls of the manor. Trying to remember—or perhaps trying to forget—which room had belonged to Oliver Blake. Which of those rooms on the second floor had he been sleeping in when Oliver had appeared and held a knife to his throat? Which of those windows had he considered jumping from after Oliver's head had cracked against the bedpost? Which of those walls held the priest hole he had hidden in, and the passage that had allowed him to escape?

He pulls his gaze away from the row of dark glass. With luck, Eva's brother will finish the restoration of the house soon and sell it to some wealthy nobleman with a love for remote and windblown places.

"And you've not... changed your mind?" Finn asks, feeling his heart quicken slightly.

"Changed my mind?" Eva snorts. "Of course not. Don't be mad." Her sudden indignance makes him smile. That ship in the bay, the secret they are keeping from her family, it all feels easier to carry with Eva at his side. Strange that it might feel that way when her presence makes the stakes that much higher.

There's an impossible faultlessness to her place in their firelit cottage. A sense of her belonging, in spite of every piece of logic and reason. One night, with firelight pouring through the window, and her latest attempt at a bread loaf sitting charred and fragrant on the table between them, he'd looked up from his soup bowl and been almost surprised to find her sitting there opposite him. Had been overcome with a need to make this forever. With his soup spoon still in his hand, he'd garbled out a request for her to become his wife, before he lost his nerve. Eva had given him a smile that said she'd been waiting an eternity for him to do it.

He bends his head to find her lips. Knows he ought to tell her of the ship beyond the house. She will see it, no doubt, when they head back to Longstone. And she will panic at Henry Ward's nearness to her family; will panic at the thought of what he might be planning.

Is his former captain here merely to mete out the punishment he feels Finn has escaped? As much as he wishes things were that simple, Finn can't quite make himself believe it. Henry Ward had returned to Northumberland at the same time as the Blakes. He had been well acquainted with Eva's late mother, Abigail. Henry Ward is intertwined with Eva's family in a way Finn can't quite make out.

And then, of course, there is the slightly sickening fact that if all Ward wanted was to see him dead, it would be an easy enough thing to achieve.

And so just for now, he says nothing to Eva. Lets them have this fleeting moment, eye to eye, before they return to being hunted.

# CHAPTER FOUR

Nathan's headache is not helped by the wailing of the baby coming from the nursery upstairs. He rubs his eyes and gulps his wine. Winces at its harshness.

On the other side of the dining table, his brother-in-law's eyes drift upwards. "No doubt the poor lad's due a feeding," Edwin says irritably. "I'll have strong words with his mother when she dares show herself."

Nathan puts his glass down a little too heavily. Crimson droplets slosh over the side and bead on the surface of the table. This is far from the first time Harriet has disappeared from the house for hours on end. These days, his sister seems to always be either locked away in her workroom, or wandering around the island on her own private journeys. Lost in thoughts she has no mind to share. Harriet's eyes have taken on a distant look of late; sometimes Nathan guesses she is merely lost in thoughts of her paintings. Other times, it is as though her mind has landed somewhere impossibly far away. His youngest sister has always been something of a mystery to him, but Lindisfarne seems to have drawn her further into herself. He knows how much she misses London; how much she had railed against coming here. He worries for her sometimes. And he knows she would not welcome his concerns.

Nathan glances at Theodora beside him, to gauge whether she has registered the conversation. She has a pencil in one hand and a piece of bread in the other, and is hunched over the table, scribbling furiously on crumb-covered paper. He catches a handful of words: *fairies* and *moon* and, inexplicably, *big furry seal suit*. He can tell from the faraway look in her eyes that her imagination has taken her far away. Good.

"I've a good mind to go and fetch her," Edwin says tersely, slicing his meat into slivers. "That Miss Mitchell, she's a bad influence."

Nathan feels something flip in his chest. He had not realised Harriet was with Julia Mitchell. Not that he can pretend to be surprised. As far as he knows, Julia is Harriet's only friend in this place. "You ought to forbid Harriet from seeing her," he tells Edwin stiffly. "She's not to be trusted."

Several weeks ago, Nathan had discovered Julia's two brothers hiding in the roof of Highfield House. Men on the run after their bloody clash with dragoons at a Jacobite protest in York. After Nathan had thrown them from the house, Julia had sent them to hide away on Longstone, out of sight of the authorities. Nathan has been painfully deliberate in staying away from her ever since. He wonders distantly if the men are still on Longstone. He had been tempted to ask Eva about it, but had not wanted her to think his talkativeness meant she was forgiven.

Some treacherous part of him misses being around Julia.

He misses the brightness of her, the way her smile lights the dark corners of a room. But those things mean nothing when she had found it so easy to deceive him and his family.

He tosses back another mouthful of wine. Coughs as it sears his throat. "Thea," he says. "Eat your dinner."

Theodora glances up from the page, her blue eyes wide. She looks slightly bewildered at having found herself at the dinner table.

She spears a piece of roast beef with her fork and brings it to her mouth, without relinquishing her pencil. "Oh," she says around a mouthful, "I didn't get to read Auntie Eva my story."

Nathan slices his potatoes. "You can read it to me later. And please don't speak with your mouth full."

"You might have asked Eva to stay for dinner," says Edwin, not looking up from his plate.

Nathan hums noncommittally. He knows it was rude to send his sister away, especially with the smell of roasting meat floating up the staircase. But his anger is still far too raw to sit down to a meal with her. "Well. I was not quite yet in the mood to celebrate with her and her husband-to-be."

Edwin raises his eyebrows. "Husband-to-be? Is that so?" He chuckles, chasing down his meat with a mouthful of wine. "I have to say, I expected her to turn up back here with her tail between her legs and go chasing after Walton for forgiveness." He puts down his glass. "Probably for the best you didn't ask them to stay. That heathen of hers probably has no idea how to use a fork."

Nathan lowers his eyes. Says nothing.

In spite of himself, there's a tucked-away part of him that is happy for Eva. As much as he did not want to admit it, he had seen the grief in her eyes when she told him she had agreed to marry Matthew Walton. He had done his best to ignore it, knowing the marriage was what the family needed. And while Eva latching herself to Longstone and the lightkeeper is not the life he had imagined—or hoped for—for his sister, he cannot deny that when he saw her today, there was a glow in her eyes he is not sure he has ever seen before.

A thunderous knock at the door echoes into the dining room. Knowing Mrs Brodie is busy in the kitchen, Nathan pushes back his chair and gets to his feet. Strides down the hall.

He opens the door, heart jolting. There is Julia Mitchell, arm wrapped around Harriet as though keeping her afloat. Harriet's cheeks are pink, blonde snarls of hair clinging to her face and her bonnet swinging in one hand. Nathan can smell liquor on her.

"I lost my key," she says. She laughs, but there is no humour in it.

"I see," Nathan says tautly. His gaze is drawn to Julia, to her copper-green eyes and the unruly red curls escaping from beneath her cap. She looks away quickly, as though scorched by his scrutiny.

"Nathan," says Harriet, her voice syrupy, "are you not going to thank Julia for seeing me home?"

"Your son needs you, Harriet," Nathan snaps. "And dinner is on the table. Although I'd suggest tidying yourself first."

Julia nudges Harriet over the doorstep and she sidles past Nathan, heading precariously for the staircase. Nathan looks back at Julia. Meets her eyes for a moment.

"I'm sorry," Julia says. "She came to see me as I was closing the curiosity shop. We went upstairs and I offered her a drink. She must have refilled her glass when I wasn't looking. I didn't realise how much she'd had until she got up to leave."

Nathan wants to berate her. Wants to blame her for depositing his sister on his doorstep in such a state. But he can see the concern in Julia's eyes. And though he struggles to see beneath Harriet's brittle shell sometimes, he knows her well enough to be sure this was all her own doing.

But there is nothing else to say. He gives a terse nod and closes the door, ignoring the way his heart is hammering.

# CHAPTER FIVE

This morning, the blank canvas feels as though it is mocking her. It has been more than a month since Harriet has even dipped her brush in paint.

The last piece she had begun, she had destroyed. Barely recalls doing it. She remembers little beyond anger, frustration, her thoughts distorted by one too many glasses of Edwin's whisky. When she had looked back at her canvas, it had been covered in angry whorls of black paint that had buried the sunlit scene she had spent so many hours crafting. She had stared at it for a long time with an odd sense of detachment, trying to make sense of why she had done it. And the answers, well, they are a little too frightening to look at in great detail. There are pieces of herself she would rather keep out of the light.

For five weeks, Harriet has let the frustration of the blank canvas swallow her. Has let herself be consumed by it, morbidly content in her inaction, her inability to conjure up any image worth realising. But today, things have changed. A letter. Arrived from London, from her dearest friend Isabelle. Harriet has read the excitable, curling script so many times she knows it by heart.

*My patrons, Lord and Lady Baillieu were visiting from Paris last week and I told them about you and your work. They were most curious, and I took the liberty of showing them your seascape I so proudly hang in my workroom. Needless to say, the Lord and Lady were most impressed and they have expressed a wish to see more of your pieces. They would very much like to meet you.*

And then, the letters becoming rounder and more elaborate, as though Isabelle carried as much excitement at the prospect as Harriet did:

*I would so love you to accompany me to Paris when I attend the Baillieus' next salon in April. Do say you will be back from the wilds of Northumberland by then and will be able to join me!*

Harriet's childhood painting tutor, Madame Octavia, had introduced her to Isabelle and the other artists in her circle. Though Harriet had been barely sixteen at the time, they had taken her under their wings, welcomed her into their clique. Given her the praise and encouragement she needed to begin to believe in herself as an artist.

Once a fortnight, the group would gather in each other's homes—in chandeliered drawing rooms and garden sheds, and dank kitchens that reeked of old ale and tallow. Wherever they met, it did not matter. The group straddled class and gender lines, drawn together by a shared passion for their art. Peering over wine glasses and through clouds of pipe smoke, they would share their work, critique each other's paintings, discuss their inspiration.

When Harriet was among the group, it did not matter that she was a woman, or that she was not yet even twenty. Or

that Edwin never allowed them to gather beneath his roof—
and would grumble endlessly when she returned home with
smoke on her clothes, light-headed with wine and ideas. All
that mattered were the brushstrokes, the colours, the tools,
the plans. And the sense of freedom that came with it all.

In the company of Isabelle—beautiful, talented Isabelle;
all dark hair and curves, who painted portraits as though she
were looking into another's soul—Harriet felt able to voice
pieces of the things that lingered in the dark recesses of her
mind. Her anger at Nathan for wrangling her into the
marriage that suited him best. Anger at herself for blindly
accepting. The way her husband and son so often feel like
strangers. And the way there was not a single cell in her body
that had ever wanted a husband at all.

Isabelle, eight years older than Harriet, was never fazed by
her scandalous admissions. She just listened and nodded and
let a moment of silence pass to craft her answers before she
opened her mouth.

*I know how it feels to be different,* Isabelle would say. *I know
what it is to feel as though you do not fit in.*

Isabelle had turned not fitting in into an artform. After
several years of unhappy marriage, she was now living apart
from her husband, spared the marriage market on account of
her promise to support herself. And what a dazzling job she
was doing at that, with a paint-filled garret in Lambeth and
her portraits hung in the salons of one of the wealthiest
families in France.

Isabelle is everything Harriet aspires to be. She misses her
with an intensity so deep it almost feels like a physical thing.

This opportunity she has dangled in front of her, it's a
piece of that dream, that unconstrained life. It feels too

impossible, like it belongs to someone else.

Harriet knows the journey to Paris will not be cheap. The cost is well within her husband's reach, she is sure. But she knows Edwin despises her artists' group, with their disdain for social norms and their elaborate, outlandish ambitions. Knows he believes he deserves a sainthood for allowing her to attend their gatherings. How she will convince him to part with the money and let her flit off to Paris with Isabelle, she has no thought. Not that that is as pressing an issue as the blank canvas in front of her. The sum will matter little if she has nothing new to show the Baillieus.

She closes her eyes. Imagines her work on display at Lady Baillieu's salon. Sees people discussing, admiring. *Such fine use of colour. An intriguing perspective.* Sees a life in which she is more than just mother, wife, trapped on an island.

Perhaps, she thinks, she will have to paint under an assumed name, pretend a man had done the work. The letter from Isabelle had not discussed such details. Harriet knows her evocative landscapes are far outside the scope of the still lifes and domestic scenes expected of a female artist. But if she is to paint under a man's name, so be it. Having her work on display would still be the greatest of thrills.

She reaches for her notebook and pencil.

In a room above her head, her son Thomas wails. She feels instinctive dread tighten her muscles. Does her best to block out the sound. She puts the pencil to the page. Tries to let her imagination, her inspiration, guide her. The baby shrieks. The sketch refuses to find its shape.

Footsteps creak across the upstairs passage. Down the staircase. Thomas's howling gets louder, and there is a knock at the door of her workroom.

Harriet supposes it was inevitable. But she knows that, as she pulls open the door, the look she gives Thomas's nurse is sour and unwelcoming.

"I'm sorry to disturb you, Mrs Whitley," says Jenny, eyes lowered. "He's ready for a feed."

Of course he is. Harriet's hand tightens around the pencil. She can't help the tug of resentment. Has she not given enough of her body to this child?

She takes the baby, giving Jenny a brusque nod. There's an apologetic look in the nurse's eyes that makes Harriet faintly guilty. Quiet and loyal Jenny, who had long ago buried her own son and husband, has been with them since Thomas's birth six months ago. Harriet knows she would never have survived this long without Jenny's knowledge, her support, her patient encouragement. But that does nothing to quell her irritation at being disturbed. Every now and then, she sees a look in Jenny's eyes that suggests she is afraid of her. And what an odd thing that is, Harriet thinks, given the woman is more than twice her age, with endlessly more wisdom. An odd thing, but strangely thrilling nonetheless.

She carries the baby upstairs. Not once has she ever brought Thomas into her workroom. And she never plans to do so. She wishes she could keep her husband out too, but that is far more difficult, given he has control of his own two legs.

She sits in the chair in the corner of her bedroom with Thomas at her breast. Hears footsteps down the passage. The door creaks open. Edwin goes to the washstand and empties the jug into the basin. His shirtsleeves are rolled up and his coal-coloured hair clings to his neck. He splashes his face, sloughing away the dust of the renovations.

Harriet watches him curiously, trying to read his mood. It's a difficult thing, given how little she knows him, even after a year and half of marriage. Sometimes—often—he feels more like a headmaster than a husband. And they seem to have come to a wordless agreement that things will run more smoothly between them if they keep the more jagged parts of their personalities hidden from each other. But right now, she needs him. Or rather, she needs his money.

"Have you finished fixing that broken window in Eva's room?" she asks, with as much sweetness as she can muster.

Edwin turns to face her, eyebrows raised in surprise. Water drips off his sharp chin and he reaches for the cloth beside the basin to dry his cheeks. "Yes," he says. "I've put a second coat of paint on the dining room wall too."

"You've been busy this morning."

He looks at her, something tentative in his eyes. He seems caught off guard by her sudden interest in his work. Faintly suspicious. No doubt he suspects she is trying to make up for appearing on the doorstep like a vagrant last night. Which, she supposes, she is.

"You ought to come and see it once Thomas is fed," Edwin says, as though agreeing to take part in this game she has begun to play. "The colour is quite lovely. I think you will like it."

"All right." She lifts the baby onto her shoulder and uses her free hand to lace her stays.

Edwin looks down at their son, rubbing a hand across his downy blond hair. "That's quite a mop he's growing."

Thomas opens his mouth and fountains a trail of vomit down Harriet's shoulder. Edwin wipes at it with the cloth. "You were not at breakfast this morning," he says to her.

"Have you eaten today?"

Harriet bites back an irritated retort. She knows Edwin, twelve years her senior, looks upon her as little more than a girl. A fragile, delicate thing in desperate need of guidance. But perhaps he might trust her enough to determine on her own when she is hungry. "I shall eat later."

He gives a murmur of displeasure. "What's in your hand?"

Harriet had not realised she was still carrying Isabelle's letter. It is crumpled in her clenched fist, tucked in behind the baby's back as though it has become a part of herself she is unable to detach from. "A letter," she tells Edwin. "From London." She knows there is no need to say more. She has few acquaintances in the capital beyond the members of her artists' circle. Certainly none that would write to her.

"Ah," says Edwin, that single half-grunted syllable enough to convey his every thought about whichever peculiar soul had written her the letter, and whatever it is they might want.

Harriet stands, planting Thomas on her hip. She will not speak of Paris yet. She needs time to wrangle herself back into her husband's good graces after plundering Julia's liquor stores last night. She gives him the girlish smile she knows appeases him. "Why not show me the dining room?"

31

# CHAPTER SIX

"Nor'-westerly wind," says Finn, climbing down the steps at the front of the cottage. The sea is restless and gunmetal grey, the afternoon air cold and briny. "Perfect conditions for learning to tack."

"As long as you're not in any hurry to get to Lindisfarne." Eva gathers her skirts in her fist as she passes the rockpools in front of the house. "And you don't mind me sailing around in circles."

"I'm never in any hurry to get to Lindisfarne." Finn chuckles. "In a hurry to leave, usually, so welcoming are the villagers."

Eva grins. Looks over her shoulder at him as she navigates over the rocks towards the jetty. "Well, that is what you get for stealing their coal. And for betrothing yourself to a suspected government spy."

He laughs. Then nods towards the empty mooring post on one side of the jetty. "I see Michael has left again. Thought the bloody fool was out here to hide."

Eva knows Julia Mitchell's brother Michael has been making regular visits to either the mainland or Holy Island—these days, the longboat is gone more often than it is here. For what purpose she does not know for certain, though she can guess well enough. She has little doubt that Michael is still deeply entrenched in the Jacobite cause, despite the hangman's noose already having been tied for him.

"Seems two months in the attic at my family's house and he's had enough of hiding," says Eva.

"I don't like it." Finn turns up the collar of his greatcoat against the wind. "It's dangerous. Feels like it's only a matter of time before the redcoats are at our door."

Eva shares his annoyance. Harbouring Jacobite criminals is risky. Every time Michael leaves the sanctuary of Longstone, he is putting them in greater danger. Still, she knows selflessness is not high on the Mitchells' list of qualities.

"I heard the Jacobites are going south," Finn tells her. "Planning to take Newcastle."

Eva feels a pull of unease. With the exception of Michael and his brother being crammed around their supper table, they have so far managed to avoid entangling themselves in the Jacobite Rising. At the thought of the conflict coming as close as Newcastle, Eva feels distinctly on edge. "Do you think that's where Michael is headed?" she asks.

"Could be," says Finn. "But they're saying the militia's close to securing to the town. If he's on his way down there to fight, I don't think he's much to look forward to."

Michael and his brother Angus have been on Longstone for more than a month, and have not yet made any mention of leaving. Eva knows they are waiting for news of their elder brother, Hugh, before they head to London to hide away in the city. She doesn't begrudge them that. But it has felt far too crowded in the Longstone cottage, with sleeping pallets rolled up in corners and empty crates crammed around the table to compensate for the lack of chairs. A single bedroom for them all to navigate as they take turns keeping the light.

Nonetheless, there has been something thrilling about sneaking around Longstone with Finn, trying to snatch a scrap of privacy. A kiss without witnesses, a moment alone in the overcrowded cottage. A mouthful of wine in the dim light of the shed, hidden between piles of earth-fragrant peat.

Eva appreciates the irony that it might feel so congested in a place of such dazzling remoteness. But her courtship with Finn has always been a slightly backwards thing. They had been keeping the light as near strangers, had spent the night on Longstone together before they even knew each other's name.

Finn steps into the skiff. "Right then," he says, offering her his hand, "get in the boat, lass." He unties the mooring rope as she climbs aboard. "I'll row her clear of the island and then she's all yours. You can take us into this wind over to Lindisfarne."

Eva looks back at the island as Finn rows out into the sea. It's a sight she still struggles to believe is real: their stone cottage rising from the rock as if it had always been a part of it; the towering needle of the firebasket just beyond. Mirrored planes of rockpools, whorls of white water, and then sea, and sea, and sea. To the north-west lies Lindisfarne; and beyond the black rock crenelations of the other Farne Islands is the mainland village of Bamburgh, the silhouette of its castle like stacked dice on the horizon.

Finn slides the oars from the oarlocks and settles them at his feet, the boat tilting rhythmically on the swell. He nods towards the lines. "Haul in the sheets to get her moving, then we'll bring her close to the wind."

Eva frowns in concentration as she tugs on the ropes, opening the sloop's mainsail. It thwacks noisily before tightening. The boat begins to fly out in the direction of the open ocean.

"Good." Finn nods. "Now bring her into the wind."

Eva leans carefully on the tiller, feeling the boat shift beneath her. Wind tears into the sail, making it drum and flutter loudly. She grits her teeth in frustration. "This always seems far easier when we're talking it through at the supper table."

Finn chuckles, leaning back against the gunwale to watch her. "Aye, but it's quite useless information at the supper table, I've found." He nods towards the thundering sail. "How do we fix it?"

"We're too close to the wind," Eva says. "We need to fall off a little. Back the way we came."

He grins. "Seems there's hope for you after all."

Tentatively, she guides the boat off the wind, feeling it fall into a gentle rhythm. And she lets herself breathe.

The life she is building here is at once overwhelming and impossibly simple; a life of callused palms and wet skirt hems, and arms turned muscular from hauling the firebasket into the sky. A life in which she has learnt to bake bread, to pull bones from fish, to drink water straight from the sky. A life far beyond the one she imagined she would live.

A life which, if she is able to look past the fear of Henry Ward, has made her desperately happy.

As they skirt the south-eastern tip of Holy Island, Eva sees Finn's eyes pull northward. She knows he is looking towards Emmanuel Head. Looking for that dark outline of Ward's ship.

Despite the shock that had rattled through her when she had caught sight of the *Eagle* on their way back to Longstone earlier in the week, she knows she cannot be surprised that Ward is here. She has been waiting for more than a month for him to show himself. Glimpsing his ship had almost been a relief—had taken away the element of surprise. Still, knowing where the ship is, and knowing exactly what Ward plans to do to her and Finn—and her family—is another thing entirely.

Eva shuffles across the bench and lets Finn take the tiller as they make their way towards the Lindisfarne anchorage. A thick bank of clouds billows across the sun, turning the water to ink. A large brigantine lies at anchor on the edge of the bay, a single longboat cutting a steady line from its hull towards the shore.

Finn eases the skiff up to the rickety wooden jetty. It thuds softly against the moorings between an armada of tiny fishing boats. He secures the mooring ropes and climbs out of the boat. Offers Eva his hand. She keeps a hold of it as she walks down the jetty and across the beach. Her shoes crunch over the dried rafts of seaweed as they pass the tiny wooden fishermen's huts. A waft of seaweed and herrings hangs on the air.

She feels the heads turn, eyes pulled away from the brig in the bay. Eva knows she is not imagining the whispers, the murmurs, the gossip. She hears her name, half-whispered. Knows everyone is aware of her sinful life, living out on

Longstone with Finn Murray.

"Something I can do for you?" Finn calls to an older woman who is passing with a basket on her hip. She is watching them openly, her expression wavering between curiosity and derision.

She puts her head down and hurries away. Eva hides a smile.

Finn puts a protective hand to the back of her neck. "Shall I see you to the house?" he asks.

"No. It's all right. You go to the market. I'll meet you back here later this afternoon."

While Eva has little hope of resurrecting things with Nathan right now, she is determined not to drift apart from her sister. Harriet had been in such a terrible state when Eva had left for Longstone, and now that Nathan has permitted her back through the door of Highfield House—however reluctantly—she plans to make up for lost time with her.

Finn meets her eyes. "Be careful."

"And you." She hates the thought of letting him out of her sight while they are so close to Ward and the *Eagle*. Nonetheless, she knows they are in far less danger here in the village than they are in the deep isolation of Longstone.

Finn kisses her cheek—for the benefit of the onlookers, Eva is sure—then she turns and follows the coast path through rolling dunes towards the house.


"Well now." Harriet looks up from her plate of toast as Eva appears in the dining room. "Look what the tide dragged in." She is alone at the vast expanse of the table, picking at her breakfast, though it is well past noon. Today she is back to her usual polished self, in a pale pink woollen dress, her blonde curls held high on her head with a fine pearl-studded comb. She lifts a teacup to her lips with delicate fingers.

Eva tries to flatten her windblown hair with her palm. As she slides into the chair opposite her sister, she glimpses the streak of ash on her skirts. How had she not noticed that on the way here? She tries ineffectually to scrub it away with her thumb.

A chaos of hammering spills down from upstairs, making the lamp above the table sway. The dining room, Eva realises, has been painted the colour of eggshells, the large fireplace blackened and polished. The piney scent of paint still hangs faintly on the air. It's one of the few improvements she has seen to the house since the restorations had begun. She nods towards the freshly painted walls. "The colour is nice."

Harriet smiles wryly. "Edwin thinks so too. I hoped he might have managed something a little more interesting."

Eva lets her comment slide. "I'm sorry I've not come more often." She raises her voice to be heard over the thumping. "It's just—"

"Oh I know," says Harriet airily. "Nathan's being an utter beast. I don't blame you." She lifts the lid of the teapot to inspect its contents. "I'll have Mrs Brodie fetch you a cup."

"No, it's all right. Perhaps a walk instead?"

Harriet laughs. "You wish to leave before Nathan catches you here?" She nibbles at her toast, then places her half-eaten slice back on the plate. "Very well. This racket is driving me mad anyway."

Wrapped in cloaks against the bracing autumn air, they follow the winding coast towards the village. Wind bends the grass of the dunes, catching the wings of a flock of pintails and carrying them back into the sky. Eva finds herself glancing sideways at her sister, trying to see behind her eyes. She can see no hint of the despair she saw in Harriet the day she had fled to Longstone. But she knows better than to believe it is not there. Knows Harriet is adept at quashing the chaos down under a pristine and polished surface.

She wants to ask her outright how she is faring. If she is happy. If life on Lindisfarne has become bearable. Uncomfortably, Eva realises she knows the answers to these questions. And she has no thought of how to make them otherwise.

"Are you painting?" she asks instead.

Harriet doesn't look at her. "Why would I not be painting?"

Eva debates whether to mention the ruined canvas. Decides against it. Instead, she asks, "What are you working on?"

Harriet is silent for a moment and Eva wonders what she is thinking. "I'm in between pieces," she says finally. "Waiting for inspiration to strike, I suppose."

"I'm sure it will come if you give it time." Eva wonders if Nathan has said anything to Harriet about her betrothal to Finn. Harriet has always been lost in her own existence, but Eva is still surprised they have made it through a scrap of toast, a cup of tea, and a mile of walking without her sister mentioning such life-changing news.

As Eva opens her mouth to speak, Harriet says, "I hear you shan't be skulking back to Highfield House with your tail between your legs."

Eva smiles to herself. She knows this is as close to a word of congratulations as she is ever likely to get from her sister. "No," she says. "I shan't."

Harriet watches her feet for several paces. She gathers her skirts in her fist and tiptoes around a mud puddle. "I was glad you went, you know."

Eva looks up at her. "You were?"

"Yes. Well. Not for me. I would have much preferred to have you around." Her voice is suddenly thin. "But for your sake, I'm glad you went."

Eva gives her a short smile. "I'm glad I went too. Rather, I'm glad I found the courage to go."

Harriet hums, yanking at her cloak as it entangles itself on a withered hunk of gorse. "Are you certain about it though?" she asks, keeping her eyes down. "Living that way for the rest of your days? It's not... well, it is hardly the kind of life you are accustomed to, is it."

Eva feels a flicker of irritation. "I am not sure the life I am accustomed to has ever made me happy."

"Still. Are you going to be any happier condemning yourself to a penniless life on an island the size of a rock?" Eva glares, but her icy look seems to barely penetrate Harriet's cool exterior. "And I'm sorry, Evie, but I know for a fact that you would rather die than wash your own bedclothes. And I also know you can barely cook a piece of toast. Are you really going to—"

"I can see what you are trying to do, Harriet," Eva snaps. "And you shan't talk me out of it. I have made my decision and I could not be happier about it. If Finn and I are to spend our lives penniless and eating burnt toast, then so be it."

"I am not trying to talk you out of anything. I already told you I was glad you went." Harriet shrugs. "I thought they were quite reasonable questions."

Eva grabs her arm to silence her as they step into the

village. People are gathering around the hill at the bottom of the castle, eyes on the ramparts, chatter in the air. A pistol shot sounds from within the castle grounds.

Eva feels suddenly hot. The panic that has been at her edges since finding the *Eagle* threatens to rise. But this is not Henry Ward's doing, at least as far as she can tell. She hurries towards the water, trying to get a glimpse of the castle. A steady stream of onlookers is filtering in from the village. Two dragoons burst through the castle gates, a woman among them she guesses is one of their wives. Another pistol shot echoes in the cold air.

Eva catches sight of Joseph Holland on the edge of the water. She knows him a friend of her brother's—and she also knows him to be one of the government spies who are using Highfield House. She elbows her way towards him, tugging Harriet along behind her. A woman tears past, thumping into her shoulder.

"What happened?" Eva asks Holland.

"Jacobites," he says, folding his arms across his thick chest. "Taken the castle." He keeps his voice low. "They're saying it was the master of that brig out in the bay. Errington. I reckon Forster sent him over from Bamburgh."

Eva nods. She knows much of the village of Bamburgh, just across the water, is owned by Thomas Forster, a Jacobite commander.

"The guard's saying he let the fellow in to see the barber and Errington pulled his pistol," Holland tells her. "Seems he and his mate have taken charge of the place." He nods in the direction of the two soldiers who are hurrying towards the water. "Threw the redcoats out."

Eva looks up at the ramparts. "There were only two

soldiers in the castle?"

"Aye. Looks like the rest of the garrison was off duty."

"Why?" she demands. "With all that's happening in Newcastle, how could they not have been expecting an attack?"

Holland smiles wryly, but doesn't respond. Eva glances out across the water, half expecting to see the anchorage filling with ships carrying Jacobite reinforcements. But beyond the large brig she had seen on their arrival— Errington's vessel, she realises now—there is little in the water beyond fishing boats and Finn's small skiff.

She feels distinctly uneasy. And painfully aware of the Jacobite criminals hidden away in her cottage. She finds herself glancing around the thickening crowd in search of Finn, needing the reassurance of his presence. She sees no sign of him.

"We ought to go back to the house," she tells Harriet.

"Don't be mad. This is the most excitement the place has seen in weeks." There's a shine in Harriet's eyes, a crooked half-smile on her lips. She lets out a private laugh. "I thought you were the adventurous type now."

"There's a difference between adventurousness and foolishness."

"Honestly, Evie, you do have a way of making everything so dismal. What are you afraid is going to happen? Some bloodthirsty Scotsman is going to come tearing out of the castle and throw you over his shoulder?" She laughs to herself. "That would be a thing to witness."

Eva grits her teeth. Turns away before she's tempted to wish such a fate upon her sister.

Harriet sees him on the edge of the crowd; a man who should not be here.

He is the brother of Julia Mitchell, and a known Jacobite with the shooting of a soldier to his name. Harriet had assumed he and his brother were hiding away on Longstone, in an attempt to keep their necks unbroken.

His head is down and a large cocked hat is pulled low over his face, but she has no difficulty recognising him, with a flame-coloured queue hanging down his neck, and coppery bristles covering his cheeks and chin. Little wonder Julia had shipped her brothers out to Longstone to hide them from the authorities. The Mitchells have about as much hope of blending into a crowd as a man with two heads.

Julia's brother makes his way through the throng, heading towards the water, as though trying to find a better vantage point. Curious, Harriet finds herself following him. She fancies seeing the look on Julia's face when she tells her her criminal of a brother is strolling about Lindisfarne in sight of the castle guards. Harriet has always had a desire to stir things up. Life is far more interesting that way.

As though feeling Harriet's eyes on him, he turns. His eyes catch hers. It's a knowing look, somehow. Does he remember her from the night he was dragged out of Highfield House by her husband? Perhaps. Either way, that look tells her he knows he has been recognised. It is a powerful feeling. Because Harriet knows he will not soon forget her.

"Where did you go?" Eva demands when she returns.

"Nowhere." She could tell her, of course, that one of her Longstone hideaways is strolling around the village, just to see lose her mind. But Harriet is more interested in the man who is standing at her sister's side now, a protective hand to the back of her neck. He's tall, broad shouldered, towers over Eva. And though there is a gaping disparity between his colourless sailor's slops and her neat wool skirts, there's a strange compatibility to them that takes Harriet by surprise. Eva's fingers brush lightly against his, the motion seeming so instinctive she is almost unaware of it. She takes a step closer to him, as though steadied by his presence. There's a practised ease between Eva and her lightkeeper, Harriet realises, as though they have already lived their entire lives together. The sight of them strikes her with a violent and unexpected stab of jealousy.

It's Harriet's own presence that flusters Eva, clearly ruffled at this colliding of the two disparate parts of her life. Pink cheeked, she garbles out introductions, accompanied by an over-enthusiastic wave of her hand.

Harriet looks Finn Murray up and down, inspecting him openly. In spite of his slops and tarred greatcoat, and apparent inability to use a razor, he is not quite as wild and unkempt as she had imagined. His beard is trimmed close to his chin, light brown hair pulled back neatly, a faded blue neck cloth tied at his throat. There's a half-smile on his face, as though he is well aware of the examination she is subjecting him to. "A pleasure to meet you, Mr Murray," Harriet says smoothly. "You've come just in time. It seems Evie is rather concerned about wayward Scotsmen whisking her away to their lair."

The lightkeeper chuckles. "Is she just?" He catches Eva's eye and gives her a private smile.

"We'll see you back to the house, Harriet," she says

crisply. "You shouldn't be on your own. Not with all that's going on."

"I hardly think any Jacobite rebels will be blockading the path to Emmanuel Head," says Harriet with a dull laugh. But her mind is racing with thoughts of Julia's escaped brother, with the castle siege, with the man who is to be her sister's husband, and she realises suddenly that she does not wish to be alone with her own thoughts. A stolen glass of Edwin's whisky and a few hours in front of her notebook are what she needs to calm her jealousy; calm her desperate need to appear on Julia's doorstep and create drama for the sake of something to do. Julia is her only friend in this place, and Harriet does not want to lose her out of her own petty need to cause trouble. She closes her eyes, hit with a pang of self-loathing.

Perhaps when she returns home, she can funnel these unwelcome emotions into a piece of art that is actually worth looking at. Or at least more than a scribbled-out sketch. And so she capitulates to Eva's motherly objections and allows herself to be escorted back to Highfield House.

# CHAPTER SEVEN

Rain is thumping steadily against the windows of Harriet's workroom. She has given up on trying to paint, and is standing with her forehead to the pane, watching trails of water carve their crooked path down the glass. Beyond the window, the sea slaps hard against the embankment.

It's during the high tide that escape feels the most unobtainable. It's a foolish notion, Harriet knows, because she is just as trapped here whether the tide is high or low. But somehow, when the steppingstones of the Pilgrims' Way vanish beneath the water, cutting Holy Island off from the mainland, it heightens her sense of hopelessness. As though her paintings—and her dreams—will sooner be washed away than make it to a salon in Paris.

She takes her cloak from the back of her chair and slides it on over her shoulders. Never mind the rain. Yesterday, Edwin had forbidden her from leaving the house, convinced more Jacobites were about to land on Lindisfarne with guns ablaze. Now word has come that the redcoats have taken back the castle, he has unbolted the doors. And Harriet is not about to be constrained by a little filthy weather. She pulls up the hood of her cloak and slips out the front door before anyone can stop her. Cold air blasts away her sluggishness.

Wind is howling across the island, gathering the rain into a squall and tossing the high tide up over the beach. Harriet presses a hand to her hood, trying ineffectually to hold it in place. After a moment, she gives up. Allows herself to enjoy the feel of the wind making chaos of her hair. Sea spray mixes with rain on her cheeks.

She looks about her as she walks; at the hazy pall of the sea, the blown yellow tussocks of grass that cover the dunes. She tries to commit this silvery, windswept landscape to memory. It's the natural world she wants to paint; wants to capture the infuriating beauty of this island, her prison. But everything she has sketched or imagined so far feels so derivative and commonplace. Meagre attempts at matching Lorrain's perfection of nature. Godly images that feel hollow and inauthentic. Even the seascape she had gifted to Isabelle, the piece that had captured the attention of her friend's wealthy French sponsors, is full of other people's ideas.

How proud Harriet had been when she had first seen her piece hanging in Isabelle's studio. She had told herself she was special; that it meant she held pride of place in Isabelle's heart. Perilous thoughts. She chases them away before they lead her into dangerous places.

Harriet's skirts are soaked by the time she reaches the curiosity shop, her waterlogged cloak heavy on her shoulders. Half the island is caked to her shoes.

Julia is unlocking the front door as she approaches. "What are you doing out in this weather, you madwoman?" She holds the door open with one arm.

Harriet stands in the doorway and steps out of her muddy shoes. Rain drips from her hair and trickles down the back of her neck.

"I'm surprised your keepers let you visit me after your little effort last week," says Julia. Her ginger cat peeks past Harriet, contemplating a dash out into the rain. Julia scoops it under her arm.

Harriet smiles crookedly. "I'm sorry. You know I can't hold my liquor."

"I do now, aye."

She's a little embarrassed, yes. Knows working her way through Julia's whisky and turning up back at the house without her key had not been her finest moment. But Harriet has seen her husband and brother in their cups on far more than one occasion. And she is fairly certain it has never caused the sky to fall in.

"May I stay?" she asks with a coy smile.

"What do you think, Minerva?" Julia says to the cat. "Shall we give her another chance?" The cat squirms out of her arms and stalks off across the shop with its tail in the air. Julia snorts. "Hideous thing." She looks back at Harriet. "Stay. But you're only having tea this time." She pulls her pocketbook out of her apron and empties the coins onto the counter.

Harriet slings off her sodden cloak and hangs it over a chair that's sitting in the corner of the shop, pushed up against an overflowing bookshelf. She stands in front of the newly lit fire. Holds her hands close to the flames for a moment, then pulls the pins out of her windblown hair and sets them on the mantel. She rakes her fingers through the wet tangles. "I think Nathan was a little pleased to see you the other evening."

Julia doesn't look up from the coins she is counting. "I'm sure. He looked simply overjoyed at my turning up on your doorstep."

Harriet ignores her sarcasm. She wrangles her thick blonde curls into a fresh plait. "You ought to come for a visit."

"Why, exactly? To anger your brother again? I don't think so."

"Don't let his foul mood bother you," Harriet says, pinning up her hair. "He's just bent out of shape because Evie's gone flitting off with the lightkeeper instead of marrying the fop he picked out for her."

Julia snorts. "I think there's a little more to his anger at me than that. It's slightly more than a *foul mood*, wouldn't you say?"

Harriet turns towards a loud creak coming from the cellar. She plants her hands on her hips in mock outrage. "Julia Mitchell. Do you have a gentleman visitor down there?"

Julia smiles wryly. "I think my creaky old shop has your imagination running. Nothing more scandalous than that."

"I thought perhaps that was why you did not wish to visit Nathan," Harriet teases. "Because your interests had turned elsewhere."

"Ha. I wish it were that—" Julia slams down the coins and rushes towards the door. She throws it open and reaches out to grab the arm of the man who is approaching. It's Julia's brother, Harriet realises with a jolt. The man she had seen skulking through the crowd the day of the castle siege. She is almost glad he is here. The temptation to tell Julia she had seen him would have been too great for her to resist. Besides, this way she will get to see the ensuing confrontation. Because while Harriet is pleased the man is here, she can tell Julia is anything but.

She yanks her brother into the shop and locks the door behind them. "What in hell are you doing?" she hisses, ushering him away from the window. "You know you can't be here! What if someone sees you?"

"Calm yourself," her brother says coolly. He takes off his cocked black hat and shakes the water from it. "This weather's far too hideous for anyone to be out. No one saw me."

"People have windows," Julia snaps.

Her brother glides past her comment. "I've just come to make sure you and Bobby are safe."

Julia folds her arms. "We were safe until my criminal of a brother decided to grace us with his presence."

His eyes shift to Harriet, catching the amused half-smile on her lips. "I recognise you."

"I should think so," she says. "Given I saw you being led out of my house in disgrace."

"Ah yes. You're one of them. The Blakes." Harriet had expected him to look ashamed, but he studies her with something close to fascination. He turns to his sister. "Didn't know you were friends with their kind, Jul."

Julia narrows her eyes in response.

"How about a drink then?" he asks.

Julia hesitates for a moment, and Harriet can tell she is debating whether to throw her brother straight back out into the rain. "Upstairs," she says finally.

Harriet is not sure whether the invitation is extended to her as well, but she has no intention of leaving. This is the most interesting thing to have happened here in weeks. Far more interesting than the siege of the castle that had barely lasted long enough for those two useless Jacobites to get through the door. She follows Julia and her brother up the creaking wooden staircase, leaving damp footprints in her wake.

Julia's tiny living quarters are marginally neater than the shop, with two narrow beds shoved up against a wall, the table at the other end of the space still filled with teacups and half-eaten bowls of porridge. The air is thick and warm with woodsmoke.

Julia's brother sinks into a chair at the table, long legs splayed. "Where's Bobby?" he asks, taking the spoon from one of the porridge bowls and scooping up the cold leftovers.

"He's at the dame school," Julia snaps. "Thank God." She throws a log on the simmering fire and pokes it back to life. "I've spent long enough explaining why you're hiding away. I don't fancy telling him why you've decided to behave like such a fool." She bends down for the kettle and hangs it on the hook above the flames.

"How about something stronger?" says her brother.

"At ten in the morning?" Julia shrugs resignedly. "Do as you wish." She takes out two fresh teacups, spearing Harriet with a sharp look. "*You're* only having tea."

Harriet smiles in amusement. "Yes ma'am."

A loud knock sounds at the door of the shop. "Anyone there?" calls an irritated male voice. "You open or not?"

Julia huffs, clearly flustered. She tosses a cloth at Harriet. "Make the tea," she orders. "And don't touch any more of my damn whisky." She charges down into the shop, the tinkle of the bell above the door echoing up the staircase.

Her brother watches after her with the faintest of smiles on his face. He turns back to Harriet. "Highfield House. It's not where I recognise you from. I saw you here on Lindisfarne the day of the siege."

Harriet spoons tea into the pot. "Which one are you?"

He chuckles. "I'm Michael."

"Shouldn't you be hiding away on Longstone with my sister?"

"I should, aye."

"But?"

"But there are pressing matters here on Lindisfarne."

She snorts. "The siege at the castle? Sounds like it all came to nothing."

"Aye." Something dark falls over Michael's eyes. "Should never have happened like that. Communication between the English Jacobites... it's not what it ought to be. Errington clearly expected reinforcements. But not a single soul came to support him, even with Forster just across the water. Now the poor bastard's locked up in Berwick."

*Listen*, thinks Harriet. *Observe. Gather the pieces.* "Is that why you were on Holy Island the day of the siege?" she asks. "Because you thought support was coming too? And you wished to join them?"

He hesitates, as though debating whether to trust her. Then he seems to remember that she already knows exactly who he is and what he has done, and that there is little point being so slippery. "I saw Errington's brig approaching from Longstone," he says. "Could hardly sit back and not find out what was happening, could I?"

"Seems like that's exactly what you ought to have done."

"And am I to hide away on Longstone and not do my part

to help the Rising succeed?"

Harriet puts a hand to her hip, taking him in. He's a flat-faced bear of a man, with wide shoulders and cheeks sprayed with freckles. The same shrewd green eyes as his sister. He's a fool, certainly, to be strolling about here where anyone could see him. But there is something almost admirable about his passion. It's a cause she cares little about—at least beyond the information she can gather for her own hazy purposes—but she likes his determination to succeed in the face of the odds stacked against him. In a strange way, he reminds her of herself. Or at least the person she wants to be.

"Sounds to me like you've already done plenty," she says. "Is that not why you're hiding away on Longstone in the first place?"

Michael doesn't answer, and Harriet wonders if the stories about him shooting a dragoon are true. He reaches down to pet Julia's cat, but it stalks away from his reach and leaps up onto one of the beds. Turns in a circle before settling down among the blankets.

Rain patters softly against the narrow window. Harriet thinks of the fragments that had spilled out from the spies' meeting the night she had stood with her ear pressed to the parlour door. "If you want to do your part, you're in the wrong place," she tells Michael. "The Jacobites are mustering on Lesbury Common." Somewhere at the back of her mind, she knows she ought not have let this information out. Of course, he will demand to know where she heard such things. But inexplicably, the passion with which he speaks makes her want to help him. And the look of faint surprise on his face makes it worth it. It's a look beyond Edwin's condescension, beyond the thinly veiled pity she had seen in Eva's eyes when

53

they had last met. A look that suggests she has something of value to impart. When, Harriet wonders, did anyone last look at her like that? Certainly not since she had left London and her artists' circle.

"Lesbury Common," Michael repeats. "And how exactly do you know that?"

"I hear things. Just like everyone else does." She doesn't look at him as she takes the boiling kettle from the hook and fills the teapot.

Michael chuckles. "I see." He goes to the cupboard and pours himself a cannikin of whisky. Holds the bottle up to Harriet in offering.

"I'm under strict instructions to only have tea."

"So I hear. But you don't strike me as a woman who takes orders."

Harriet smiles to herself. She wants to be that woman, of course. That woman who doesn't take orders, she has her paintings hung in French salons and does not bend to the will of her husband. But that woman feels impossibly far away. "Well," she says, "in any case, it's a little early for me."

"Is it?" Michael empties his cup in one mouthful and refills it. "Your sister and her dearly beloved have Angus and me keeping the light at all hours. Hardly know if I'm coming or going. Or what the hell time it is."

"Seems a fair trade," says Harriet. "Given they're risking their own backsides by hiding you from the redcoats."

Michael peers at her over the top of his cup. "How do you know where the Jacobites are mustering?" There's a faint look of suspicion in his eyes, and Harriet begins to regret her comment. "Is it because your family is spying for the government like everyone says?"

She snorts. "Don't be foolish. If we were, do you really think I would tell you what I know? More to the point, do you really think a woman would be privy to that information?"

Michael shrugs. "Plenty of the Jacobite spies and informants are women. Why should the government side be any different?"

Harriet lets out a laugh that sounds faintly hysterical. "I told you, I just hear things. I listen. It's a valuable skill—one you ought to try sometime." Michael chuckles, but Harriet is saved by Julia's footsteps striding back up the stairs.

"Just sold that dress sword for a small fortune," she tells them. "Told the fool it once belonged to the Earl of Carlisle. He's decided it will make a fine wedding gift for his son."

Michael empties his cannikin. "I'm glad to see your morals as a businesswoman have not gone begging."

Julia takes the teacup Harriet has filled for her and sinks into a chair opposite her brother. "Why are you here?" she asks him.

"I told you, I came to see that you and Bobby are safe."

She shakes her head. "Don't lie to me, Michael. Tell me what you're up to. Are there Jacobites meeting on Lindisfarne? Or have you come from another meeting in Bamburgh?"

Michael turns his empty cannikin around between his fingers. Harriet can tell he is reluctant to speak—but is it because he doesn't trust her? Or because he wishes to keep his plans from his sister?

He nods towards Harriet. "You ought to watch yourself around this one, Jul. Don't you know there's talk of her lot spying for Geordie?" There's a teasing tone to his voice, but

Harriet knows not to take his words lightly. Her heart begins to quicken. She knows she should not have mentioned Lesbury. Knows that in her own need for validation, she has added fuel to the rumours about her family. If only she were as good at thinking as she is at listening.

"And don't you know better than to believe gossip, Michael?" Julia gives Harriet apologetic eyes. "Do you really think if Harriet's family were spies, they'd be mad enough to set themselves up on the biggest house on the island?" She gets to her feet and begins to gather up the breakfast dishes. Tosses them into the trough beside the hearth. "Besides, I've better judgement than that." Harriet can tell she is on edge. "I'd not be friends with her if I thought there was an inch of truth to the rumours."

"You know he can't truly believe them, Julia," says Harriet, peering sidelong at Michael. "If he did, he would not be hiding out on Longstone in my sister's company."

"Well. Perhaps that was not my wisest of choices." Michael gives Harriet a look that seems almost conspiratorial. And perhaps he had not previously believed the rumours about the Blakes. But perhaps her comments have given him pause. Made him wonder if there is truth to what everyone says about her family.

Harriet prays he does not tell Julia of her comment about Lesbury Common. Her family are not spies, of course. But that would be a difficult thing to explain if Julia was to ask questions. The Mitchells can never know what Highfield House is being used for. Even if she could trust them not to reveal such a thing to the rest of the village, it would put an end to Harriet's friendship with Julia. Would remove the last threads of trust between the two families.

"That's enough, Michael," Julia snaps. "Not only do you put me and Bobby in danger by showing up at our door, you also have the nerve to make accusations against my friend?" She plants a hand on her hip and glares at him. "It's time for you to leave."

Harriet expects a retaliation, but Michael just stands and kisses his sister's cheek. "Take care, Jul. Tell Bobby I'm thinking of him." He glances back at Harriet, then seems to decide against speaking. He is down the stairs and out the door without another word.

# CHAPTER EIGHT

Eva opens her eyes to flickering darkness. The light of the firebasket seeps through the gap in the shutters, casting a dim gold thread across the bedroom. She feels restless. Achy with the sleeplessness that has plagued her since she spotted Henry Ward's ship beyond Highfield House. She can tell she has not been asleep for long. Guesses it close to midnight. A few hours before she and Finn will take the watch from the Mitchells.

They had returned from Holy Island two days ago to find Michael back in the cottage, refusing to speak of where he had been. Finn had dished out a warning for him to stay hidden or leave; Eva doubts it will have little effect. But now the redcoats have reclaimed Lindisfarne Castle, and put a stop to the attack on Newcastle, her concerns over harbouring the two Jacobites have lessened. Or rather, they have been overtaken by her ever-present fear of Henry Ward.

She slips out of the blankets and navigates around the edges of the crowded room. With the Mitchells here, they have moved Finn's bed from the living area into the bedroom, beside the creaking old mattress he had slept on as a child. He is snoring lightly in the old sagging bed, and Eva is careful not to wake him as she passes.

She peeks through the gap in the shutters, needing a glimpse at the sea. She sees little but the blaze of the basket and the deep darkness beyond, and the absence of ships' lights goes some way to steadying her unease.

It's the anticipation, she thinks, that is hardest to carry. The knowledge that Ward had deliberately let them escape his ship so they might suffer through this almost unbearable uncertainty. He had wanted them to worry, to live each moment with one eye on the sea—and he has succeeded.

There is a part of her that wants to see Henry Ward again. Wants answers to the questions he had planted in her mind the night she had been aboard his ship. How had he known her mother? Why has he come back to Northumberland now? And what part—if any—had he played in her family fleeing Lindisfarne?

Nathan had claimed Abigail had taken them from the island out of grief over Oliver's death. But Eva is certain there are pieces she is missing. They had left Holy Island on foot in the middle of the night, taking nothing but the clothes on their backs. Abigail was logical, clear-headed; not the kind of woman to tear her children from their beds and race into the rising tide of the Pilgrims' Way without the most pressing of reasons.

Then again, the mother Eva knew would never have invited a man like Henry Ward into her home, so perhaps the woman she remembers is only a fragment of who Abigail Blake really was.

She creeps back across the room. Muffled voices come from the other side of the door.

"...to fight," she hears. Her curiosity piqued, she tiptoes towards the door and presses her ear against it. "I've heard word," she hears Michael say, "that the Jacobite army is gathering on Lesbury Common."

"Word from who?" Angus sounds doubtful.

"It doesn't matter. But I trust it's more than a rumour." A chair squeaks noisily. "We can make it to Lesbury in a day."

"Don't be mad," says Angus. "If we're caught, we'll swing."

"Once we re-join the army, we'll be protected. A day's ride," Michael is saying. "If that."

"That's a day too long," Angus snaps. "We know the redcoats are active up in these parts. I've not spent this long hiding just to do something foolish like this."

"You're a bloody coward. Hiding away when the cause needs you." There is silence, then the groaning of floorboards, a pacing back and forth. "We can't just sit back and do nothing," Michael snaps. "Look what happened on Lindisfarne. A prime opportunity lost."

Angus scoffs. "All the more reason to stay away from the rebel army. The English Jacobites are a bloody shambles. I can tell that even from out here."

"Do you truly imagine the two of us are so desperately wanted by the redcoats that they'll recognise and hunt us down the minute we set foot on the mainland?"

"It's not a risk I'm willing to take."

The pacing stops, punctuated by the crack of a log breaking in the grate. "I've heard other rumours," Michael says after a moment.

"About what?"

His voice drops, and Eva can barely make out his words. "We can't stay here. I don't know if we can trust her. This talk about her family… Maybe we were too quick to dismiss it."

Something tightens in Eva's stomach.

"We've been here weeks, man," Angus hisses. "Do you not think if she planned to turn us in, she might have done so already?" He laughs humourlessly. "I'm sure the two of them can't wait to be rid of us."

"What if she's already sent word to the authorities?" Michael's voice is an angry hiss. "What if it's just a matter of time before dragoons turn up on the doorstep?"

Angus snorts. "You're far too distrusting. Besides, Julia would never have brought us out here if she thought it would put us in danger."

"I don't think Julia knows as much as she thinks she does. Or else she's damn good at pretending otherwise."

"You're mad," Angus says again. "If you want to risk your life by re-joining the rebels, I can't stop you. But don't expect me to join you."

The men fall silent, and Eva tiptoes back towards the bed. Just what, she wonders, has Michael Mitchell heard? Rumours of her family spying for the government have been circulating since they returned to Holy Island almost four months ago. Surely Michael has heard them before now, given how often he is away from Longstone. There must be something else that has sparked his suspicions. Has someone discovered Highfield House is being used by government spies? Eva wishes she had managed to get a little more out of Nathan the last time they had spoken.

The smaller bed creaks.

"Evie," says Finn, leaning up on his elbow. "Is something the matter?"

She lets out a breath she hadn't realised she was holding, and slips into bed beside him.

"Careful now," he says lightly, "you know I'm not to be trusted."

Eva smiles into the darkness. "Yes you are."

He chuckles. "Well. You've been warned. If you don't make it to your wedding day with your good name intact, I can't be held responsible."

Eva laughs softly, sinking into the warmth of his body. "Two minutes," she says. "I'll just stay for two minutes." With his arm wrapped around her and his breath in her hair, she feels her heartbeat slow. Feels a little of the tension drain from her shoulders. "Michael has decided he doesn't trust me," she murmurs. "He seems convinced my family are spies, and that I'm planning to turn him in at any moment."

"Is that so?" Finn chuckles against her shoulder. He pushes aside her hair and kisses the back of her neck. "Hopefully that will inspire him to get the hell out of our house."

# CHAPTER NINE

Watching her sister marry the lightkeeper makes Harriet feel as though she's drowning. Perhaps it's the close, fragrant church air; a smell of old, cold stone and earth. Perhaps the cloying presence of her own husband, his long legs stretched out in front of him as though to prevent her from escaping. Perhaps Nathan's surliness that is souring the air.

Harriet is surprised he had not changed his mind about attending. She had assumed his pride and anger would get the better of him. After all the effort he had put into securing Matthew Walton as Eva's husband, it must be a real slap in the face to see her marrying a man who has decided to attend his own wedding wearing a mud-coloured coat with mismatching buttons.

For a while, it had been refreshing to see some true emotion beneath Nathan's forced congeniality. But his saltiness is beginning to grow thin.

Eva looks impossibly happy. Standing at the altar with her lightkeeper and his chaotic buttons has made her blissfully ignorant to the look of displeasure on Nathan's face.

Harriet could not for a second have imagined Eva agreeing to a life like this; a man like this. During her long engagement to Matthew Walton, she had planned out every inch of her wedding ceremony: her lace-trimmed sack gown, the bride's pie and wedding cake, the flowers the attendants would wear in their hair. And here she is wearing nothing more elaborate than her blue woollen day dress and a ribbon at her throat, speaking her vows in a near-empty church, with the German Ocean thrashing beyond salt-speckled windows.

Harriet supposes stranger things have happened. Although she can't think of many.

She's happy for her sister. Of course she is; of course she is. But she can't shake the disappointment that Eva won't be there around the dinner table to save her when Nathan, Edwin and Matthew Walton launch into their next tobacco-fuelled diatribe. Then again, Harriet is fairly certain that Eva's marriage to this man the sea washed up has put an end to Walton joining Nathan and Edwin around the dinner table at all.

But the thing is done. Eva has pledged to honour, serve and obey, and live a life lit by the Longstone light.

Harriet feels hollow. Cold. She is glad when Theodora leaps to her feet and accosts the newlyweds, giving her space to sneak out into the churchyard. Heartfelt congratulations feel a little difficult to conjure up right now.

She finds herself wandering between the crooked teeth of the graves behind the church, desperate for a distraction. Her father lies somewhere in these grounds; the churchyard closest to where he had grown up. She walks the rows of weather-worn headstones, taking in the names; one tragic story of loss after another. Her father was in the earth before she was born, and he feels suitably distant and unknown. Throughout her life, Harriet has made her own image of him, cobbled together from the stories told to her by Nathan, by their mother. She wonders if there is any accuracy to the image of him she has in her head.

She finds him in the far corner of the churchyard, behind a veil of long grass.

Samuel Blake, beloved husband and father, departed this life December 8th, 1694.

Harriet's chest clenches like a fist. She feels suddenly breathless. Unmoored, like the earth is falling out from under her.

"Harriet?" Edwin's voice seems to pull her from the edge of a chasm. He is standing outside the church, an expectant look on his face. "Are you not going to come inside and congratulate your sister?"

The earth feels unsteady as she crosses the damp grass back to the church. She feels oddly outside herself as she pulls Eva into an embrace, kissing one cheek, then the other. Holding out a polite hand for her new brother-in-law. She hears herself murmur well-wishes in a voice that does not sound like her own.

"Are you all right, Harriet?" asks Eva, frowning.

"Yes, of course." She forces a smile. Wraps a hand around the top of the pew to steady herself.

She is barely watching as Eva and Finn make their goodbyes and head into the village. Barely listening as Edwin urges them towards the wagon, in order to make the low tide.

"Nathan," she says. "Come with me."

Her brother frowns in question, but follows her into the

churchyard.

"The tide…" says Edwin again.

Harriet ignores him. She stares back down at Samuel Blake's headstone, eyes on the carved words as though she might somehow find a way to alter them.

Nathan bends down, yanking out the long tussocks of grass that obscure the grave.

"Did you know?" Harriet asks him.

"Know what? That Father was buried here? Yes, of course. I—"

"The date," she snaps. "Look at the date."

Nathan turns back to the headstone, his inhalation audible as the realisation swings at him. "It's a mistake, surely."

"How could it be a mistake? Mother would never have let that happen." But in that instant, Harriet realises she knows nothing of what her mother would have allowed. Her mother had spent Harriet's entire life peddling lies.

Because Samuel Blake, beloved husband and father, was lying in the earth a year and half before she was born.

# CHAPTER TEN

"There are church records, perhaps," Nathan is saying as the wagon sighs across the sand back towards Holy Island. Sea licks and sloshes at the wheels, making Edwin tut with impatience. "They may be able to confirm Father's date of death."

Harriet is barely listening. She feels completely unravelled, like she has no idea of who she is. But has she ever? She has never wanted to look too deeply at her own inner workings, for fear of what she might uncover. And now, with this knowledge—or rather, lack thereof—she feels even more afraid to examine who she truly is.

"Nathan is right," says Edwin, his eyes drawn away from the water as the coach rattles onto the island. "This could be an error..."

Harriet smiles wryly. Shakes her head. She knows deep within herself that this is no error. As bewildering as this realisation is, there is also a sense of things falling into place.

Because she has always felt as though she was on the

fringe of this family. Though, as children, Eva and Nathan had both doted on her, she has never felt truly able to connect with them. She and Eva are so strikingly different that their conversations rarely do more than scratch the surface. When she had seen her sister the day of the siege, it had not even crossed Harriet's mind to tell her about the Paris salon. And she is fairly certain Nathan has never seen her as anything more than a bothersome child, to be married off as briskly as possible, and turned into someone else's problem.

"It's no error," she says finally. She feels it with a certainty that reaches her bones. She looks out the window at the spiralling mound of Lindisfarne Castle, her eyes blurring over at the too-familiar sight. "Do not bother hunting down the records, Nathan. They will tell you the same thing."

They sit in silence for the rest of the journey. And when the hired wagon deposits them outside Highfield House, Harriet is quick to make her way inside and down towards her workroom.

She hears footsteps behind her and silently wills Edwin to leave. She cannot find room to entertain him right now. She knows she will say something she will regret. And she also knows she will not regret it much.

She is surprised to hear Nathan call her name. She cannot remember the last time her brother had sought her out like this. She and Nathan have never had any great need for one another's company. She looks up at him, sure her surprise is showing in her eyes.

"I just..." He clears his throat. "I just wanted to say... None of this matters, Harriet." He shakes his head. Rubs the back of his neck. "I mean... Of course it matters. But it does not change who you are to us."

His words are so painfully awkward and genuine that they make Harriet's throat tighten. Tears gather behind her eyes, catching her by surprise. She cannot remember the last time she cried. She blinks them away hurriedly, unwilling to let her brother see them.

Nathan is right; this does not change who she is because she has always felt like an outsider. But she appreciates this from her brother. Half-brother. The reality of it stings. She flashes him a short smile. A faint nod. And then she disappears into the sanctuary of her workroom to prevent her tears from spilling.

Nathan knows he ought to have realised this earlier. Ought to have been old enough to recognise the canyon of months between his father's death and his sister's birth.

He remembers his father's death vividly. Remembers him taking to his bed with a sudden illness; remembers his mother's fear that the smallpox would spread through the household. He remembers the burning clothes and the heady smell of smoking herbs billowing at every window. And he remembers watching that lonely coffin being lowered into the ground behind St Aiden's, in the town where Samuel had grown up. More than anything, he remembers the painful hollow that had taken root inside him when he had seen the empty chair at the head of the table. He had assumed it had all happened not long before Oliver's death. Not long before they had made their hurried escape from Holy Island.

Harriet was born mere months after they arrived in London. Nathan has clear memories of her as an infant. Of building a new life in the capital with his mother and sisters. But youth had made his memories run into each other. Made time distort. The lie his mother had told the world, of Harriet being Samuel Blake's daughter, was one he had never stopped to question.

He sinks into the chair in his study. Stares out the window and lets his eyes lose focus as they take in the ink-dark sea. He pulls off his wig and tosses it on the desk beside the pounce pot. Unties his hair and rakes his fingers through it. It feels limp and oily beneath his touch.

He had woken up dreading the day, fearing he might poison Eva's wedding with this anger he is unable to shake. Nowhere in his wildest of thoughts had he imagined it might turn out like this.

But with the knowledge that Harriet's father is not his own, it feels strangely obvious. He feels foolish for having overlooked such a thing for the past two decades.

A knock at the door startles him.

"Who is it?"

"You've a visitor, Mr Blake," says Mrs Brodie from the hallway. "Mr Holland is waiting for you downstairs."

Something tightens in Nathan's stomach. Joseph Holland comes to the house for one reason alone these days: to deliver messages that will be passed between the government spies. Nathan knows he can expect visits from men posing as workers over the next few days. They will collect the messages Holland has left behind, and Nathan will spend the rest of the week drowning in worry, terrified that someone from the village has caught wind of what is taking place at Highfield House.

He wonders if Mrs Brodie is beginning to get suspicious

of all these visitors. Beginning to recognise that these so-called workers never do so much as lift a hammer. He realises he has no idea where his housekeeper's alliances lie, and what she would do if she did have any suspicions. Perhaps she, like many Northumbrians, is hedging her bets; lending support to whichever side appears to be on top.

He wonders, for not the first time, if it is too dangerous to have outside help in the house. The thought is chased by the one that always follows it: that letting Mrs Brodie go would likely raise even more distrust among the villagers. And, perhaps more pressingly, that they would be utterly at sea without her, given his family can barely boil water with all their cooking skills combined.

Tying his hair off his shoulders but ignoring the wig, Nathan makes his way down to the parlour.

Holland is still dressed in an enormous tarred greatcoat, a knitted cap pulled down low on his round head. His chin is covered in grey bristles, cheeks red with cold. A folded page is tucked into one of his meaty hands. At the sight of Nathan, he nods in greeting and hands over the missive. Nathan tucks it into the pocket of his waistcoat. The letter is sealed to prevent prying eyes, but even if it wasn't, he has never had an ounce of interest in what is inside the spies' intelligence. The Jacobite Rising is a calamity he wants to stay as far away from as possible.

Not that that has turned out so well for him thus far.

"You look exhausted, Blake," says Holland. "I hope all this business isn't getting to you. You know my men are as discreet as possible. The last thing I want is to put your family in danger."

"I know. And I appreciate it." Nathan chuckles dryly. "My

exhaustion's not your doing, Holland. It's just been... quite a day."

"Don't suppose there'd be a glass of that fine brandy of yours on offer?"

Nathan goes to the liquor cabinet. "That's the best idea I've heard in ages." He pulls out two glasses and fills them generously.

Holland shrugs off his greatcoat and tosses it over the back of the armchair, sending a mildly unpleasant smell of herrings into the air. He takes a glass with nod of thanks. Smiles at Nathan. "You know this good stuff is the only reason I seek out your company." He gulps down a mouthful. "Far better than the swill on offer among the fishing fleet."

Despite his tatty, unrefined appearance, Nathan knows Joseph Holland is not a man to be underestimated. When he had first arrived back on Lindisfarne, Nathan had foolishly assumed Holland to be a simple fisherman. But of course, he now knows him to be deeply entrenched in the anti-Jacobite cause, with contacts high up in the government.

Nathan sinks into an armchair and gestures for Holland to sit opposite. For a moment, the two men drink in silence, the fire popping steadily between them. Holland says, "I saw your sister in town with Julia Mitchell."

Nathan swallows another mouthful. "Yes."

"You know the Mitchells have Jacobite leanings," says Holland. "Julia's father fought at Dunkeld. And word is her brothers went to fight for the Duke of Ormonde."

Nathan keeps his gaze level. He knows all too well about the Mitchells' Jacobite leanings. He had heard it from Julia's own mouth, even before they had found her brothers hiding in the roof. To Holland, he says, "I've heard the rumours.

They are hardly newsworthy, are they? There are plenty of families in this part of the country with Jacobite sympathies."

Holland hums to himself, clearly irritated at Nathan's apparent apathy. "I don't want her anywhere near this house," he says. "It's too dangerous." From his tone of voice, Nathan can tell this is not merely a suggestion.

"Why?" he pushes. "What do you know of her?" He is suddenly afraid of the answer. He has heard countless stories about the terror Cotesworth and his men have inflicted on Jacobites in other parts of Northumbria: houses raided and people interrogated. Catholics, and anyone else suspected of Jacobite sympathies, thrown behind bars. He couldn't bear to see that happen to Julia and her son.

He peers at Holland, trying to see behind his eyes. Is he simply conscious of the Mitchells' Jacobite leanings, or does he suspect Julia's direct involvement in the cause?

"I'd keep Miss Mitchell away from your sister too, if I were you," says Holland, sidestepping Nathan's question. He stretches tree-trunk legs out in front of him. "You know she has quite the reputation." He chuckles. "Seems she's not too fussy about who she lets warm her bedclothes. It don't look so good for your sister to be seen in her company."

Nathan feels the back of his neck heat. It's part anger, he realises—both timeworn rage at Julia, and at Holland for speaking about her so freely, so crassly. And it's part something else entirely. Something far more primal, that catches him by surprise.

Since he was a child, he has struggled with physical contact, and his aversion to human touch means such visceral thoughts are few and far between. The only other woman he had ever desired like this had been his late wife, Sarah. There is something more than a little unwelcome about deceitful Julia triggering these same extraordinary feelings.

The chaos of thoughts roils up inside him and he gulps hurriedly at his brandy. Narrowly avoids a coughing fit. "Believe me," he tells Holland, "keeping Julia Mitchell away from this family is very much my intention."

# CHAPTER ELEVEN

"So tell me," says Finn, "was this fine establishment where you always dreamt of spending your wedding night?"

Eva laughs. "Since I was a girl." She shuffles her chair closer to the table so her thigh is pressed against his. He smells the sea on her. Feels the warmth of her body.

It's a sorry looking place as far as lodging houses go, with crooked tables and liquor on the air, though Finn has been in plenty worse. If he'd ever given any thought to the matter in the past, he would never have imagined bringing his bride to such a place, but the tiny village of Bamburgh has few better options. Nonetheless, there's a fire roaring in the grate in the corner of the dining room, and dishes of beef stew floating out from the kitchen that are making his mouth water.

This is a place he knows well. And a place he's sure Eva has not forgotten. He'd first kissed her in a room upstairs. Had made a mess of things then; let her go to protect his secrets. And he never plans on doing that again.

Two dishes of food land on the table in front of them. Eva

nods her thanks to the barmaid. Her eyes are shining in the glow of the candle in the centre of the table, wine and firelight colouring her cheeks pink. She looks happy, Finn thinks. Impossibly, fiercely happy. There's still a part of him that's afraid she might disappear. That he might wake alone in his cottage after a doze he had not meant to fall into, and find she was nothing but a liquor-fuelled dream.

Eva leans close, her lips to his ear so he can hear her over the raucous chatter in the dining room. It's busy tonight, with cloaked travellers and sailors in tarred greatcoats marching in and out of the door. Blasts of cold air make the flames in the grate dance. "In any case," she says, a shiver going through him at the feel of her breath on his skin, "I'm just glad not to be spending my wedding night elbow to elbow with Michael and Angus."

Finn chuckles as he picks up his spoon. "I don't think I'll be missing them too much either." He slides his free hand over her knee. Two months of having her in the cottage beside him and it's taken the restraint of a monk not to crawl into her bed. Getting through their supper with their bodies pressed against each other like this is a supreme exercise in self-control. But after all she has given up to become his wife, the least he can do is let her finish her food before he carts her off upstairs.

He knows she's relieved that her brother did not recognise him today. Finn is relieved too, a little, though he knows his worry is unfounded. Too much time has passed, surely, for Nathan Blake to have any inkling of who he is.

"What in hell are you doing here, Finn?" He looks up to see two of the farmhands he had been working with in Berwick last week. "Thought you only showed your face off

Longstone in the daylight," says Arthur, the older of the two men.

Finn chuckles. Gives them what he's sure is a ridiculously large grin. "Aye well. Special circumstances. This fine lass has just let me make her my wife."

Arthur belts a fat palm into the table, and Eva grabs at her cup of wine before it's upended in her lap. "Well then!" He bellows at the barmaid, "Another round over here, lass. Quick now." Arthur and his friend pull up stools and plonk themselves at the table. Finn wraps an arm around Eva's shoulder and mouths a silent apology. She smiles.

"I hope you know what you've got yourself into, lass," says Arthur. "They say he's a right troublemaker. Got no manners neither."

Eva sips her wine and gives Finn a smile over the top of her cup. "I shall consider myself warned."

Arthur looks up at the barmaid as she deposits four cannikins of whisky on the table.

"Tuppence." She holds her palm out flat towards him.

"No, no," he says, "no charge for these, all right, my love? Finn has just made this lovely lass his wife."

The barmaid snorts. Plants her free hand on her hip. She looks worn through with annoyance. "When you bring a bride in here, Arthur, you can have your drinks for free." She holds her outstretched hand under his nose. "Tuppence."

Arthur grumbles to himself and hunts around in his coat for his coin pouch.

Finn chuckles. "You're a right generous soul, Arthur."

"Don't mind her," Arthur tells him, nodding after the barmaid as she disappears with his coins in her fist. "She's just churned up cos of them ships in the bay. She reckons the rebels are going to storm the castle like they did on Lindisfarne. I told her she ought to expect such things in a Jacobite town like this."

The smile disappears from Eva's face. "What ships in the bay?"

Arthur shrugs as he tosses back his whisky. "Don't know who they belong to. Came in an hour or so ago. Probably here on Forster's bidding." He grins at her. "Or pirates, maybe."

Eva pushes back her chair. "Excuse me," she says. "I need a little air."

Finn catches up to her as she reaches the door. He takes her hand. "Ward has no idea we're here."

"You don't know that. He could have followed us." Eva steps out into the narrow lamplit street and hurries towards the bay, tugging him along beside her. The sea is sighing gently against the sand, lines of white water shimmering in the moonlight. Eva charges out onto the beach, squinting into the darkness. Several smaller boats, theirs among them, sit on the sand high above the waterline, the outline of two large brigs visible in the deeper ocean. Lamps glow atop their masts, casting silvery circles on the sea.

Finn joins Eva at the water's edge, pressing a hand to the small of her back. "Neither of those ships are Ward's," he says.

Eva scrubs a hand across her eyes. Nods. Finn watches her shoulders sink forward as she lets out a long breath in relief. "Your friend was probably right about them being Forster's ships." She looks up at him, her face shadowed in the moonlight. "I'm sorry. I did not mean to run off like a madwoman. I just... I worry for you. I worry about whatever it is he is planning."

Finn wraps his arms around her waist and pulls her close. "I think we're both entitled to a little madness." He tucks a strand of hair behind her ear and grins. "Besides, any excuse to get rid of Arthur."

It is late, thick dark, when he wakes. He sees her at the window, peeking through the curtains, the shape of her lit only by moonlight. She has her cloak tugged around her body, her dark hair hanging loose and tangled down her back. He's struck almost breathless by love for her, fresh need for her. Most of all, by a longing to protect her from Henry Ward, and the threat he has come to represent.

"Eva," he says. She turns. "Don't. Not tonight. Please."

For a brief moment, she hesitates, then makes her way back towards the bed. She lets her cloak fall to the floor and climbs beneath the blanket. Shuffles in so her body is pressed to his. Skin to skin, his lips find hers, and he pulls her close.

"It's all right," says Finn, breaking the kiss and finding her eyes in the darkness. "Everything will be all right. You know that, aye?"

Eva nods, entangling her legs with his, as though attempting to tether him to her. "Yes," she murmurs. "Of course. Everything will be all right."

But she has left the curtains open a crack, Finn realises, as if keeping a constant eye out for that danger he is unable to take away.

# CHAPTER TWELVE

"How are you?" Edwin asks. It's early morning; Harriet can tell from the pale blue light creeping through the gap in the curtains. She had come to bed just a few hours ago. Has barely slept. A dawn chorus of birds is bawling outside the window.

She can tell from the expression on her husband's face that he is surprised to see her awake. Usually, she is only roused with some difficulty by Jenny when Thomas wakes and begins screeching to be fed. Last night, though, her thoughts had been racing far too violently to sleep.

She feels completely unmoored. Feels more out of place here than she ever has; lying in bed beside a husband she barely knows, in this house that belonged to a man who is not her father.

Edwin is propped up on one elbow, looking down at her with a frown of concentration, as though he is studying a new specimen of plant life. His face looks sharper than usual, thanks to the dark hair hanging loose on his shoulders. It's beginning to thin, Harriet notices, with a vague sense of detachment.

"I'm fine," she says. Before she can roll over, putting her back to him, he reaches out and presses a hand to her bare wrist. It's a tentative move, uncertain. There is rarely any incidental touching between them—Edwin had put an end to any attempt at romance in the early days of their marriage when it became clear his stilted affection was not going to be reciprocated.

"Harriet," he says gently. "Please. Do not shut me out."

Though she rarely enjoys his touch, there is something strangely comforting about his nearness right now. Something steadying about the feel of his rough craftsman's skin against her own. Something that reminds her of the way life used to be, back when she was still Samuel Blake's daughter.

Instead of rolling over, she sits up in bed. Allows him to keep a hold of her. "I am not shutting you out," she says. "There is just nothing to say."

"Nothing to say?" He sounds incredulous. But why, she wonders? Because between the two of them, there is always nothing to say. How can she tell Edwin how she feels, and who she is, when she barely knows that herself?

"I imagine you feel cheated," Harriet says finally.

Edwin raises his thin black eyebrows. "Cheated?"

"Yes. You married me thinking I was the daughter of a wealthy English merchant. And now your son could have any bastard's blood in his veins."

Edwin sits up and leans back against the bed head, releasing his grip on Harriet's wrist. He examines his thumbnail. "Well. That is not something anyone needs to know, is it." His voice is clipped.

Harriet nods silently. She knows this comment is meant for her benefit as much as his own. A promise that this shameful piece of her heritage might be kept away from gossiping ears.

She would confess such a thing to her artist friends, Harriet thinks distantly. They would not judge her. Isabelle would tell her to pour the pain and uncertainty into her paintings, commit them to her canvas. Harriet had tried to do such a thing last night, but had found herself paralysed with the mounting pressure of her lack of inspiration. She has become too adept at pushing things to the back of her mind to take any value from her pain.

"When do you imagine we might be back in London?" she asks suddenly.

She catches a flicker of irritation in Edwin's eyes at the change of subject. But he says, "There's still much to do on the house. But perhaps by the spring."

The spring feels impossibly distant; an entire north-England winter to crawl through first. But this is the first time she has ever succeeded in chiselling a possible date out of her husband. Spring—with luck she will be back in time to join Isabelle on her trip to Paris.

"I should like to be gone as soon as possible," Edwin says, "given the unrest up here. But I cannot leave Nathan to finish the restorations on his own. And he seems hell-bent on making the work far harder than it needs to be. He seems completely unable to finish one job before beginning the next."

"He does, yes." This is her chance now, Harriet realises. Now she has Edwin's sympathy, and they have come to rest in agreement of the futility of Nathan's restoration project. "My friend Isabelle showed one of my paintings to her sponsors," she blurts. "They wish to meet with me. In Paris. In April."

Her heart has struck up suddenly in a rapid cadence, and what a joy that is. A long-forgotten thing. How can it be, she wonders distantly, that she might have made it through spies and sieges, and the knowledge that she is not her father's daughter, with barely a ghost of a reaction. How cold and empty she must be. But this; speaking of this dream—and doing so to her husband, who could shatter it with a single word—this is where she feels alive.

"I see," Edwin murmurs. He hates the idea, Harriet can tell. But he has not yet shut it down completely. Whether out of mere sympathy for her, or whether he is truly considering it, she cannot be certain. "I do not think this the right time or place to discuss this, do you?"

"Why not?" she demands. But he is saved from answering by the shriek of their son, as though the two of them have been conspiring for it to be exactly this way all along.

Nathan finds himself pacing his study.

He is worried for Harriet. Since learning the news of her father three days ago, she has been more withdrawn than usual. Has spent even more time in her workroom, and even less time with her family. Though she is doing her best to pretend she is unaffected by her discovery, Nathan can tell the knowledge, or rather, the uncertainty, has cut her deeply.

He needs to tell Eva. He knows Harriet would benefit

from a visit from her sister. And in any case, the news of Harriet's parentage is something Eva ought to know.

But getting the news to her is something of a challenge.

An irritating voice at the back of his head tells him it is no challenge at all; tells him that Julia will no doubt happily sail over to Longstone and bring Eva back to see Harriet.

No. There must be another option.

Perhaps he could go to the harbour and pay a fisherman to visit Longstone. And then what? Is he to expect Eva to climb into a boat with a near stranger? He can hardly expect that of her after all that happened with Donald Macauley. No doubt if he were to make the journey over alongside the fisherman, she would be more inclined to come back with them. But a boat trip to Longstone is top of the list of things he desperately wishes to avoid—narrowly beating out a visit to Julia Mitchell.

Perhaps he could wait until Eva comes to Highfield House of her own accord. But he can hardly hold his breath waiting for that to happen. He had made it through her entire wedding without cracking a smile. She is hardly going to be rushing back here for more brotherly kindness. And Harriet could use Eva's company sooner rather than later.

Dammit to hell, he knows Julia is his only option.

He pushes open the door of the curiosity shop. Julia is standing by the shelves, hunting through a collection of books while she chats to the elderly couple beside her. She is a chaos of colour, in striped green and white skirts and a pink neckerchief, her red hair bundled in a knot high on her head. She looks over and meets Nathan's eye for a second, before turning back to the customers. Nathan hovers by the door, watching as she pulls a book from the shelf.

He finds his gaze darting around the shop. Searching for what, he wonders? Jacobite pamphlets pinned to the wall? A rebel soldier hiding behind the bookshelf? He knows he is being ridiculous. But Joseph Holland's words have got under his skin.

"Ah. Here it is. I knew it was there somewhere." Julia smiles warmly as she passes the book to the older woman. Her husband hands over the payment and Julia thanks them as they make their way out the door. Nathan shuffles awkwardly aside to let them by.

Julia's smile evaporates as she turns to look at him. "I'm surprised to see you here."

"Yes. Well." He clears his throat. "I need your help."

She folds her arms. "Do you just?"

Nathan hesitates. Each of the fifty-seven times he had played this conversation out in his head during the walk into the village, Julia had been far more acquiescing than this. Far less terse. He had imagined she would leap at the opportunity to help him, in an attempt to make up for the way she had betrayed him and his family. He realises he has made something of a miscalculation.

He ploughs on. "I need to get a message to my sister on Longstone. Something has happened with Harriet. And I think Eva ought to know about it."

Julia's eyes soften. She unfolds her arms. "With Harriet? Is she all right?"

From her words, Nathan guesses Harriet has said nothing to Julia about her recent discovery. And of course, he will not be the one to tell her. "She has not been herself of late," he says instead. "And I think she would benefit from a visit from her sister." He looks Julia square in the eyes, ignoring the treacherous fishtailing in his chest. "Will you take word to Eva? Ask her to come back to Lindisfarne with you?"

Julia gives him the faintest of smiles. "Of course."

Eva is checking the lobster pots at the edge of the jetty when she sees the boat cutting towards Longstone. She stands quickly, blind to the wave that recoils off the edge of the island and soaks the hem of her skirts. But it is not one of Ward's longboats.

It is the little fishing dory that belongs to Julia Mitchell.

Eva lowers the lobster pots back into the water and watches with folded arms as Julia approaches the moorings.

"Your brothers are inside," she says brusquely.

Julia stays aboard the dory, one hand pressed to the post of the jetty. "Nathan sent me," she says, ignoring Eva's sharpness. "He's asked me to bring you back to Holy Island. Something has happened with Harriet."

Eva knocks on the door of her sister's workroom. Steps inside tentatively.

Harriet glances up from her notebook. She looks pale, her blue eyes underlined in shadow. A teacup sits on the table beside her, along with an untouched plate of bread and cheese.

"Shouldn't you be galivanting around Longstone with your new husband?" she asks.

Eva hovers just inside the door. From where she stands, she can glimpse the scribbled-out sketches on the pages of the book. They remind her of the angry scrawls Harriet had left across her last painting. "Nathan told me what happened. I'm worried about you."

"Why?" Harriet turns back to her notebook.

"What do you mean, why?" When her sister doesn't reply, Eva walks up to the table in frustration. "Can we at least have a conversation?"

"What is there to say?" Harriet puts the pencil down anyway. Her eyes stay fixed to the page.

What is there to say, Eva realises? Nothing will change this. And she is sure nothing is going to make it any easier for Harriet. She goes to the window and pushes on the sash to let a little fresh air into the stuffy room.

"Leave that," Harriet barks.

Eva steps away obediently. She perches on the edge of the faded armchair. "I am glad you're working," she says, nodding towards the notebook.

"Why would I not be working?"

Eva picks at a loose thread on her shortjacket. "I saw what you did to your last piece."

"Oh. That."

Eva waits, but nothing more is forthcoming. "What made you do it?"

Harriet shrugs, without looking at her. "It was no good. The colours were all wrong. Unfixable. Best to just start again." Her words are thin.

"And this piece?" Eva asks. "Are you happier with it?"

"There is no piece yet," Harriet says tautly.

Eva swallows a sigh. She can practically feel the wall of ice her sister has erected around herself. Harriet picks her pencil back up and begins to sketch lightly. Eva follows the movement of the pencil. Watches the faint outline of a willow tree appear on the page. It's an enchanting ability that Harriet has, she thinks; to make images come to life on the page like this. A gift no one else in the family shares. Eva finds herself wondering if she had inherited it from her father.

"How is your little island?" Harriet asks after a moment.

"It's beautiful," says Eva. "The way the sea changes colour with the light, and the way the tide reshapes the place… It's magical." She smiles to herself. "And the sound of the birds is like nothing you've ever heard before. I think it would inspire you. Perhaps I can take you back with me one day. I would like you to see it."

"Yes. Perhaps." Harriet shades a faint shadow beneath the willow. After a moment, she says, "It is just… the not knowing." Her words are so airy and insubstantial that it takes Eva a moment to realise she is finally speaking of her father. "Having no thought of where I really come from. Of who my father might be. How can I have any sense of who I am?"

And Eva's chest squeezes with dread. She feels hot and she feels cold at once, and she forces herself to keep the gasp of her understanding silent. Because it is no mystery, she realises then. It's sickening and inevitable. And it is no mystery at all.

# CHAPTER THIRTEEN

Eva says nothing to Harriet. She says nothing to Julia when she takes her back to Longstone that evening. But as Finn is shovelling coal into the firebasket, she is pacing, pacing in front of him, her stomach in knots and the words she has kept in all day spilling out without pause.

"I ought to have known it the moment I heard about Harriet's discovery," she says, her fingers entangled in the fine wool of her shawl. "How could I have been so blind?" She thinks of the night she had spent on Henry Ward's ship. Thinks of how fondly Ward had spoken of her mother. Thinks of the look in his eyes when he had mentioned Abigail Blake's name. "And the way he looks, Finn. His eyes. His hair. That unnatural beauty. That is all Harriet." She stops pacing. "I'm right, aren't I."

Finn secures the chain to the hook. "I would imagine so, aye."

Eva looks up at the flickering light, feeling it warm her cheeks. The sea clops against the edge of the island, a constant rush in her ears.

The realisation is turning her stomach. The realisation that Henry Ward had shared her mother's bed. That her sister has his blood running through her.

"Do you think..." She fades out, unable to finish the sentence. Tries again. "Do you think he forced her?" The words are bitter on her tongue.

Finn tilts his head; doesn't speak at once. Perhaps he is debating which would be worse: for her mother to have been forced into Ward's bed, or for her to have gone there willingly.

"The truth, Finn," she says.

He sighs. Looks up at the dancing light. "I was just a lad. So I don't know for sure. But when I saw Ward and your mother together, they seemed... Well. It seemed as though she enjoyed his company. She welcomed him into the house. Dressed up when he came to see her."

Eva nods faintly. She sits on the edge of the island, warmed by the glow of the firebasket. The sea reaches for the toes of her shoes. Somewhere in the darkness she can hear the throaty wail of a seal.

Finn sits beside her, reaches an arm around her shoulder. "All right?"

Eva hugs her knees. "When I was aboard Ward's ship, he told me I was just like my mother. I denied it, but I knew he was right. At least, I thought he was. I always believed Mother and I were so alike. Rigid. Followers of the rules." She shakes her head. "But for her to have invited a man like Henry Ward into our home... For her to have had a child with him... It's as though there was a completely different side to her that I never knew about."

Finn catches her eye and smiles crookedly. "I've never known you to be one to follow the rules."

"Perhaps I am like my mother after all." She leans her head against his shoulder, feeling it rise and fall with breath.

"Will you tell Harriet?" he asks.

For long moments, she doesn't speak. "No," she says finally. "I can't. No one can know. What if I told her and she decided to seek Ward out? There is so much he could tell her. About Oliver..." The words leave a dull ache in her chest. Around Finn, she never speaks her brother's name.

He nods slowly, not looking at her. "Aye, he could. But do you really think it's something you ought to keep from her?"

Eva stares out across the dark sea. On the edge of her vision, a volley of sparks flutter down from the firebasket and disappear on the water. Somewhere in the back of her mind, she knows Finn is right. But the thought of her family finding out what he did to Oliver is unthinkable.

"She cannot know," she says finally. "We cannot take that risk." She closes her eyes, trying to push away the nagging of her conscience. "Besides, I am doing her a favour. If I were Henry Ward's daughter, there is no way I would want to know about it."

Theodora is staring out the window, not paying the slightest bit of attention to her Latin text. Nathan can't quite find the energy to pull her back to the task at hand. At least when she is looking out the window, he is saved from hearing about how much she hates Latin.

Suddenly, she gasps with delight. "Bobby's here!" She flings down her quill, splattering ink across the page. She leaps up from Nathan's desk and presses her forehead against the glass.

"Theodora—" he begins, but she is already off down the stairs. And, he realises when he gets to the entrance hall, she has already opened the front door to Bobby and Julia. Before he can get a word out, she and Bobby tear into the dunes.

Nathan sighs. It's time he had strong words with his daughter about acting like less of a wildling, especially when he is attempting to teach her his questionable Latin grammar. Begrudgingly, he tries to remember when she has ever looked quite so free and happy. Certainly not since her mother died.

Steeling himself, he looks back at Julia. She is holding a large wooden box in her arms. "Why are you here?" he asks. The words come out cold and unfeeling, and he is unsure if he furiously regrets them, or if he is proud of himself for managing them.

Julia holds out the box. "This is for you. An apology of sorts. I've been wanting to give it to you for some time, but I figured I had best wait until your anger at me had settled somewhat." There's a faint glimmer in her eyes, the freckles on her pale cheeks pronounced in the sunlight.

"I see," says Nathan. "And you think my anger at you has settled?"

Julia doesn't falter. "I think I did you a favour by sailing out to Longstone to fetch Eva in the middle of my workday. So the least you can do is take the box."

Holland's warning echoes in Nathan's head. He knows the spies working for the government have little trust for Julia Mitchell—for reasons he does not want to explore. What he does not know, is what they will do if they catch sight of her at Highfield House.

Nathan takes the box, half out of curiosity, and half out of a need to get her off the property—both for her sake and his own. He lifts the lid and peers inside. And he feels something shift in his chest. Inside is a telescope, a six-draw piece of brass and wood, just like the one his father had given him when he was a child. He had seen it in Julia's curiosity shop last month. A metal stand is folded up beneath it.

"You seemed fond of it when you saw it in my shop that day," she says. "I would like you to have it."

Nathan swallows heavily. He'd had no idea Julia had even seen him looking at the thing. He holds it back out to her. "That's kind of you. But I cannot take it."

"Why not?" she asks, before he can get a hand to the door to close it.

"Because I really think it best that you have nothing to do with this family going forward." The words are hard to get out.

"You needn't have anything to do with me. You just need take the telescope."

"No. I can't." He pushes the box back into her arms, careful not to make contact with her.

She flashes him a smile, as though the words he has been grinding out have not even registered. "Bobby and I will leave you be. And I will put the telescope out by the cart shed. Best you take it inside before the weather turns and ruins it."

Nathan goes back upstairs, churning out a rote scolding to Theodora about not running off like a rabbit, and letting Mrs Brodie answer the door. His heart is not really in it. He sends her off to finish her Latin and returns to the dressing room to begin putting the fireplace back together. The damn thing has been in pieces for more than a fortnight. After a few minutes, he climbs to his feet and goes to the window. Looks down at the cart shed.

Julia has done as she promised. There is the telescope, the box leaning up against the padlocked door. The sight of it makes Nathan shake his head in frustration, but he can't deny there's some small part of him that is pleased to see it.

He goes out to the cart shed and collects the box, then tucks it beneath the desk in his study. It will rain tonight, he thinks. And there's no point letting a fine piece of equipment like this get destroyed.

# CHAPTER FOURTEEN

It has become a game, Harriet realises. A sickening, pointless game of letting her eyes drift over every man in the congregation and wondering if he might be her father. Perhaps it's that grizzly fisherman in the corner, with the cap pulled low and a devious look in his eyes. Perhaps the too-righteous husband of the woman who owns the fruit stall, sitting front and centre, nodding along to the pastor's dreary words.

She forces herself to stop. Nothing good can come of this. She knows the chance of her father—whoever he may be—sitting in this church with her is impossibly small. And even if it wasn't, she could hardly just approach the man and accost him with such news.

Still, she wonders. More about her mother than her father. Had she let him willingly into her bed? Had she done so in some twisted act of grief over her husband, dead for less than a year before Harriet was conceived? Or had she welcomed Samuel Blake's death? Her mother suddenly feels like as much of a stranger as her father.

Harriet glances at Edwin beside her. He is nodding along routinely to the sermon, but the glazed look in his eyes tells her his thoughts are far away. Ought she prod at the issue of Paris? Instinctively, she feels that this will make him even less likely to agree to it. No doubt he is waiting for the news of her parentage to become old, and then he can turn her down without looking like too much of a bastard.

Harriet closes her eyes. Tries to breathe deeply. She hates sitting here among these cold, unyielding walls, with the frozen stone eyes of saints bearing down on her. It feels as though they can read her every sinful thought. Something that feels like dread rolls around inside her.

When the service finishes, she makes her way out of the church, her hand pressed dutifully into the crook of Edwin's arm. Jenny trails them silently, Thomas asleep on her shoulder. The morning is grey and cold, with just a thin rim of gold lining the bank of cloud above the ocean. Gulls swarm low, in perfect synchronicity, over the crumbling stone walls at the back of the churchyard.

Movement in the ruins of the monastery behind the church catches Harriet's eye. Michael Mitchell is standing in one corner of the old priory, his cocked hat pulled low. It's the most brazen of moves—almost as though he is daring the people of Holy Island to catch him and turn him in, just to find out where their alliances lie. Michael is deliberate in catching Harriet's eye. She tries to turn away, but his intense gaze spears her. With a brisk nod, he gestures to her to join him.

He's mad, surely. Does he truly expect she can just disengage herself from her husband and sidle into conversation with a wanted man? And does he not realise his own damn sister is here among this crowd? Still, Harriet supposes, for all this foolishness, whatever he wants must be important.

She murmurs to Edwin about hanging back to speak with the priest. Her husband releases her arm without a word.

Harriet waits until the crowd has dispersed and the door of the church has closed. Then she steps into the long shadows of the priory. Old stone towers rise up on either side of them, swallowing the meagre threads of sunlight. "Julia is right," she snorts. "You're a fool. Do you not know there are government spies on the island?"

He smiles faintly. "You would know." Harriet snorts. She turns to leave, but Michael snatches her wrist. "Wait. I've been thinking about you."

She raises her eyebrows. "Have you just?"

"Not in that manner," Michael says witheringly. "I've been thinking about why you told me about Lesbury Common. It was a dangerous thing to do. You're either a fool, or you have little loyalty to your family."

The words strike her. Because she realises they are true. How can she claim to have loyalty to her family when she had so carelessly revealed a secret that could put them in danger? Almost as though a part of her had known all along that she was the ill-fitting piece. The curly-haired blonde child of a man who is not Samuel Blake.

"Either way," Michael continues, not waiting for her to speak, "I could use your services."

"What do you mean, my services?"

He slips a piece of paper into her hand. "Read it," he says. "And think about it. I'll make it worth your while."

Harriet waits until she is safely tucked away in her workroom that evening before opening Michael's letter. It's little more than a scrawled note, containing a time and a place. One o'clock tomorrow morning, at an address she does not recognise. She ought to feed the note into the lamp, of course; see this foolishness burn to ash. But instead she crushes it between her fingers, indecision swaying inside her.

Something urges her to go. To hear what Michael Mitchell has to say—and why, of all things, he needs to say it to her. *I will make it worth your while;* what had he meant by that?

It's madness, of course, to even be thinking of traipsing across the island in the middle of the night, especially at the bidding of someone she barely knows. Michael is a known Jacobite; there is every chance he is leading her into a trap. But she has always found it hard to conjure up the fear she knows she ought to feel. When Julia had been sneaking around Highfield House to visit her brothers, Harriet had had no qualms about venturing into the night to confront the intruder. She had been far more intrigued at the prospect of some excitement than fearful of what might happen to her. Sometimes she finds it difficult to place any great value on her own life.

By midnight, the house is quiet. Harriet opens the door of her workroom and listens. No sound of movement, beyond a clock ticking steadily in the parlour and the shift of wood as the fire in the kitchen dies away. She pulls on the cloak she had hung over the back of her chair and takes the lamp from the mantel.

The night is clear and cold, with a dinted moon rippling its light off the water. Lamps glow atop the masts of the ship that has been moored beyond the house for the past weeks.

Harriet walks carefully over the uneven grass, the lantern held out in front of her. She feels a dull swirling in her belly, something that hints at a thrill, at excitement. A thrill at what, she wonders? The prospect of being caught? Of defying her husband? Of taking a step closer to that woman who does not follow orders?

The address on Michael's note is at the other end of the village to Julia's curiosity shop. Harriet keeps to the edges of the town, careful to avoid the anchorage and tavern. She knows that if any of the villagers saw her creeping around by lamplight, they would be even more inclined to believe her family were spies. A group of fishermen pass, laughing loudly, and Harriet darts into an alley, pressing herself against the wall until they are gone.

She reaches a small stone cottage on the corner of Marygate. Wooden shutters are closed over the windows, but a thin thread of smoke is rising from the chimney. Harriet taps lightly on the door, edgy with anticipation. She glances over her shoulder. The street is empty, save for a fox that scuttles down a dark alleyway and disappears.

The door creaks open to reveal a dark-haired young woman. She is unfamiliar—and on this island that is something of a novelty. Harriet has not seen her at church— a Catholic, perhaps, and in that case, almost certainly a Jacobite. Michael's lover? Or just someone willing to help further the Jacobite cause? She is dressed in a dark woollen dress and shawl, as though she is trying to blend into the night, her hair scraped back in a severe bun. The single candle in her hand casts shadows over her cheeks and gives her a faintly hunted expression.

"Did Michael send for you?" she asks brusquely. Her Northumbrian accent is thick and harsh, and Harriet has to concentrate hard to catch her meaning. She nods.

The woman gestures for Harriet to follow her into the cottage. She leads her through a narrow passage, closed doors on either side and the salty stench of tallow thick in the air. She shoulders open the door to the kitchen. It is small and cramped, with a single table in the centre cluttered with stacked wooden bowls and a half-eaten loaf of bread. Firelight glows in the range, the air thick with the smell of old boiled meat.

Michael Mitchell is sitting at a chair with his long legs stretched out and his hat sitting on the table in front of him. He is wearing the same dark greatcoat he had appeared in at Julia's shop. Harriet is surprised to see him alone. She had half expected to be walking into a Jacobite meeting.

"You came," says Michael.

"You sound surprised."

"A little."

Harriet stands with her back pressed to the cold stone wall. "Are you not worried I've brought the redcoats with me? Or that I'm going to tell every soul I meet where you're hiding?"

"And are you not worried I might have some fellow Jacobites tucked away in the corners ready to come after your family?"

"I suppose I ought to be, yes." Michael's words about her being disloyal to her family echo in Harriet's head. There's a truth to them, no doubt. Is that why she has come here tonight? To create trouble for the family she has begun to feel so detached from? The answer is an uncomfortable one, and she pushes the thought away quickly.

The dark-haired woman steps into the kitchen and places the candle on the sideboard. She looks at Harriet with slightly narrowed eyes.

Michael drums his fingers against the table top. "I know you're not a spy. I told you, I've had time to think about it. If you were, you would not have said a word about where the Jacobites were gathering. I've heard others speaking about Lesbury Common since. The rebels are waiting there for directions from France or Scotland. I think it's like you said; you just overheard something." He shifts forward in his chair to eye her. "And I think you just like to cause trouble. Stir things up."

"Is that why you wished to speak to me?"

Michael exchanges glances with the dark-haired woman. "I need to get to Lesbury," he tells Harriet. "To re-join the rebels."

"I thought you were waiting for your older brother."

Something passes across Michael's eyes. "Well. As much as I hate to say it, the prospect of Hugh returning seems less and less likely with each day. And I'm a wanted man now. I know it's dangerous for me to be strolling around the place, especially now the redcoats are so active in these parts."

Harriet snorts. "That did not seem to bother you much before."

Michael ignores her comment. "I need your help to get to Lesbury."

"My help?" She raises her eyebrows.

"Aye. It's dangerous for me to make the journey on my own. I can't take the chance that I might be recognised. But if were to make the journey with you, I'd be under less scrutiny."

Harriet frowns. "Why?"

"You'll pose as my wife," says Michael matter-of-factly. "The redcoats will be on the lookout for men on their way to join the rebel army. But they'll never suspect that a man travelling with his wife is headed for Lesbury Common. You'll be the perfect cover for me."

Harriet doesn't speak at once. She had not expected this. On the other side of the room, the other woman stands with her back to the door, studying Harriet with a look of open distrust.

Harriet sits at the table. Michael's request is laughable. But she cannot deny she is curious. "And how exactly do you propose I return to Lindisfarne once I've deposited you into the hands of the rebels?"

"Anne will accompany us," Michael says, nodding to the other woman. "She can pose as your lady's maid. And she will be able to drive the wagon back to Lindisfarne."

Harriet's eyes meet Anne's for a second, then she turns back to Michael. "If that is the case, why do you need me? Why not just take her?"

"It's a long journey back, and you'll be travelling late at night. Safer for there to be two of you." His lips quirk. "I'm not a complete bastard, regardless of what you might have heard about me. I don't want either of you to get in trouble."

"And you do not think two women travelling alone will raise suspicions?"

"Not if we have our stories prepared," Anne speaks up. Harriet turns to her in interest. "Why do you think so many women are working for the Jacobite cause? Because we don't arouse as much suspicion. If the redcoats stop us, we'll tell them your husband has died and you're on the way home to your family."

Harriet smiles crookedly. "It sounds as though you have done this before." When Anne doesn't respond, she leans back in her chair and looks at Michael. She ought to have shut this down already. Ought to have laughed in Michael Mitchell's face and marched right out of the house. But she finds herself saying, "Why should I do this for you? I hardly know you. And all I do know of you is that you're a violent man and a liar."

The smile doesn't leave Michael's lips. "Harsh. But probably fair." He reaches into his pocket and produces a coin pouch. Sets it on the table in front of him. "I can pay you."

Harriet straightens. "Well. Why did you not tell me that before?"

"I suppose I wanted to see if you would do it out of the kindness of your heart."

Harriet snorts. "I'm not an idiot. And I'm afraid there's little kindness in my heart."

"One guinea and ten," he says.

Her heart skips. One guinea and ten. Enough, she imagines, to get her to Paris. But she senses Michael's desperation.

"Two guineas," she says.

"One and fifteen." And at once, Harriet's mind is racing. Thoughts of her paintings on the Baillieus' walls, thoughts of being in Paris with Isabelle—thoughts of being somewhere other than this cursed island. There is no way she will make the journey to Lesbury and back without Edwin noticing, of course. But what is the worst he could do to her? Yes, he could strike her, cause physical pain, but such a thing would only be temporary. He could declare he was washing his hands of her and leave her to her own devices—and what a blissful outcome that would be. Really, she thinks, the worst he could do would be to take her upstairs and put another child inside her. She wonders if he is more or less likely to do so if he is angry with her. Even that would almost be worth it if she has the means to make Paris a reality.

Thoughts of Thomas tug at the back of her mind. He will be without his mother for a day or more. Jenny will care for him; feed him—milk and flour from the pap boat, like Harriet has pushed for in the past. Best she begin to sever his reliance on her. After all, she cannot take him with her to Paris.

She lets Michael see none of her racing thoughts. Lets him see nothing but a cool façade of indifference. "I will think about it," she says.

Irritation flickers across Michael's eyes. "Think quickly," he snaps. "The army won't stay there forever. When you've made up your mind, leave word with Anne."

# CHAPTER FIFTEEN

"If I did not know better," says Julia, picking her way across the mudflats towards Nathan, "I would say you had come here looking for me."

Nathan plants his boots in the damp sand at the top of Saint Cuthbert's Island. "I hardly think so. My daughter likes this part of Lindisfarne the best. Nothing more than that." He knows there's a hollowness to his words. Because when Theodora had asked to be taken out to the islet off the coast of the village, Nathan's first thoughts had been of Julia. He has seen her and her son out here on many occasions. Knew there was more than a small chance they might run into one another. He had found himself agreeing to Thea's request anyway.

He trudges down the sandy embankment towards Julia. Slate-coloured clouds weigh on the horizon, and the cold air smells of rain. He can feel his cheeks reddening in the wind. Can taste the sea on his lips.

Julia gives him a half smile. "It does not suit you, you

know. This rudeness. It sounds very forced."

Nathan doesn't speak at once. Because the truth is, it feels forced as well. He hates confrontation, hates rudeness. Is uncomfortable with anything other than easy cordiality. But given the way Julia has deceived him in the past, he knows he needs to keep his guard up. It is too dangerous not to. Both in regard to Holland's warning—and in regard to his own traitorous heart.

"Well," he says, avoiding her comment, "I do suspect Theodora wished to come down here in the hope she might see Bobby." The two children have already scrambled onto the islet and are pointing and laughing at the diving seals.

"Aye," says Julia. "They do seem rather fond of one another." Nathan realises he is standing close to her; close enough to count the pale explosion of freckles on her cheeks. He is strangely comfortable at her nearness, he realises. That fact in itself makes him uneasy.

Theodora bounds over the rocks on the edge of the island. "Stay out of the water, Thea," Nathan calls. "It's far too cold for wet feet." His daughter ignores him, scrambling up the outcrop on hands and knees, giving them a fine view of her underskirts and stockings. Nathan rubs his eyes.

"I hope you took the telescope in out of the rain," says Julia. "It's quite a high-quality piece. At least, the fellow who sold it to me assured me it was. I hope he wasn't trying to swindle me."

"It is a high-quality piece," Nathan agrees stiffly. "I shall return it to your shop when I have a free moment."

Julia smiles to herself. "You do that." She bends down to pick up a seashell, running her gloved finger over its pearly surface. She tucks it into the pocket of her cloak. "How is

Harriet?" she asks. "I've not seen her in more than a week. I'm a little concerned about her."

Nathan hesitates. Some selfish part of him is pleased Harriet has not been spending her time with Julia. Another part knows it would do his sister good to see her friend. Tentatively, he asks, "Has she told you…"

Julia catches the hood of her cloak before the wind whips it off her head. "She's not told me anything. I only gathered something was amiss after you sent me to fetch Eva."

Nathan nods stiltedly. "Well. I am sure Harriet will speak with you when she is ready."

Julia's gaze drifts past him to a figure making his way down the hill towards them. Nathan's stomach dives at the sight of Joseph Holland. He knows it will do neither of them any good if Holland sees him and Julia together. He is about to make his excuses when Julia says, "I'd best go." Her jaw tightens, her eyes hardening at the sight of Holland. "Bobby!" she calls. "Come on, now. Quickly." When her son doesn't turn, she gathers her skirts in her fist and strides across the mudflats towards him, barely reacting when a wave jolts off the edge of the island and washes over her shoes. Nathan stares after her, baffled by her unease. Holland has his eyes on Julia, yes, but there is no way she ought to know that.

Unless she has somehow caught wind of Holland's position. Unless the men spying for the government are not as well hidden as they believe.

Nathan's heart begins to bang against his ribs. What would such a thing mean for the safety of his family? If Jacobite sympathisers like Julia have somehow learnt of Holland's role, there is every chance they might also have learnt that the government spies are using Highfield House.

If Julia knew such a thing, surely she would not have spoken to him so genially today. Surely she would not have helped him by sailing out to Longstone. Surely she would not have given him the telescope.

Unless she was playing him like she has done in the past.

Nathan rubs his eyes, feeling the beginnings of a headache. If he is honest with himself, he had been pleased to find Julia on the beach today. But he knows that was foolish. Knows he must be stronger than that. He will not, he tells himself firmly, allow her to mislead him a second time.

"I thought it was your intention to keep Miss Mitchell away from your family," says Holland, his footsteps crunching across dried seaweed as he makes his way towards Nathan.

Nathan folds his arms. "It's a small island. Sometimes running into her cannot be helped."

Holland hums noncommittally. For a moment, Nathan considers telling him of his suspicions that the government spies may not be as hidden as they believe. The moment the thought arrives, he dismisses it. Untrustworthy though she may be, he cannot put Julia and her son in danger like that. Besides, Holland and the other spies have been careful. Discreet. And Nathan is certain his family has been too. If anyone has come to learn what the house is being used for, he cannot make sense of how.

"Is that why you're here?" he asks Holland. "To warn me away from her? Because I can assure you, there's no need."

Holland chuckles humourlessly. "Are you certain about that?"

Nathan shoots him a glare. "Perfectly."

"I saw you while I was up on the Heugh," says Holland,

nodding towards the hill behind the ruins of the monastery. He stops speaking for a moment as Julia charges past, dragging Bobby along behind her. "Miss Mitchell," he says with a nod. She gives him a strained smile of greeting and hurries away, ignoring Nathan. When she is gone, Holland says, "We need the house for another meeting. Tomorrow evening."

"As you wish." Nathan knows there is no point in arguing.

Holland gives him a nod of thanks. "I appreciate it, Blake," he says, clapping Nathan on the shoulder, as if he had even a hint of a say in the matter.

Eva finds Nathan striding back up the hill from Saint Cuthbert's Island. Theodora is just ahead of him, pink-cheeked and windblown, with her woollen bonnet pulled almost to her eyebrows. The hems of her blue checked skirts are sodden and tangled around her legs. At the sight of her aunt, she bounds forward and throws her arms around Eva's waist.

Nathan doesn't look particularly pleased to see her. "Planned to accost me did you?" he asks.

Eva ignores his sharpness. "I went to the house. Edwin told me you had taken Thea out here."

"I was looking for selkies," Theodora puts in. "Magic seals."

Nathan raises his eyebrows. "Where on earth did you hear about selkies? Did Bobby tell you?"

"No," she says airily. "Mrs Brodie did. After Miss Jenny took me and Thomas to see the seals one day. And then I had cocoa."

"I see."

Eva eyes her brother. His hands are dug deep into the pockets of his greatcoat, a faint frown creasing the bridge of his nose. "Are you all right?" she asks. "You seem bothered."

"I'm fine." He doesn't look at her.

"Are you sure?"

"What do you want, Eva?" he says tautly.

She reaches for her niece's hand. "I thought perhaps I might resume Thea's lessons?"

"Yes!" Theodora sings, before Nathan can speak. "But no arithmetic. Just reading and writing."

Nathan manages a half-smile. "It seems your niece has spoken." He gives Theodora a pointed look. "But she will do arithmetic too. And Latin."

Theodora screws up her nose.

"You shall have to come to the house," Nathan tells Eva, watching his feet. "I'll not be taking her all the way out to you."

Eva gives a short laugh. "I figured. I'm learning to sail," she tells him. "I shall be able to come on my own before too long. At least as soon as I can come about without ending up right back where I started."

"I see," says Nathan, her meagre attempt at humour either ignored or unregistered.

"Bobby hates arithmetic too," Theodora says suddenly. "At school, he has to do the mul-ta-pa-cation tables." She speaks the word out carefully. "But they also do reading and writing. He said I should come too, but Papa won't let me."

"Is that so?" Eva looks sideways at her brother. "I wonder why that is."

Nathan ignores her.

"I'm writing a story," Theodora announces. "About the fisherman's wife who asked the selkie to take her to the moon. Mrs Brodie told me all about her. I'm putting her in my own story. But I'm giving her a better ending. I'll read it to you in our next lesson." She pauses for breath. "Can we have it tomorrow?"

"Of course." Eva releases her hand and Theodora runs ahead into the open grassland behind the village.

Nathan watches after her. "I'd forgotten those tales," he says. "About the selkies. I suppose you were too young to remember folk tales like that." He digs his hands into his pockets. "Perhaps I ought to have a word with Mrs. Brodie. Ask her not to speak to Thea about such things. I know there's talk of the... old ways up here. Do you think I ought to be concerned about her getting carried away with such ideas? Folk tales and superstitions and the like drifting down from Scotland. I'd hate for her to get lost in them."

Eva laughs, buoyed by his attempt at conversation. "You've a very imaginative daughter, Nathan. As you well know. Only you could make such a thing a cause for concern. Just because she is writing stories and listening to folk tales does not mean she is about to lose herself in the old ways."

"Mm." He does not sound convinced.

"Why not send her to the dame school?" Eva asks. "I'm sure such a thing would be good for her. Better than sitting around in that creaking old mansion all day. Need I remind you that you did not want Thea in the house at all."

"Believe me, I do not need to be reminded," Nathan snaps. "And I'd say you lost any input you might have had in Thea's upbringing when you absconded across the sea."

"Absconded across the sea?" Eva shakes her head. "You're impossible. And offensive."

"I'm sorry," he says, not sounding sorry in the slightest.

"How long are you planning on holding this grudge for?" asks Eva. "Because the thing is done. Finn and I are married. And nothing is going to change that. I hoped marrying for love would not cost me a brother."

Nathan looks at her witheringly. "That's a fine attempt at guilting me, Eva. I thought you above such things." He walks with his eyes down for several paces. Finally, he says, "I can't send Thea to the dame school. Not while there are so many people here who do not trust our family. I hate the thought of leaving my daughter with people I'm not sure would have her best interests at heart."

Eva nods. She understands, of course. How could she not? But surely Nathan is holding on too tightly. Seeing danger where there is none. She dares to say, "I suspected it was because you did not want Thea around Julia Mitchell's son."

"Well. That too."

Eva sees something flicker across his eyes at the mention of Julia. The sight of it tugs at her chest. She knows how rare it is for Nathan to be drawn to someone the way he was to Julia. She regrets that he had been deceived by her as he had.

"I think you're right to stay away from Miss Mitchell," she tells him. "But I don't think that's a good enough reason to keep Thea away from school..." The last words of the sentence are strangled, but she does her best not to let Nathan see her sudden unease. She tries to hide the way her eyes pull towards the man striding up the hill from the anchorage.

He is impossible not to notice. Striking and sculpted

Henry Ward, who walks in giant strides and spills confidence, has the kind of charisma that draws eyes and stops conversations. At the sight of him, any doubts Eva had had about Harriet's parentage fall away. Because there in Henry Ward is her sister's beauty. It was not found in plain and mousy Abigail, or rugged and red-cheeked Samuel Blake.

Eva lowers her eyes and pulls up the hood of her cloak, praying Ward doesn't see her.

Once, Henry Ward had shown her kindness. When he had learnt she was Abigail Blake's daughter, he had taken her to his dinner table and lavished her with care and attention. But she is sure all of that kindness was erased when she helped Finn escape his ship.

What is Ward doing here on Holy Island? Panic rushes through her at the thought of her husband, waiting for her at the Lindisfarne anchorage. She knows Finn will be aware—knows he is always on the lookout for Ward. But all it would take would be a stray pistol shot. A moment of diverted attention for Ward to get what he has been seeking.

No. There has to be more to it. If Ward merely wanted Finn dead, he has had ample opportunity to see the thing done. But this knowledge goes far from reassuring her. Because the sight of Ward, who has given almost all his looks to his daughter, reminds Eva that he is inexorably linked to her own family. In ways she is only just beginning to untangle. Does he know about Harriet? Is that what this is about?

"Eva? What is it?" Nathan follows her gaze. He glances at Ward, but looks away without comment. Nathan has heard of Henry Ward, of course. Eva had told her brother all about him after she had returned from his ship several weeks ago. But Nathan has not seen Ward for twenty years—if, indeed, ever. Surely he has no idea who the man in front of them is.

But now she sees Harriet in Henry Ward, it seems impossible that her brother cannot. Still, she reminds herself, to Nathan, the man in the tricorn hat striding up the street with two of his crewmen is a stranger, barely worth a passing glance. And it is best that it stays that way. Eva does not want her family drawn into this sorry business she and Finn have with Ward. At least no more than they are already.

"I'd best get back to the anchorage," she says, forcing herself to keep her voice level. "I do not wish to keep Finn waiting." She is suddenly desperate to get back to Longstone as quickly as possible. She flashes Nathan a strained smile. "I shall see Thea for her lesson tomorrow at noon."

Nathan watches Eva disappear towards the anchorage, then he strides back towards the house at the same brisk pace, calling Theodora to keep up with him. He desperately hopes his sister had not registered the look of horror on his face.

He dares a glance over his shoulder. Watches the man in the cocked hat disappear into the tavern, flanked by two others. The door thumps shut behind them.

Nathan knows he ought not be surprised to see him. But every time he glimpses Henry Ward's face, he cannot help but be filled with dread.

# CHAPTER SIXTEEN

"Why are we walking so fast, Papa?" Theodora whines. "Slow down."

Nathan reaches out to grab her hand. The physical contact sends an unpleasant jolt through him, but it has the intended effect of making her skip to keep up with him. Her narrow fingers curl tightly around his gloved hand.

He cannot bear for Ward to see him. Worse, he cannot bear for Ward to see Theodora; to see that which Nathan holds most dear. That which would fell him the hardest if it was taken from him.

He touches a hand to his forehead. Even through the thick leather of his gloves, his skin feels hot and cold at once; dread mixed with the icy wind. Dead and alive. The swirling in his belly is telling him to let go of Thea's hand, but he is physically unable to. It feels as though he must keep hold of her forever, forever, forever, because how easily Henry Ward might take her if he untethered himself from her. At the sight of Ward walking through the village, the threats he has made feel all too real.

Beyond the town, the land opens out to gold-tinged grassland. In the fading daylight, Nathan feels intensely vulnerable. Insignificant in the expanse of this openness; and beside him, tiny Thea, the height of fragility. His heart is thumping hard, goaded on by his daughter's tight grip on his hand. There's a smile on her lips—he knows she is enjoying the rare contact. Knows she has no thought of the chaos roiling inside him.

He feels watched. He whips his head around, trying to catch sight of the eyes he can sense boring into him. Nothing, of course. Just his imagination charging. As it so often is, this part of the island is almost impossibly empty.

He knows he shouldn't be carrying this alone. Eva has had her own run-in with Henry Ward, and so, apparently, has her husband. He ought to tell them of his own dealings with the man. The demands Ward has made. But things have gone too far for that. He is too deep into the charade to dig himself out of it now.

He shakes his head wryly to himself. He had cursed Julia for her lies and deceit. Is he really any better?

They step through the front door of the house, and Nathan lets himself breathe. He releases Theodora's hand and locks the front door. And before he can really understand what he is doing, he is marching up to his study and pulling that damn box out from under his desk. Setting the telescope up at his study window.

In the early-evening light, the first stars are beginning to glitter, and he angles the telescope to catch their glow. He lowers his eye to the lens and pulls in a long breath. A little of the tension in his muscles evaporates.

There is something oddly calming about peering through the glass into the oceanic depths of space. Somehow, the sight of the stars that the telescope pulls from the blackness dulls the panic, fades out the image of Theodora in Ward's grasp. Against the enormity of the night sky, and cradled behind locked doors, Nathan feels blissfully insignificant. And so does Henry Ward.

"What's that, Papa?" Theodora is standing in the doorway, chewing the end of her plait. He had not heard her approach.

"Come and look," he tells her.

She hurries towards him. He angles the barrel towards the waning moon, its peaks and valleys stark against the darkening sky. He guides Theodora to stand in front of him and peer through the eyepiece. A faint murmur escapes her.

"Oh," she says. "The moon." When she looks back at him, her eyes are wide and her lips parted in a look of entrancement.

Nathan smiles to himself. He had had the same reaction when his father had first set the telescope up for him, and he had peeked out into the night through this very same window.

"Can you see all the peaks and depressions on the moon?" he asks his daughter. "As if someone has scooped out spoonfuls of it?"

Theodora nods, her eye still to the glass.

"Some people think some rocks crashed into it," he tells her. "And that's how all the holes got there."

She looks over her shoulder at him. "Maybe the fisherman's wife did it after the selkie sent her to live there."

He chuckles. "My nanny used to tell me stories about the selkies when I was a boy," he says. It's a memory that had been frayed and distant until he had heard Theodora speak of

117

the old folk tales that afternoon. A memory of windblown hair and muddy boots, and legs aching from running the dunes. Of being an island child who believed in the shape-shifting selkies and spoke with the rounded vowels borrowed from the Scots. A part of himself he had forgotten. Certainly, his mother had never sought to remind him of it. Once they had left Holy Island, she had barely spoken of the place. Running the dunes with folk tales in his head had been replaced by arithmetic tutors and cricket matches. Later, by the rigidity of a business degree at Cambridge. Coffee house debates about unemployment figures and Britain's involvement in Continental wars. A merchant enterprise; a wife, a daughter. And then grief and failure that had stripped the last of the magic from the world.

But, "I remember hearing about the selkies taking off their seal suits and turning into real people," he tells Theodora. "Although I never heard of them living on the moon."

Theodora giggles as she looks up from the telescope. "The selkies don't live on the moon. Only the fisherman's wife who asked the selkie for a wish. Mrs Brodie told me about her. Her house wasn't big enough and she wanted a castle on the moon. Mrs Brodie said she got lonely there after a while and wanted to come home. But in my story, she likes it, and she decides to live there forever. Look." She nudges him gently towards the telescope, pulling her hand away from his shoulder quickly. "That mountain on the side looks just like a castle where she might live."

Nathan smiles faintly. "You know these are just stories, don't you? The selkies are not real."

Theodora laughs. "Of course I do. Don't be silly, Papa." She presses her eye back to the lens. And though his problems have rarely felt more weighted, Nathan feels an immense pull of gratitude for Julia's telescope, and the space it has given him to breathe.

# CHAPTER SEVENTEEN

Finn scrawls the tide times in his logbook, his pencil scratching across the page. Eva is pacing the living space, her stockinged feet sighing against the floorboards.

"Do you think Ward knows about Harriet?" she asks. "Do you think that's why he came to Northumberland in the first place? Do you think that's why I saw him on Holy Island today?"

Finn leans back in his chair, following her with his eyes. Her fingers are intertwined in her worn yellow shawl, dark hair hanging loose down her back as she marches from the sideboard to the doorway and back again. She is making it hard for him to concentrate.

Finn puts down his pencil. He wraps his hands around his teacup, listening to the wind rattle the open shutters. A blaze of firelight is pouring through the window and casting long shadows across the cottage. He can hear faint snoring coming from the Mitchells behind the closed door of the bedroom. The spring watch open on the table beside him tells him it's a couple of hours from dawn.

Though he is doing his best to stay calm, he can't deny he is on edge. Longstone is feeling far from the place of isolation it has done for the past five years. But he is fairly certain it is not Henry Ward's daughter that has brought him back to Lindisfarne. "If he knows about her, and wants to meet her, why would he wait twenty years to do so?" He shakes his head. "I don't think this is about Harriet. But I do think it's about your family. It's too much of a coincidence that he would appear now, at the same time you all returned."

Eva nods slowly, her eyes glassy as she stares into the grate. A log breaks open, sending sparks flying up the chimney. "You're right." A frown creases the bridge of her nose. "He has been in Northumberland for more than a month. If he wanted to see Harriet, surely he would have done so already." She sits opposite him and begins bouncing her knees up and down. Finn presses a hand to her thigh and she stops jolting. Picks up her teacup. He wishes he could take the rest of her anxiety away as easily.

"And you've not told her who her father is?" he asks.

Eva puts her cup down without taking a sip. "How can I?" She is suddenly defensive. "What if she seeks him out and he tells her everything?" She shakes her head in frustration. "You of all people ought to understand why I cannot say anything!"

Finn nods. It's a conversation he does not want to get into again. Of course he understands.

He wants to go to her, hold her, promise her everything be all right. Promise her that Ward will not hurt them. But Eva is far too involved in this, far too aware, far too intelligent, to accept his empty assurances. He hates that he cannot protect her. And while having her on Longstone with him is every dream he never knew he had, he hates that he has brought her here to live a life so full of worry.

He stares out the window, past the glow of the firebasket to the inky plain of the sea. Lights out there, but they are far too low in the water to be Ward's ship. Lindisfarne fishermen, no doubt, out for the herrings that swarm at night, threading between the rocky outcrops of the Farnes in the glow of the firebasket.

He scrawls in the log: *fishermen sighted.*

He had started keeping the logbook when he had returned to Longstone five years ago after almost fifteen years of living a rootless, transitory life. Back then, in the wake of his father's death, the loneliness of the island had weighed on him, and the log had been a way to fill the empty hours of firelit night. A way of reminding himself that the rest of the world was still out there. Now, it has become a daily habit to record the high and low tides, the weather, the ships that pass the island. He is also well aware that by doing so, he is tracking the days in which Henry Ward has not come for him. Recording yet another day he has survived.

A part of him wants to leave this place. Climb into the skiff with Eva and sail somewhere Ward will never find them. He has made the Longstone light his responsibility, but he does not want it to cost him his life. Nor does he want to condemn himself to a life of running, of constantly looking over his shoulder. Of waiting for Henry Ward to spill his most damaging of secrets.

Finn knows Ward wants to punish him for Oliver's death. But what is he waiting for? Is his marriage to Eva somehow protecting him? Perhaps Ward is unwilling to send his crewmen to Longstone and put Abigail's daughter in the line of fire. But Ward has had plenty of opportunity to come after Finn alone. Times when he has been on the mainland; times when Eva has been away on Lindisfarne.

Perhaps he is simply not as important to Ward as he might have imagined.

Either way, he has had enough of waiting. He thinks of Eva standing at the window on their wedding night; thinks of the fear in her eyes when she had looked out over the water in search of Ward's ship. He does not want this to be his life. And more than anything, he does not want it to be Eva's.

At the first hint of dawn, Eva throws the Mitchells out of the bedroom and climbs into bed. She falls asleep quickly. Finn's eyes are heavy with sleeplessness, but he knows if he is to catch hold of Henry Ward—and if he is to do so without his wife knowing—he needs to leave now. Eva will be awake again in a few hours, ready to go to Holy Island for her niece's lessons. With luck he can make it there and back without her having any inkling of it.

"You going somewhere?" asks Angus, as Finn reappears in the living area, tugging on his coat.

"Nowhere of any importance," he says. And in case it didn't sound suspicious enough, he adds, "Not a word to Eva."

Navy blue sea fringes Holy Island in the early morning, the pale stripe of dawn glowing on the horizon. Cold wind skims the water, promising an early winter. Finn shivers, turning up the collar of his greatcoat and flexing his frozen fingers. He sails past the village, out towards Emmanuel

Head, where the *Eagle* is moored. He looks up at the barque. He can see a man on anchor watch, but the dark portholes suggest only a skeleton crew is aboard. He knows there is a good chance Ward and his crew are still in the village tavern.

Finn has vivid memories of Ward's privateering crew spending long nights in sordid drinking holes. Whenever the captain had allowed it, they would disappear into the taverns dotted along the coast of east England and the Spanish Netherlands. As a child, he had stayed aboard the ship with a cleaning rag in hand and list of hideous chores to complete. He can still conjure up the smell of beeswax polish, the stench of the congealing stew in the galley; the scrapes and slops as he emptied the vats into the sea.

He takes the skiff back to the village and secures it to the jetty. In the early morning, the first of the fishermen are bustling around the huts, arms loaded with bundled nets. Finn feels their eyes on him, but he keeps walking with his head down, making it clear he is in no mood for questions.

His footsteps echo across the cobbles as he approaches the tavern. Drunken laughter bounces between stone walls. Two men stumble past him, crooked with drink; another sits slumped against the outside wall. Finn pushes open the door. He is greeted with a fog of stale smoke, air thick with liquor and sweat. Men laugh and chatter loudly.

Finn hopes Ward is here among his crewmen. Far safer to confront him in the village than in the privacy of his ship.

The moment he steps inside, he catches sight of Ward standing at the back of the tavern. He seems locked in a heated conversation with a greying, narrow-faced man. The man has a faint familiarity to him, and Finn guesses him a long-time member of Ward's crew.

Ward turns towards Finn, as though sensing his arrival. Their eyes meet. Ward makes his way towards him, picking his black tricorn hat up from the large table in the centre of the tavern as he passes. He nods towards a smaller unused table at the back of the room.

"I thought you and your crew would be more discreet than this," Finn says, following. "Now that you've turned to piracy."

"And I thought you would be wiser than to seek me out." Ward is dressed in a dark waistcoat with silver buttons, his ornate white shirtsleeves buttoned neatly at his wrists. The faint red webs in the corners of his eyes hint at a long night, though his clothes are unstained and his greying hair is tied back in a neat queue. He pulls out a rickety chair and stiffly lowers himself onto it.

Finn slides onto the chair opposite. "I figured you're unlikely to shoot me with so many witnesses."

Ward's eyes dart momentarily to his crewman at the back of the tavern, then he looks back at Finn. "From what I hear, I don't imagine there would be all that many people on this island too distraught over your death. You've a reputation for being somewhat light-fingered. It seems folks are not all that willing to have their hard-earned coal used to keep the Longstone firebasket burning."

Finn smiles wryly. "I'm sure they're not." In truth, he knows Henry Ward is unlikely to shoot him at all; at least, not here in a cold-blooded murder. If he is to kill him, it will be done according to the laws of his ship's articles: a hanging from his yardarm, or a keel-hauling in the lightless water beneath the ship. "What of you?" he asks. "Are you not worried about being caught? You know they love to see pirates hanging over the Thames these days."

Ward sits upright in his chair, his spine rigid against the backrest. He folds his hands neatly on the table in front of him. "Well. Some risks are worth taking. In any case, we sailed over from San Salvador without engagement. So it's safe to say the authorities are not on our tail."

"What risks?" Finn pushes. "Why leave the Caribbean? Why come to Northumberland, of all places?"

"Because I have matters to attend to here."

"And your crew is happy to sit about in the bay for weeks on end? Are they not craving action?"

Ward smiles thinly. "Hence the long night in the tavern."

Finn leans back in his chair, considering. Back when he was Ward's cabin boy, he'd had a strong rapport with his captain. There had been trust between them; openness. Ward had filled the gap left by the father Finn had never seen eye to eye with. The father he had fled Longstone to get away from.

Ward had taught Finn to make a three-masted barque bend to his commands. To fire a pistol with striking accuracy. To stand on deck with a quadrant to his eye and trace a path through the sea by starlight. And he had made it clear that Finn could always come to him with his questions. His fears. That grand, polished great cabin had never been inaccessible, even if it did manage to instil in him a sense of awe. Somehow, under Ward's guidance, Finn had never felt afraid. Even with French gunfire roaring around his ears, he had felt steadied by Henry Ward's presence. If they were to die, Ward had always said, they would do so for their country. And what greater honour there was than that?

Finn had believed those words as a child. Ward had led

him to foolishly trust in his own invincibility. But now, he sees the hollowness of that refrain his captain had spouted. He has been far too close to death by Henry Ward's hand to believe that dying will come without fear.

While he knows, of course, that there is no chance of rebuilding the trust he and Ward had once shared, he wonders if he can at least get his former captain to open up a little. Speak in something more than riddles.

"Why piracy?" Finn asks. "You were always so adamant that we only attack enemy ships. No conflict without a letter of marque, was that not what you always said?"

"The war with France is over," Ward says evenly. "There's no role for privateers. It leaves men like me with few options, wouldn't you say?"

"Find yourself a nice little cottage to retire in and leave us all alone."

Ward gives a short laugh that disappears quickly. "I'm glad you're here, Finn," he says suddenly. "There's something I would like to speak to you about."

Finn raises his eyebrows. "If that's the case, why did you not send your thugs to collect me like last time?"

Ward ignores the barbed question. He waves a hand towards the bar. Moments later, two cannikins of whisky appear on the table. He nudges one towards Finn. "Here. I suppose you're to be congratulated on your marriage. You and your new wife are the source of much gossip here on Lindisfarne."

"I'm sure." Finn turns the cup around in his hand, without drinking. "I didn't imagine my marriage to Eva would be something you wished to celebrate."

Ward brings his cannikin to his lips. "Well. Had things not

happened the way they did between you and Oliver, it would have brought me much joy to see you marrying Eva Blake. But if Abigail knew Eva had married the man who killed her brother, it would destroy her."

Finn bristles. He knows Ward is right, and the truth of it is an ache. "Eva's mother is dead," he says tautly. "What she would think is of no consequence." But he can't make himself believe his own words. He knows Oliver's death has been at the forefront of Eva's mind since she learnt who Harriet's father is. He knows she is afraid of what Henry Ward could tell her family. But he also knows there is more to it than that. He can see it in her eyes sometimes. He can tell she thinks of her mother, of Oliver. Thinks of the betrayal she has committed by marrying him.

He cannot let Ward see his doubt. Ward had always taught him to find a man's weakness. Finn knows it is no secret that Eva is his. But what of Ward? Had Abigail Blake been his weakness? Had he loved her? Had she loved him?

He can feel Ward studying him. "Does Eva know you're here?" he asks.

"Of course not. She'd skin me alive for being so foolish."

"She's a wise lass." Ward tosses back the rest of his whisky. "Why are you here, Finn? Is it to try and convince me to pardon you, now you've tied yourself to Abigail's daughter?"

"No." Finn looks at him squarely. He's had enough of dancing around the issue. "I want to know why you're here on Lindisfarne. I know it's no coincidence you appeared at the same time as Eva's family. And what do you want with me that makes you so pleased to see me?" He does not dare speak of Harriet. He knows there is a good chance Ward is unaware of her existence. And he is not about to plant the idea in his head.

"My business on Lindisfarne is none of your concern."

"Of course it's my concern," Finn hisses. "Eva is my wife. And you clearly want something from her family."

Ward leans back in his chair, rubbing his shorn chin. His refusal to give a straight answer is all the confirmation Finn needs.

"Where d'you find all these men?" he asks, inclining his head towards the large table in the middle of the tavern. Despite the pink dawn filtering through the windows, there are at least twenty or thirty men still lolling around the tavern with tankards in hand. No doubt most of them belong to Ward's crew. Finn wonders how many more men are crammed between decks on the *Eagle*.

"I've spent some time in Nassau," Ward says. "New Providence."

Finn snorts. "Henry Ward in the Republic of Pirates. Never thought I'd see the day."

"I imagine you'd be quite intrigued by the place," says Ward with a thin smile. "Most of the men there were once privateers, like ourselves. Turned to piracy because peacetime has left them with little choice. The men have drawn up their own articles of agreement to live by. Crews vote on who is to lead their ships. They treat one another with much more civility than most of the sorry souls here in enlightened England. A rather fascinating social experiment, you might say."

"A social experiment? For privateers who are unwilling to accept that their privateering days are over?"

Ward chuckles. "Something like that. In any case, Nassau

is the easiest place to fill a ship. At least if you're a captain with a notable reputation." There's a forced bravado to Ward's words, Finn realises. A hint of uncertainty he has never heard from him before. It catches him by surprise.

"And did these men know when they signed with you that there would be no action to be had?" he asks. "Outside the tavern, at least?"

The corner of Ward's lips tilt up, but it's a hollow smile. "They jumped at the chance, lad. I can offer them something that no one else can."

"And what is that?"

"Immunity. From the British government at least."

"Immunity?" Finn repeats, incredulous. "How?"

"That is for my crew alone to know." He leans forward. "Although I am willing to extend that invitation to you."

Finn lets out a short laugh. "Are you just? A few weeks ago, you were determined to see me dead. Now you're offering me a place in your crew?"

"Call it a truce. I am willing to overlook the punishment due to you for Oliver's death, in exchange—"

"—for me leaving Eva behind," Finn finishes, the pieces falling into place. Something tightens in his stomach. He supposes he can't be surprised at this. But that does nothing to dull the sting of the blow.

Ward's arctic-blue eyes spear Finn's. "It's what Abigail would have wanted. Nothing will bring her son back, but at least she would be spared the knowledge of her daughter spending her life with Oliver's killer."

Finn's fingers tighten around his cup. "I've done nothing but treat her well, Ward. I'd never dream of doing otherwise."

"That's hardly the issue. As you well know."

Finn grits his teeth until pain shoots through his jaw. "You truly think I will agree to this?"

"I would at least think you would have the brains to consider it. A better offer, surely, than sleeping with one eye open, wondering when I might see fit to deliver the punishment you have so far escaped." Ward gives him a knowing smile. "Surely that is not the life you wish for for your wife."

Henry Ward's words are tinged with bluster, yes, but that does nothing to take away their impact. Because for not the first time in his life, Finn feels as though his captain has the ability to look inside him and read his every thought.

Sunlight is pouring over the horizon by the time he returns to Longstone. His body is aching with exhaustion, and though his thoughts are rattling, he is craving sleep. He leaves his damp, sea-scented greatcoat in the living quarters and slips back into the bedroom. Is relieved to see Eva breathing deeply with sleep.

As he slips under the blanket, she opens her eyes. "You're just coming to bed now?"

"Aye. I wasn't tired yet."

She sits up on her elbow, reaching out a hand for him. Her hair is tangled around her face, her thin nightshift sliding off one shoulder. "You're cold. Have you been out?"

"Just to empty the basket." The lie stings, and he curses himself for it. But it's for the best, he tells himself. Eva would tear him apart for going to see Ward, but it is more than that. Of all things, he does not want her to know of the offer his former captain has made him. It will anger her, cause her to act rashly. But perhaps, worst of all, it will cause her to question whether Ward is right to be asking for this. Whether her marriage to him is a betrayal to her family she ought never have agreed to.

For a horrifying moment, she is silent, as though turning his answer over in her mind. "Get some sleep," she says finally, sliding back beneath the blanket and pulling it to her neck. "I told Nathan I'd be there for Thea's lesson at noon."

# CHAPTER EIGHTEEN

Eva senses movement in the corner of her eye. She stops walking. She whirls around, catching nothing but the blurred figure of a roe deer darting into the dunes behind Highfield House. She quickens her stride toward the manor.

As she walks, gripping tight fistfuls of her skirts, she cannot shake the feeling she is being watched. Deep billowed clouds are low on the horizon, sucking the light from the day and adding to her unease.

Eva pushes back the hood of her cloak to open up her vision. "Henry Ward," she hears herself say, "if you're there, show yourself."

Silence, of course. Wind sighs through the grass, meeting the constant lash of the sea. She feels like a fool. Henry Ward is not the kind of man to crouch in wait in the undergrowth. He is a man who will show himself at the very moment he chooses to. She puts her head down and hurries towards the house.

"Eva. Good." Edwin staggers out the shed at the back of

the property, arms overloaded with timber. "Nathan told me you were coming today."

Eva raises her eyebrows. She is not sure her brother-in-law has ever been pleased to see her before. Although she can't deny that, after the troubling walk across the island, there is a part of her that is glad to see him too. "Is something the matter?" she asks.

"I need you to speak with Harriet," Edwin says, resting the wood against the wall of the house beside withered brown threads of ivy. "She has this outlandish idea about travelling to Paris to show her paintings."

"Why is that an outlandish idea? She is very talented. So her tutor used to say, anyway."

Edwin sighs. "I'm sure. But you know what she's like. Given the chance, this will take over her life. It's not healthy for a person to be so single-minded. And these artistic types she associates with, they're not good for her. They fill her mind with all sorts of fanciful ideas." He shakes his head, as though catching himself about to run away with his thoughts. "I need you to talk her out of it."

"You're the one who does not wish her to do it. Why do you not talk her out of it?" She pulls her cloak tight around her body. "I think it would be a good thing for her. And I think her work deserves a little recognition."

Edwin sighs wearily, as though expecting such a response. "This is not the time for her to be doing such things," he says. "This business with her father... it has upset her. I can tell. Not that she would ever admit such a thing to me." He sounds faintly regretful.

Eva wonders distantly what he would think if knew his wife was the daughter of a man like Henry Ward. She knows how much Edwin Whitley prides himself on his good name.

He digs the key to the front door from his pocket and opens it, gesturing for Eva to enter. "She listens to you," he says. "At least, she listens to you more than she listens to me. Perhaps you might consider speaking with her? Please? I would appreciate it."

Eva gives him a small nod—a gesture signifying the conversation is over, rather than any agreement to his request. He murmurs his thanks, then gathers up the timber and clatters into the house behind her.

Theodora thunders down the stairs and rushes at Eva, grabbing her hand and tugging her into the parlour. Harriet is inside, perched on the edge of the settle. At the sight of her, Eva's stomach knots.

"Sit down," Theodora orders. "I'm going to perform a reading of my story."

Eva sits obediently beside her sister.

Finn is right. She ought to tell Harriet about her father. Right now. Of course she should. But with the knowledge of who Ward is, and the terrible truths he could reveal, her precious new life has begun to feel fragile. Eva is all too aware of how easily it could be taken away. She knows that if the truth of Oliver's death came out, she would be forced to choose between her husband and her family. Nonetheless, she is aware that keeping this knowledge from Harriet is the height of selfishness—or is it?

Because despite Harriet's self-assured façade, Eva is aware of how breakable her sister really is. She has not forgotten the sight of Harriet's ruined painting. Has not forgotten the sight of her sister slumped in the armchair with a whisky glass at her fingertips to take away reality. What would the knowledge of Henry Ward do to her? Would it be any worse than the uncertainty? The question goes someway to easing Eva's guilt—though she is well aware she is making excuses.

"Wait here," Thea orders. "I have to fetch my notes." She rushes out of the room.

"Well," says Eva, giving Harriet a smile she doesn't feel, "it seems she'll do anything to get out of arithmetic these days."

"I told her she has ten minutes," says Harriet, tapping her heels edgily. "I've a lot of work to do."

"Oh," says Eva, too brightly, "you've started a new piece then?"

Harriet looks out the window. "Not yet."

"I see." Eva folds her hands in her lap. Unfolds them again, then toys with the embroidery on the edge of her bodice.

"What?" Harriet demands.

"What?" Eva echoes.

"You keep looking at me. Do you have something to say?"

"No."

"Then stop it. You're driving me mad."

Eva had not realised how many sideways glances she had been giving her sister. But sitting here with Harriet, all she can see in her is Henry Ward. "Thea," she calls desperately. "Are you ready?"

"Almost. I just have to put my costume on. And fetch Papa."

"Papa is working," Eva calls back. "You'll have to read it to him another time. Quickly now." She starts to gnaw on a fingernail, a habit she had left behind in childhood.

"You're acting strangely," says Harriet accusingly.

"No I'm not."

Harriet snorts.

"Edwin told me about your plan to go to Paris," Eva blurts. She had not intended to go near such a thing. But it is better than the silence.

Harriet smiles wryly. "Let me guess. He sent you to do his bidding. Talk me out of it."

Eva doesn't answer at once. "He is just worried about you," she says finally. "He does not think now is the best time for you to be thinking of such things."

Harriet hums. "So he is not going to give me the money I need then. She twines a loose strand of hair around her finger. "I have to say, I expected such a thing from him. But not you."

"I'm not going to try and talk you out of it," Eva hisses, taken aback by Harriet's aggressiveness. "If you must know, I told him I thought it would be good for you. I just thought you ought to know what he asked of me."

"Is that so?" Harriet's words sound full of doubt, full of accusation.

"What is the matter with you?" Eva demands. She regrets the comment the moment it is out, but her sister is utterly infuriating. She did not mean to get into this argument, but somehow this feels safer. It's old, well-worn ground, if more bitter than usual.

Theodora struts into the room. She has a worn grey blanket wrapped around her shoulders and crown of sea thrift on her head, a wad of crumpled papers in her fist. Eva has never been more relieved to see her.

"Well, this is an interesting costume, Thea," says Eva.

Harriet wants to smack that forced brightness right out of her. She's surprised by her sudden fury at her sister. Or perhaps she's not. Because really, honestly, she has been angry at Eva for weeks. Furious at her for flying out of their lives and leaving Harriet to face her starched and stilted marriage alone.

This was not how it was supposed to be. This life as Edwin's wife, it was supposed to be tolerable because she had Eva beside her. Nathan and Edwin and Matthew would gallivant around the coffee houses, and she and Eva would hide themselves away to gossip about their beastly, uptight husbands, and everything would be all right.

"I'm a selkie," says Theodora. "Half a seal and half a girl."

Eva gives her a stiff smile, painfully obvious in not looking Harriet's way. "Very good. Read us the story then."

Eva is impossibly twitchy today. Harriet does not like it. It makes her feel there is something her sister is hiding.

Theodora looks down at the papers in her hand, the blanket sliding from her shoulders and pooling at her feet. She picks it up awkwardly with one hand and drapes it back over her shoulder. "Once upon a time," she begins, "there was an old man and his wife who lived by the sea. The man was a fisherman, and one day he rescued a seal who was trapped in his net. But it was not just a seal. It was a magical selkie who turned into a lady when she climbed out of the water."

Harriet sighs, louder than she had intended, and receives a brisk kick in the foot from Eva. She grits her teeth.

Being around her sister, Harriet realises, it makes her feel abandoned. Betrayed. And beneath it all is that which Harriet has been doing her best not to acknowledge: that thick, searing pull of jealousy.

Because impossibly, unfathomably, Harriet wishes she were Eva.

She cannot believe she feels this way. As soon as she was old enough to do more than trail after her like a blindly doting little sister, Harriet had seen Eva as dour and dull. A rigid follower of the rules, dreamless and hemmed-in by expectation. That fact that her colourless sister might be living this impossible sea-drenched life is too much to take in. Especially when Harriet knows that Eva also has the kind of love that Harriet will never have. Can never have.

Eva has told her none of this, of course. But she doesn't need to. Harriet can see it in her eyes. Can see it in the way she and Finn exchange those wordless, doting glances when they think no one is watching. It makes something burn in Harriet's chest; a thorny mix of jealousy and grief.

At least, she thinks, she is still capable of feeling something.

"And on the moon," says Theodora, "the fisherman's wife found mountains that looked like a castle. And holes that were made when a rock crashed into it."

Suddenly the thought comes to her, fervent and fierce. Harriet covers her mouth to silence her gasp. The images fly at her: the rise of the dented moon, with its peaks and valleys. Its depressions and shadows. This, she thinks, will be her unique way of putting the natural world to the canvas. She will build on the work of Maria Eimmart, whose depictions of the planets she had once seen in her brother's study. She will paint the moon, the stars, the planets. Track the changing hues of the night sky.

The moment Theodora's story is finished, Harriet races to her workroom. She throws open her notebook and begins scrawling furiously.

The piece takes shape at once: the globe of the full moon, silver-gold on the horizon, shedding its light on the water as it rises. Night, she thinks—that is far more her style than the sun-streaked vista she had attempted last time. As her pencil moves without pause, a weight is lifted from her shoulders— that irrational fear that she might never find inspiration again. The fear that these interminable months on Lindisfarne might have drained the creativity out of her. She thinks of the other pieces that will follow this one: a collection of starlit landscapes. Eclipses. Comets. Fresh and new and daring. Enough to provoke discussion at the salons of Lord and Lady Baillieu—especially if they are signed with the name of a woman.

So Edwin will not give her the money she needs. It is no surprise, of course. Nor is it a surprise that she has found out this way: through her sister rather than direct from her husband's mouth. But it is no matter. She does not need him. She just needs to find the courage to take that journey to Lesbury with Michael Mitchell—and then she can go about bringing her dream to life.

"I'm concerned," Nathan says, voice low, "that people may be aware of Joseph Holland's involvement with the government." He and Edwin are clustered together at the top of the dining table, beneath a fug of pipe smoke. He can hear faint murmurs coming from the spies' meeting in the parlour. Before the meeting had begun, Nathan had gone from room to room, closing all the curtains in the house. Then he had decided that that made things look far too suspicious and had gone around opening them again.

Edwin blows a line of smoke up towards the beamed ceiling. "What makes you say that?"

"Just a suspicion." Nathan takes a long draw on the pipe, willing it to take away a little of his unease. "If the Jacobites on the island know Holland is a spy, there's nothing to say they don't know what the house is being used for. And there is no saying what they would do to our family."

"If the Jacobites on the island knew Holland was a spy, he'd be dead," Edwin says matter-of-factly. "He'd probably be taken out to sea and thrown overboard. They'd make it look like a fishing accident."

Nathan winces at Edwin's bluntness. He is not sure he agrees. Surely the fact that Holland is alive does not necessarily mean the Jacobites are ignorant to what he is doing. Deceit might come easy to people like Julia Mitchell, but he suspects that murder does not.

Edwin leans back in his chair. "You ought to have discussed it with me before you agreed to let the spies use the house in the first place."

Nathan brings his pipe to his lips. This is far from the first time Edwin has raised the issue. He does not regret his decision. Letting the spies use the house had saved Eva from suspicion at best—and death by hanging at worst. It had been a decision he had not had to think on.

The thud of the door knocker echoes through the house, making him jump. He leaps to his feet, racing towards the door before Mrs Brodie can get there. He had not expected anyone else for Holland's meeting—but he had also been deliberate in not asking too many questions.

Julia stands on the doorstep, clutching her son's hand. Nathan's heart begins to thunder.

"What are you doing here?" he blurts.

Julia looks surprised at his outburst. She falters. "I was worried about Harriet. I thought to see how she was faring." She glances down at her son. "And if you don't mind, Bobby was eager to see Theodora."

Bobby digs a large cockle shell out of his pocket. "I found this near the anchorage this morning," he says with a gap-toothed smile. "I want to show her."

Nathan realises he is standing with his arms stretched out across the doorframe, as though to prevent them from entering the house. And in the somewhat desperate hope of preventing Joseph Holland from hearing Julia's voice.

"I'm sorry," he says hurriedly. "Harriet and Theodora are sleeping." The lie feels clumsy. Transparent. "I shall be sure to tell them you came by."

Before Julia can manage a word, the door is locked. Nathan leans his back against it, closing his eyes to gather himself. He can hear the dull murmur of voices coming unbroken from the parlour. Nothing to suggest the men inside had caught on to Julia's appearance.

He goes back to the dining room and collects his pipe from the ash tray.

"Who was that?" Edwin asks, voice low.

"Julia Mitchell. Here to see Harriet. I told her now was not a good time."

"Interesting." Edwin blows out a thin line of smoke.

"What is that supposed to mean?"

He leans back in his chair. "I think you know what that means, Nate. Don't you think it rather a coincidence that Miss Mitchell happened to arrive right when Holland and his cohort are meeting?"

"With her son," Nathan hisses, inexplicably defensive. "I hardly think she would drag her child along if she were..." *A spy*. He can't bring himself to finish the sentence, in case it solidifies his own doubts about Julia, and her ill-timed appearance. What would she even be hoping to achieve by doing such a thing? She could hardly stand with her ear to the parlour door and listen.

Then again, one step inside the house would tell her something secretive was taking place here. And perhaps that is all she wished to know.

Nathan shakes the thought away.

"Be careful around her, Nate," says Edwin. "We know her brothers are active Jacobites. It's no stretch to think that she might be as well. If she were to find out what is happening at the house, she might—"

"She'll not find out what's happening at the house," Nathan says brusquely. He rubs the back of his neck, keen to change the subject. "Where is Harriet? I hope she did not hear me sending Julia away."

"In her workroom," Edwin tells him. "She's been in there since before Eva left. It seems she's working on something new."

"I trust she has no thought of what is happening in the parlour?"

"Of course not," says Edwin. "And even if she did, I doubt she would have much of an opinion on the matter."

Harriet is not in her workroom. When Nathan returns to his study, he finds her lounged in the high-backed chair behind his desk. Her long blonde hair cascades freely over her shoulders, and she has a dark smudge across one cheek.

"May I use your telescope?" she asks.

Nathan blinks. "The telescope?" He did not even know Harriet was aware of the thing's existence.

"It's for my new painting," she explains. "Thea's story inspired me." She slides forward in the chair. "I want to paint the moon in detail, like Maria Eimmart did."

Nathan smiles faintly. It has been a long time since he has heard his sister speak with such aliveness in her voice. "Of course." He reaches beneath the desk for the box containing the telescope and sets it up at the window. "It's cloudy tonight," he says. "But clear enough to see the moon, I think." He peers through the eyepiece, angling the telescope until it catches the thin white crescent. "Ah. Yes. Quickly." He steps away and nods to Harriet to catch a glimpse of her subject before it disappears behind the clouds. "Do you see it?"

"Yes." A smile appears on her lips. She looks up and snatches her notebook and pencil from the desk. She begins to draw quickly, looking alternatively between the telescope lens and the book. Nathan watches in fascination as the familiar contours of the moon appear on the page. "It's waning tonight," he tells her. "So there is not a great deal to see. But hopefully enough to get you started. Will it show you what you need?"

"Yes. Certainly. In any case, I don't wish my piece to be a scientific representation, but an artistic one. There's no need to capture every specific detail. I just hoped looking at the real thing might give me some more inspiration."

"And has it?"

"Very much."

Nathan smiles crookedly. It is only when Harriet speaks of her art that he feels he gets a glimpse of who she truly is. The only time the façade she hides behind comes down. He is also somewhat relieved that she does not appear to have heard Julia coming to the house. Or at least, if she has, she has not bothered to raise the issue. "I shall leave you to your work," he says, taking paper and an ink pot from the drawer. "Take as much time as you need."

Harriet nods her thanks. Before he reaches the door, she says, "Nathan?"

He turns to look back at her.

Harriet leans back in the desk chair, her fingers tightening around her pencil. "I've been invited to Paris," she says. "To show my work. A nobleman and his wife are interested in sponsoring me."

Nathan's face breaks into a smile. "Harriet, that's wonderful. I'm so pleased for you." He is not surprised. As little as he knows about art, he can tell his sister is immensely talented.

She does not return his smile. "Edwin does not wish me to go," she says. "He tried to have Eva talk me out of it today. He believes my place is by his side. As Thomas's mother."

Nathan hesitates. "Well. That is hardly an unreasonable position."

Harriet gives him pleading eyes. "Will you speak with him? Try to change his mind? Please?"

Nathan sighs. He can practically see the weight that has

descended on Harriet's shoulders. The passion and lightness she had spoken with moments earlier has all but disappeared. But, "He is your husband, Harriet. The decision is his. It is not my place to interfere."

Harriet opens her mouth to speak, then decides against it. She nods shortly and slides around on the chair. Put her eye back against the glass and retreats into silence.

She stays in Nathan's study until the spies have finished their meeting. No eavesdropping tonight; she cannot risk Edwin catching her and sending her up to the bedroom like a child. Besides, the pieces of knowledge she has gathered have already come in use. She has Michael Mitchell's attention, and soon she will have his money too.

If she wants to see Paris, making the journey to Lesbury Common is her only option. Edwin and Nathan have both made that clear.

She waits until they are both in bed. Puts her notebook of lunar images on the table in her workroom. And she slips out the front door.

Overhead is the dinted shard of the moon she had been peering at so closely, now nothing more than a glow behind the clouds. It's a ghostly, faraway kind of light; one that makes her think of otherworlds, and a magic she no longer believes in. It guides her way into the village.

The town is still. The sea is rhythmic against the shoreline, and in the eerie stillness its sigh seems to echo and bounce between stone walls. The stench of drying seaweed hangs on the air.

Harriet hurries through the streets with her head lowered and her lamp held out in front of her. She knocks on the door of the house at the corner of Marygate.

Anne answers without speaking. She gives a nod that is so conspiratorial that Harriet would have laughed had she not been about to leap into something so reckless.

"You can get word to Michael?" she asks, voice low.

"Aye." Anne's eyes glow within the shadows hanging over the doorstep. There's a seriousness about her, and a heaviness Harriet recognises in herself. For not the first time, she is pricked by curiosity. What drew Anne into helping Michael Mitchell? Harriet has never seen any particular affection between them; around Michael, Anne seems just as grave and unyielding as ever. Or perhaps this is just a cover she presents to hide her true nature from outside eyes. Harriet knows all too well about that. Likely though, and this brings her no small amount of satisfaction, Anne's actions have little to do with a man—or rather, little to do with any man but James the Old Pretender. As Michael had told her, there are more than a few women who are willing to risk their own safety to advance the Jacobite cause.

Her mind leaps to Julia. She can never find out that Harriet is to help Michael re-join the rebels. Once the army mustering at Lesbury engages, there is every chance Michael will die in battle. Surely, in Julia's eyes, for Harriet to help him do so would be a far greater betrayal than her hiding her brothers in the attic of Highfield House.

But right now, she has no room for Julia's concerns, or what will happen to Michael once the Jacobite army begins to march. Right now, all she has room for are those coins in his pouch—money that will be hers once she completes this task.

It will lead her towards the life she craves with every inch of her being.

"Tell him I will do it," she says. "For the sum agreed."

"Your timing is good," Anne says brusquely. "He plans to leave tomorrow evening. Told me he can't wait any longer for you to make up your mind."

Harriet nods. As she turns to leave, Anne says:

"You are one of the Blakes, aren't you?"

Harriet smiles wryly. No, she wants to say. She is not. She never was. But that is a conversation she is not willing to go into with this near stranger. Instead, she nods.

"Interesting," says Anne. "That you're doing this."

"My family are not spies," Harriet says. "If that is what you're suggesting."

"I did not say they were. But I imagine it unlikely that a family from London might have Jacobite leanings. So I can only imagine you are doing this for other reasons." She tilts her head, as though trying to see behind Harriet's eyes. "Is it as Michael says? That you have no loyalty to your family?"

Harriet bristles at the accusation, though she knows there is more than a small grain of truth to it. She does not wish to see her family in danger, of course, but perhaps there is a part of her that wishes to defy them. Defy Edwin for his refusal to support her trip to Paris, and Nathan for refusing to speak to her husband on her behalf. Defy Eva for flitting off to Longstone and abandoning her.

"My reasons are none of your business," she says tightly.

Anne opens her mouth, as though debating whether to press the issue. After a moment, she nods. "Be here tomorrow evening," she says. "Just after sunset.

# CHAPTER NINETEEN

The sunsets are coming earlier now, as the year draws closer to winter. The sun careens towards the horizon, bathing the island in the cobalt blue of evening. Harriet has told Edwin she will not be at dinner tonight, but that she will take her meal alone in her workroom. He had not argued, just as she expected. He has been reluctant to raise his voice with her since this news of her father. At least, she supposes, it has been good for something.

Her new piece is coming alive. The first layers of paint are on the canvas, colours carefully blended to depict the unending depth of the night sky. She is not sure if the thought of the journey to Lesbury is fuelling her inspiration, or if her inspiration is fuelling her desire to complete the journey. Her desire to see Michael's coins in her hand, and her paintings hung on the Baillieus' walls.

She knows she will not make it all the way to Lesbury and back without her family noting her disappearance. But she hopes she will be far enough from Lindisfarne by the time they notice her missing that they will have no way of finding her. No doubt when she returns, Edwin will have rediscovered his will to raise his voice with her, but the money Michael is paying her will soften the blow of that. It is hard to care how Edwin will retaliate when she has the means to bring her dreams to life.

She has stowed her travelling cloak and bonnet behind the chair in her workroom, along with the lamp she will need to light her way into the village. Has forced down a few mouthfuls of the soup Mrs Brodie had brought her. But after she has wiped her pallet and set the brushes aside to dry, she does not go to the window to make her escape. Instead, almost without conscious thought, she finds her way to the nursery. And she sits with Thomas in her arms, drawn here, to him, by the pull of guilt she had hoped would not show itself. His eyes, round and blue, are piercing hers, and she is finding it impossible to look away. What is he seeing, she wonders? Does he recognise his mother, or does he see a stranger? She cannot deny he sometimes feels that way to her. An unknown entity she had never longed for, the way she knows she is supposed to. She knows well there is something wrong with her; this woman who never craved a child, or the touch of her husband's body.

She traces a finger along Thomas's smooth cheek; a gesture she has done so many times in the past, in an attempt to know her son—to recognise a little of herself in him. Perhaps it's best that she finds none—after all, why would she ever wish any of her brittle self-loathing on her child?

She pulls her eyes from his and settles him into the crib, then makes her way down into her workroom before she changes her mind.

She ties her bonnet and takes the lamp from the shelf. She keeps a candle burning on the mantel in her workroom so it might cast a little light beneath the closed door and buy her time before anyone notices her missing. She wrestles open the window. The creaking front entrance of the house is an impossibility, of course, as is creeping to the back door while Mrs Brodie is at work in the kitchen. Sea-scented air gusts inside and flutters the flame of the candle. Harriet leans out the window and lowers the lamp to the earth, then lifts her skirts to her knees and clambers over the sill. She slides, somewhat ungracefully, the short distance to the ground.

Though the sun has just disappeared, there is already an inkiness to the dusk, a silver-dark light that feels almost otherworldly. The first stars are dusted across a clear sky, beside the thin crescent moon. The roe deer are active as she makes her way through the dunes, skitting between the shadows and rustling the grass. Each soft thud of their hooves makes her heart thump a little louder. She follows the rusty glow of her lantern into the village. She feels an odd sense of detachment. A sense of being utterly outside herself. Completely removed from the life she knows. And that, she thinks, is a blissful thing. She has had quite enough of being inside her own head.

"Good evening, Mrs Whitley." Harriet whirls around. It's the pastor, of all people, his voice distrusting—or at least made that way by her own racing heart. He looks past her into the empty street, then back to meet her eyes. "What are you doing out alone at night?"

"Visiting a friend," she says, sharper than she intended. Will he go to Highfield House and tell Edwin he has seen her? Unlikely, she supposes; he has no lamp, and will not set off on the trek to Emmanuel Head without one. In any case, by the time he makes the journey up to the house, she and Michael will be on their way.

The pastor—young, but with dark, scrutinising eyes beyond his years—looks her up and down, but doesn't prod. "Mind yourself," he says finally. "And have a safe journey home."

Harriet cannot get to Anne's door quick enough. She and Michael are already in the lane beside her house. Michael is tethering a horse to a small covered wagon, while Anne stows a basket of food beneath the bench seats. Michael is dressed in a dark greatcoat and breeches; Anne in simple grey skirts befitting a maid, her dark hair tucked up beneath a white mobcap. They turn in unison towards the glow of Harriet's lantern. A satisfied smile appears on Michael's face. Anne gives her a brusque, wordless nod.

"I want the money now," Harriet murmurs. She feels on edge after her run-in with the priest. Having the coins in her pocket will go some way to steadying her, reminding her of why she is doing this.

Michael raises his eyebrows, the corner of his lips turning up into a half-smile. "I didn't realise you were so distrusting."

"You were hiding in our roof. I think it fair to say you're a man who cannot be trusted."

"Very well." He digs into his pocket and produces a pouch of coins. Hands it to Harriet. "Keep it hidden while we travel. In case we run into trouble."

Her mouth feels suddenly dry. "Is that what you expect to happen? We will run into trouble?"

"I hope not," says Michael, too lightly. "That's why I have you." He finishes securing the harness and pats the horse on its broad neck. He offers Harriet a hand to climb into the wagon, Anne scrambling up behind her without waiting for assistance. Michael swings himself into the box seat and takes up the reins. And the carriage begins to move out of the village before Harriet has a chance to regret her decision.

# CHAPTER TWENTY

Nathan is infuriated with himself over how much he loves the telescope. Of course he loves it. It's just like the one he had begged his father for back when he was a boy.

"You keep this away from Oliver, now," his father had said to him, the day he had handed Nathan the box. Had even let him hide it in the study until it was time to set it up at the window. Exploring the sky with his father—and without his coldblooded brother—are some of Nathan's most cherished childhood memories.

So yes, he wants to use the telescope. And yes, he wants to share it with his own child; give her similarly precious memories; show her places that hide beyond human comprehension. The fact that the telescope came from Julia is a fact he will just have to do his best to ignore.

After dinner, he and Theodora head out into the night. Thea is bundled into her cloak and woollen bonnet, and she holds the telescope close to her chest, carrying it like the most precious of bundles. Nathan walks with the stand in one hand

and a lamp in the other.

It's a still night; clear and cold. The sea sighing is loud against the shoreline; seems to fill all the empty spaces. Overhead, the stars are a blaze. Nathan cannot wait to lift the telescope to them and pull more pinpoints of light from the darkness. This morning, in a burst of childlike excitement, he had written to the circulating library at Cambridge and ordered copies of the Kepler star maps he remembers poring over with his father. He cannot wait to show them to Theodora; to teach her to track those glittering trails of light across the night sky.

Once they are far enough from the house that the lamps behind the windows will not dim the brilliance of the sky, Nathan blows out the lantern and lets the oceanic wash of the stars intensify. In the darkness, Theodora takes a step closer to him, stopping, instinctively, an inch from making contact. Nathan takes the telescope from her hand and settles it into the stand. He peers into it, adjusting the eyepiece to track past the pointer stars and find the blaze of Polaris.

He steps aside, and Theodora hurries to the telescope. "Do you see the bright star in the middle?" She nods. "That's the North Star. It's how ships find their way across the sea."

She looks over at her shoulder at him, slightly doubtful. "How?"

"Well... It does not move across the sky like the other stars do. And it always points to the north, you see."

"What about these stars? And these ones?"

Nathan answers her questions and guides the telescope through the darkness, pointing out the dragons and bears and winged horses the constellations paint across the sky. And then he lowers the telescope for a moment, catching the glitter of a light on the sea. Henry Ward's ship, he thinks dully. He hates that that ship, that man, is always at the forefront his mind. But how can it be any other way?

He tilts the telescope until it catches the tinderbox blaze of the Longstone light. The life Eva has made out there is something of a mystery to him, and the darkness on every side of the beacon goes little way to answering his questions.

It is past nine when they return to Highfield House. Thomas is wailing steadily from upstairs, and Nathan feels his serenity dissipate. He unties the cloak from his daughter's shoulders, the telescope and stand tucked under one arm. "Up to bed, Thea. It's getting late."

"A story?" she begs.

"A short one. I shall be up in a moment."

She gambols upstairs just as Edwin strides out from the parlour. "She's gone again, Nathan," he says, scrubbing a hand over his eyes. "The window was open in her workroom. I think she used it to leave the house." He rakes a hand through his dark hair, which hangs uncharacteristically loose on his shoulders. "I've waited here long enough, hoping she'll show herself. I need to go out and find her."

The last of Nathan's calmness evaporates. He tries to keep his own anxiety under control. The memory of Eva's disappearance is far too fresh in his mind. It had been barely two months ago that she had been forced into Donald Macauley's boat and had spent the night on Longstone.

But this, Nathan feels certain, is not the same thing. He has little doubt that Harriet's disappearance is her own doing. An act of rebellion. Anger, perhaps, that she has not been permitted her trip to Paris. Perhaps he ought to have made more of an effort to convince Edwin on her behalf.

The fact that she has left of her own accord does not ease the worry in his chest. Especially with Henry Ward's ship glowing in the bay.

"I'll come with you," he tells Edwin. He sets the telescope down carefully in the corner of the parlour, regretting that Theodora will have to go without her tales of magic and moonlight tonight.

The blackness feels thick as they head into the village. As he had made his way across the dunes with Thea and the telescope, the starlit night had felt like a thrill. Full of magic. Now, the dark feels vaguely threatening. A reminder of how much his family has stacked against them.

As much as he does not want to admit it, he knows the first place they need to go is Julia's shop.

"I'll ask at the tavern in case anyone passed her in the street," says Edwin. "You check if she's with Miss Mitchell." Nathan nods, fighting off a pull of unease. Julia will likely have questions for him, after the way he had thrown her and Bobby off his doorstep yesterday. Questions he has no thought of how to answer. The thought has his heart racing, but it is with something that is not entirely dread.

He peers through the front window into the shop. It is dark, lit only by the glowing remains of the fire. He can see the bulbous shadow of the cat curled up on the tiles by the hearth. Can see a stack of books, and what appears to be clothing, piled up upon the counter. Two chairs are crammed between the shelves beside what looks, inexplicably, to be part of an old wrought iron bed head.

Nathan goes into the alley beside the building and knocks

on the side door. Silence at first, then he hears the stairs creak. Julia pulls open the door. Her lips part at the sight of him.

"Mr Blake."

"Is Harriet here?" he asks.

"No." She tugs her shawl around her shoulders. "I've not seen her in days." Concern creases her brow. "She's missing?"

Nathan nods. "Perhaps it's too soon to worry. But… well, as you know, she has not been quite herself of late."

"Is there someone else on the island she might be visiting?" Julia asks.

He sighs. "As far as I know, you're the only person she spends her time with."

"Perhaps she's with her sister. She could have paid one of the fishermen to take her out there."

Regretfully, Nathan is well aware of this possibility. He is also well aware that he ought to have sent Edwin to the curiosity shop. Because at the thought of making a journey out to Longstone, that thumping in his chest veers a little closer to dread.

"I'm sure it's too dark to sail out there tonight," he says, a little more hopefully than he knows he ought to.

Julia strides back into the shop, making Nathan follow almost instinctively. She takes her bonnet and cloak from the counter. "I'd like to know if she is out there or not. If she is, at least we can stop worrying." She tosses her cloak over her shoulders and heads for the staircase. "I'll have to go by my friend Alice's house. Leave Bobby there. I don't fancy taking him with me at such an hour. It's not the safest of journeys in dark."

Nathan's throat is suddenly dry.

Julia looks back over her shoulder at him. "Are you

coming?"

And what can he do but say, "Of course"?

# CHAPTER TWENTY-ONE

He tries to tell himself this flimsy fishing boat is seaworthy. That there is nothing beneath the water for them to strike. That this rolling, ink-dark sea does not have the power to swallow him.

But Nathan does not believe a single word he tells himself. Outside the Lindisfarne anchorage, the sea melts into the sky and his body cannot settle into the up-and-down rhythm of the boat on the swell. He can see the faint rose of light from the mainland, and out ahead, the shipping beacon on Longstone.

He pulls in a breath, fingers wrapped tightly around the edge of his seat. Despite the cold night, his shirt is damp with sweat beneath his greatcoat. How far to Longstone? Five miles? Ten? Twenty? With the dark distorting his surroundings, it seems impossible to tell.

"Are you all right?" Julia asks from behind him.

Nathan looks over his shoulder at her. Tries for a smile he knows looks more like a grimace. "I'm not fond of the sea."

"You are living in the wrong place then, aren't you."

"I'm becoming more and more certain of that each day."

Her eyes soften in the lamplight. "It's not far. A mile more perhaps."

He nods stiffly.

"Keep your eyes on the firebasket," she says. "It may help the seasickness."

He glues his gaze to the blaze out ahead of them. And it goes someway to calming the clamouring in his belly. Unbidden, he feels a pull of gratitude towards Julia.

She has not spoken a word about his refusing her entry into the house yesterday. Perhaps she has just let the matter slide out of concern for Harriet. Or perhaps she too is afraid of what questions may arise if she goes near the issue. Nathan pushes the thoughts away. He has far too much on his mind right now to even entertain the idea of Julia spying for the Jacobites. Besides, she has done him a great favour by sailing out here to help his family. He owes her more than suspicion.

He watches her lean on the tiller. "Are you certain you know what you're doing?"

"Do you wish to take over?" she asks pointedly.

He swallows. "No. I'm sorry. I just... Have you sailed out here in the dark before?"

"Yes. Well, close to dark. Not like this," she admits. "But I can manage it. The Knavestone reef is to the north-east of Longstone. We'll come in from the south."

"The reef?" he repeats sickly.

A faint smile appears on her lips. "We shall give it a wide berth, I promise. And we can thank your sister and her husband for guiding our way."

Nathan says nothing. If it weren't for his sister and her

husband, he wouldn't be needing to make this infernal journey in the first place. "When did you learn to sail?" he asks.

Julia tucks a coil of red hair beneath her cap. "When I was a child. My older brother Hugh taught me. Of course, I thought I knew everything back then. Told him I did not need instruction." She smiles to herself. "Hugh threw me into the boat and told me to sail it without him. That sorted me out nice and quick."

Nathan gives her a faint smile that disappears quickly. "You must miss him terribly."

Julia looks up at the taut sail, as though to hide the sudden emotion in her eyes. For several moments, she doesn't speak. Perhaps debating whether to discuss her missing brother with him—or whether he will use it as another opportunity to condemn her family. "It's the uncertainly that is the worst thing," she says finally. "Not knowing if he is alive or dead. Not knowing if I will ever see him again." She lowers her eyes. "When I found myself with child, my father threw me out of his house. Hugh and his wife took me in. Kept a roof over me and Bobby's heads til I could stand on my own. I owe him a lot." She sighs. "He became obsessed with the Jacobite cause after his wife and son died. A way of giving meaning to his life, I suppose. After all he lost." Her jaw tightens. "In any case, I'm sure you have little interest in Hugh's whereabouts. My brothers have caused enough trouble for your family."

Nathan looks her in the eye. "That does not mean I wish them any ill will."

Julia doesn't answer. She turns away suddenly, as though unable to hold his gaze.

After a long silence, she brings the boat up to a small jetty

162

protruding from the island. Firelight spills over the rocks, turning the surfaces of the pools bright gold. A lamp glows through the window of the small stone cottage, but beyond the reach of the firebasket, the rest of the island seeps into darkness.

Nathan did not know what he was expecting his sister's new life to look like. He only knows it was not this. He is simultaneously appalled and awed at its remoteness; its eerie, shadowed beauty. At the responsibility Eva and Finn have made their own.

He feels an uncomfortable pull in his stomach—a tug of protectiveness towards his younger sister. He is not sure if it's a fear of Eva being out here, so vulnerable to the ocean in this tiny, towering house, or worry that she might have latched herself to this life—and the man that comes with it— thoughtlessly, too quickly, too blinded by love to turn an eye to the future.

But when Eva emerges from the cottage, expertly navigating the pools and rocky crevices, there's a look about her that says she belongs here, has always belonged here. And perhaps a part of her has always known that, even as a young child when she had slept in a bedroom with the Longstone light straining through the window.

"Nathan?" she says. "What are you doing here?"

He climbs shakily from the boat, gripping tightly to the posts of the jetty. The feel of solid rock beneath his feet is somewhat steadying, though the island feels as though it could succumb to the sea at any minute. "Good Lord, Eva," he says, "this is—" She raises her eyebrows, and it has the effect of silencing him. He swallows. "Is Harriet here?"

"Harriet? No, of course not."

Nathan feels something sink inside him. Eva glances at Finn, who has followed her out of the cottage.

"Come inside," he says. "Warm yourselves."

Nathan teeters across the dark rocks and follows Eva and Finn up the steps to their cottage, Julia close behind. Finn shoves open the door and it squeals against the floorboards. Warm air billows out into the night. Nathan is grateful for the fire blazing in the grate. Even more grateful for the bottle of whisky he spies on the sideboard. One of Julia's brothers is sitting at the table, surrounded by three empty soup bowls. He stands as they enter.

"What in hell are you doing sailing here so late at night, Jul?" he demands. "It's far too dangerous a crossing."

"Calm yourself, Angus," she says, holding her hands up to the fire to warm them. "We're here in one piece." She rubs her palms together. "Where's Michael?"

"Thought to ask you that," Finn shoots. He leans up against the door and folds his arms across his chest. "If your brother wants to use this place to hide then I suggest he damn well stays hidden."

Julia straightens suddenly. "Michael has left again?"

"Aye," says Angus. "He says he's off to another..." He eyes Nathan warily. "Well."

"Another meeting?" Julia finishes tautly. "You can trust him, Angus. If you couldn't, do you really think your neck would still be unbroken?"

She looks sideways at Nathan, and for a moment, he tries to see behind her eyes. Does she truly trust him, she wonders? Or is this all part of some game she is playing?

Eva follows Nathan's longing glance to the whisky bottle. She goes to the sideboard and clatters through it for the cups. Fear for her sister is coiled tightly at the base of her stomach. She knows Harriet has been on edge lately. Knows she is likely to behave rashly. And she also knows the villagers do not trust her family. Whether this disappearance is Harriet's own doing or not, Eva fears she is in danger.

She fills four cups—all they have in the house—and hands the cannikins around. Nathan nods his thanks. Drinks hurriedly.

"When did you last see Harriet?" Eva asks him.

"Sometime before dinner tonight," he tells her. "She said she was going to work on her painting. No one heard her leave. She must have gone out through the window."

Eva takes a sip from the fourth cup, then hands it to Finn. "I'll come back to Lindisfarne with you," she tells Nathan. "I'll help you look for her. I cannot just stay here and wait for news."

Finn empties the cup in one gulp and sets it on the table. "Wait for the slack tide," he tells Julia. "A quarter of an hour. It will make your journey back a little safer."

She nods. Crouches back beside the fire to warm her hands.

Eva goes to the bedroom to gather her things. She is not sure what is rattling her more: anxiety over Harriet's disappearance, or the prospect of the treacherous journey back to Holy Island in the dark. Finn follows her into the bedroom. Closes the door behind him. "I'm coming too. I'll take you over."

She pauses, her duffel bag in one hand and her spare shift

in the other. "No," she says. "Not to the house. I couldn't ask that of you."

"You're not asking it. I'm suggesting it. I want to help you find your sister."

She hesitates. "I do not know how long I'll be there. It could be days."

"It's no matter. Angus can keep the light. And Michael, if he ever bothers to show himself."

"What about…"

He steps closer and cups her elbow in his broad palm. Eva smells woodsmoke and ocean on his skin. "Do you not want me there?"

She lets out her breath. "Of course I do. But…" She does not want memories of Oliver's death to return to the front of his mind. And perhaps there is also a fear of what her family might see if Finn was to step back into Highfield House. Perhaps this secret they are carrying might become a little harder to keep.

He presses his rough palms to her cheeks. "I'm coming with you, Evie." He lets his hands fall and reaches for his greatcoat slung over the foot of the bed. Eva tries to catch his eye, but he is looking away, wearing a closed-off expression. And perhaps closed off is exactly what he needs to be to set foot in Highfield House again. She feels a swell of love for him, coupled with a pull of unease. "Finish packing your things," he says stiffly. "We need to catch the tide."

With the slack tide, the water is black ink, rippled orange by the firebasket. Finn glances over his shoulder at Julia's fishing boat edging away from his jetty. Once she is clear of the island, he tugs on the sheet to open the mainsail, catching the breeze. He navigates slowly around the rim of the Farnes, letting Julia follow close behind. To his right, he sees white water glowing as it breaks on the Knavestone rocks. For all the years he has lived on Longstone, he can count on one hand the number of times he has made this journey in the dark.

Eva's eyes are wide in the glow of the lamp she is clutching. "You don't think she's with Ward, do you? What if she found out about him somehow?"

Finn fears such an outcome as much as Eva does. He can't bear the thought of her family finding out the truth about the night Oliver died. If that happened, he'd have little choice but to accept Ward's offer to join his crew and disappear from their lives. It's a prospect he can't bear to follow far.

He glances over his shoulder at the firebasket. It's a strange feeling to see it from the sea like this. Unmooring, like he is heading to places he was not meant for.

Places like Highfield House.

The house is visible from far out on the water, lamps in windows glowing like moons. He has seen this house from the sea on countless occasions. How many times had he stood on the deck of the *Eagle* while Ward was inside the manor, spending his nights with Abigail Blake? It had looked just as it does now.

Though they are memories he rarely revisits voluntarily, he finds himself combing through his recollections of Ward's visits to Abigail. Whenever they had returned to England after privateering in the German Ocean, she had offered the *Eagle's* officers comfortable quarters for the night. Had the visits taken place across months or years? Had Ward and Abigail known each other before her husband had died? How long had they shared each other's bed? Finn has no thought of it. He himself had only set foot in the house on one occasion—the night that has stayed with him ever since.

It's a fresh kind of stupidity, perhaps, to be willingly stepping back into the place. But as he watches the hazy shape of Highfield House sharpen, Finn knows he has no choice. Eva must be here, therefore so must he. Not for a second had he questioned that.

That doesn't change the hollow, falling sensation in his stomach as he eases the skiff towards the beach.

Eva glances sideways at him, her fingers clenched tightly around the handle of the lantern. "You can change your mind, Finn. I'll not—"

"I'm not going to change my mind." The words come out sharper than he intended, and Eva falls silent. He flashes her an apologetic look and covers her hand with his, but doesn't trust himself to speak.

The past cannot hurt him, of course. Oliver Blake's ghost is not going to rise from the woodwork and end him. But the truth that he is hiding; that can hurt him. Worse, it can hurt Eva. And it has the power to tear them apart.

# CHAPTER TWENTY-TWO

Harriet is not sure she has ever seen darkness quite as thick as this. There is barely a thread of a moon, and the stars have disappeared behind a solid bank of cloud. Cold wind gusts through the open front of the wagon, fragrant with the smell of damp earth. All that lights the road is the flimsy lamp in front of the box seat. Still, the horse trots onwards, the rhythmic rattle of hooves lulling Harriet into something trancelike and quiet. And perhaps this is the best state to be in; a state which does not allow her to think too closely about all she is doing. About her family, who will no doubt be looking for her by now. About the son she has left behind. About what might lie in that impenetrable darkness.

There's an uncomfortable tightness in her chest. A shallowness to her breath. Fear, she realises. She tries to swallow it down. Fear is one of those gruelling emotions she does her best not to feel. And more often than not, she succeeds. Is able to detach herself from her reality enough to let the fear pass her by. But it is here now, simmering at the back of her mind like a contagion.

From the dark innards of the wagon, Harriet can just see through to the box seat. She can see Michael in profile, his features underscored by lamplight. His square jaw is set firm, eyes fixed ahead in intense focus. What is he thinking? Is he imagining the moment he will re-join the Jacobite rebels; or that moment when he has sword and pistol in hand, and it is a toss of a coin whether he will live to see the next sunrise? Or is he merely focused on the next moment ahead; the next yard of dark road; the next tug of the reins? Is he, too, afraid? Or is his passion for his cause too consuming for that?

Harriet had assumed her own passion for her cause was too. But the fear is here, thick and cloying, turning her stomach and making her fingers clench hard in her lap. Now identified, it will not lie down.

She slips a hand beneath her cloak, feeling the bulge of the coin pouch inside her stays. Coins that will make all this—and whatever fury she returns home to—worth it.

She can feel Anne's eyes on her. Dark brows, full of expression. "So what is it then?" she asks. Her voice cutting through the silence make Harriet jump. They have barely exchanged a word since they left Holy Island several hours ago. "Why are you here?"

"Pardon?" Harriet heard her perfectly; just needs a moment to craft an answer. Decide how much to share.

"Your reason for being here," says Anne, toying with the hem of her apron. "What is it?"

Harriet peeks through the front of the wagon at the barely lit road ahead. "He is paying me well," she says simply. "And I have a great need for the money."

Anne gives a short laugh. It's a judgmental sound that adds to the faint nausea in Harriet's stomach. "What need does a lady like you have for money? Your family is the wealthiest on the island."

Harriet would laugh if it weren't for the sense of dread she feels creeping up on her. If the villagers were to see the broken window panes of Highfield House, or the holes in Nathan's boots, she feels certain they would change their assessment of the situation. But she says, "That money belongs to my brother. My husband. It is not for my own purposes."

"Your own purposes. And what might those be?" Anne sounds disparaging, and Harriet desperately wishes for their old silence.

"It's of no matter," she says.

She hears another laugh come from the darkness. She can just imagine what Anne is thinking: that this polished young lady from the house on the head needs the money for silk gowns and fancy scents, and jewels to hang from her throat. When she compares her plans for Paris with the way Michael is about to risk his life, they feel barely less trivial than a new wardrobe.

She finds herself thinking of Isabelle. What will she think when Harriet tells her of this journey she has undertaken to make Paris a reality? Pride, perhaps? Admiration? Or will she scold her for leaving her son behind; leaving her husband and siblings to worry? Isabelle is far more caring than she is, Harriet knows. Far less selfless. It is part of what had drawn her to her in the first place—that glimpse of something she knows is all too lacking in herself.

Inexplicably, she feels tears prick her eyes. She blinks them away quickly.

"What of you?" she asks Anne. It feels like the silence is over, at least for now, and if they are to speak, Harriet would rather steer the conversation away from herself.

Anne lowers her voice. "I wish to play my part. And they'll not accept a woman in their army. We're consigned to running messages. Raising the next generation of men who will fight for the Stuarts."

"Would you fight for them? If you could?"

"Of course I would," Anne says, with a touch too much conviction. Enough to let Harriet see the hint of doubt beneath. Anne is quiet for a few moments, as though she too has caught a glimpse of her own uncertainty. "I think of it sometimes," she says. "Pulling on a pair of breeches and tucking my hair up under a cap. Wouldn't be the first woman to do so. But I couldn't do that to my husband. He needs me."

Anne is aware her reasons sound like an excuse, Harriet can tell from her tone of voice. And it brings her a hint of satisfaction. Still, Anne obviously has more than a hint of passion for the Jacobite cause. She wouldn't be here if she didn't. What would it feel like, Harriet wonders, to fight for something so selfless? If she is ever to place her survival upon the toss of a coin, it will be for her own purposes, not that of some distant would-be king.

"What does your husband think of you doing all this with Michael?" she asks.

Anne snorts. "I'd tell you if I thought he had any knowledge of it. Poor fool can't hold his liquor. Just have to feed him a glass or two and he'll sleep through til morning. He'll have no inkling I'm even gone."

Harriet squeezes her hands together even tighter, forcing down a swell of panic. She will have no such luxury; of that she is certain.

"And you?" asks Anne.

"My husband will know I am gone," she says. "And I shall pay for it when I return. But this is something I have to do."

Finn draws his sloop up beside Julia's fishing boat, allowing Nathan to stumble from one vessel into the other. He curses as he lands heavily in the skiff beside his sister.

"All right, Nathan?" Eva asks, the faintest hint of a smile on her lips.

"Fine." He looks over his shoulder at Julia and gives her a brisk nod. "Thank you," he says stiffly. "For taking me out there."

An unreadable look passes over Julia's lamplit face. Then she nods and tugs on the mainsail sheet. "I shall let you know if I hear anything."

Eva looks questioningly at her brother as Finn rows the skiff towards the shore. "That was rude. You might have asked her to the house."

Nathan watches Julia's boat round the point and head back towards the village. "She has Jacobite sympathies," he says. "It's too dangerous her being at the house when Holland and the other messengers could turn up at any time. Besides, when did you become her biggest supporter?"

"I just think—" Eva jolts forward as the boat crunches hard against the pebbles on the sea floor. She grabs at the gunwale to keep from falling. "What are you doing, Finn? Are you all right?"

"Sorry." He is distracted. On edge. He can feel it behind him; Highfield House. Can see it in his mind's eye: cobbled brick and stone walls, crooked chimneys, the weather-worn red tiles of the roof. Perpetual darkness behind the rows of gabled windows.

He feels the boat tilt as Nathan steps out into the shallow water. Still, he doesn't turn.

"All right?" Eva asks again, voice low.

Finn nods. Stands and leaps out of the boat in one swift movement, to prevent himself from changing his mind. He holds out his hand for Eva. She takes it, then watches him closely as he drags the skiff up onto the beach. She hangs back, letting Nathan go on to the house ahead of them.

In the moonless night, the house is a beast, candles glowing in windows and the front door thrown open, letting a blaze of light out onto the dunes. Finn forces himself to walk. To breathe evenly. To step through the front door.

Here is the foyer, hung with paintings of weatherworn lands and men in wide Elizabethan collars. There is that wide staircase Abigail Blake had looked down on him from, before leading him upstairs to her son's bedroom. The air feels thick and close, fragrant with candle wax and freshly cut wood. The faint hint of pipe smoke and the lingering mustiness of neglect. He feels it tighten his chest. Hears the blood rushing in his ears. His hand tenses around Eva's.

She glances at him. "We do not have to…"

He shakes his head faintly, silencing her. He can feel the unease pouring off her; fear over her sister, and anxiety over his being here. He had not come with her so she might feel anxious. He knows that right now, his presence is having the opposite effect to what he had intended. He presses a hand between her shoulder blades, nudging her forward. Nods. It's all right.

He follows her into a sitting room, where an enormous fire is roaring in the grate. After the icy journey across from Longstone, the room feels hot and airless. He feels the back of his neck prickle with something that is either heat or dread. Finn finds his gaze travelling around the room; to its worn embroidered armchairs and polished tea tables. A large bookshelf stands against one wall, the gold-embossed spines of the volumes tatty and faded.

He wonders if this is the room where Abigail had entertained Henry Ward and his crew. He pictures Ward reclined on the settle with his long legs stretched out in front of him, pictures his crewmen in front of the fire with glasses in their hands. And what about Abigail herself? Had she welcomed them? Drunk with them? Had she sought time alone with Ward? Or had that been all his doing?

Tonight, Harriet's husband is the only man in front of the fire. His greatcoat and hat have been tossed carelessly over the arm of the settle, his shirt half-untucked and his hair windswept and tangled. He looks a different person to the wigged and polished gentleman Finn had met at his wedding.

"The pastor saw her in the village," Edwin tells Nathan. "She told him she was going to see a friend. I assume it was a lie." He looks past Nathan to Finn and Eva. "I see you brought the cavalry." Finn feels Edwin looking him up and down, assessing him. Eva takes a step closer to him, perhaps unconsciously. Perhaps a defensive, protective move. But after a moment of consideration, Edwin says, "It was good of you both to come."

A housekeeper bustles into the room with a tray and places a large porcelain teapot on the table, along with a plate of colourless biscuits. Nathan nods his thanks and she disappears silently from the parlour.

This housekeeper, this tea tray, this cavernous, embroidered parlour—it's a reminder of the status of the family Finn has married into. A reminder—as if he needs one—of how much he does not belong here. He knows the Blakes' money is running out; Eva has told him everything. But it does not feel that way. Sometimes it is easy to forget the old wealth his wife comes from when her hair is windblown and her hands are streaked with coal dust.

Eva goes silently to the table and fills the teacups. The faint mewling of a baby floats down from the top storey.

"We ought to be out there looking for her." Edwin begins to pace. "Not sitting here drinking tea."

"You know there's little more we can do in the dark," says Nathan, taking a bottle of brandy from the cabinet and sloshing an ocean of the stuff into his cup. "We'll go out looking again at first light." He nods vaguely towards the plate of biscuits. "Please. Eat."

"No, thank you." Finn's voice comes out strained. He doesn't want to be here, making these forced, unfamiliar pleasantries. Despite the vastness of the room, the air feels too thick, too heavy, making something close in his chest like a fist. It is taking everything in him not to tear out of this house and never return.

Eva glances at him. "I'm going to try and sleep," she murmurs. "Will you join me?"

Finn nods wordlessly. They make their goodnights then, alone in the dark hallway, Eva takes his hand. Her grip is tight;

for her own sake or his, he can't quite determine. She takes a step onto the staircase.

Finn's free hand shoots out, grabbing hold of the banister. Because at once he is a child again, following Abigail Blake up these stairs, the smooth, time-worn wood of the rail beneath his palm. He hears his breathing quicken.

Eva stops walking. "Let's go back downstairs. We can—"

"No," Finn says quickly. "It's all right. Really." He starts climbing again, before she can question him. Before he can change his mind.

There are reminders. Will always be reminders. Reminders he has learnt to deal with. The faint scar on his forearm from Oliver Blake's knife. The dark shape of Holy Island, visible through the cottage window. And yes, the sky blue eyes of the woman he loves—the same eyes as her elder brother; the same eyes that had stared lifeless at him from the floor of the bedroom with the priest hole within the wall. This house is just one more reminder. It does not need to consume him.

Eva pushes open the door to what he assumes is her old bedroom. It's sparse and cold, the grate empty and the wash basin dry, as though no one has entered since she had come to live in his cottage. A chipped chest of drawers is pushed up into one corner, a worn gold-rimmed mirror sitting above the mantel. Like the rest of the rooms in the house, the walls are lined with dark wood panelling, but through the open curtains, Finn can see the faint bloom of the Longstone light.

In spite of himself, he smiles. "You can see the firebasket from here?"

Eva comes towards him. Slides her arms around his waist and looks up at him, her chin against his chest. "I may have spent a little time pining at that window." She holds him tightly, as though trying to shield him—from what? The past? The house itself? He lets himself sink into her. She stands on her tiptoes to kiss his lips. "Thank you for coming. I'm glad you're here."

At a knock on the door, she releases her grip on him, and goes to collect a jug of water from the housekeeper. She murmurs her thanks and closes the door quietly behind her, setting the jug on the washstand.

Finn sits on the edge of the bed. It groans loudly beneath his weight. "I came back here once, you know. After Oliver... I came back to see your mother."

"You did?" Eva perches beside him, kicking off her shoes and curling her legs beneath her.

"Aye. A couple of months after it happened." The beams above their heads creak softly as the house settles around them. "I'd found work on a farm in Berwick by then, but I knew I had to come back. I wanted to tell your ma what happened. How he died." He lowers his eyes. "Tell her I was sorry." They come out sounding husky, these words he has never spoken before. His visit to the house, his failed attempt at an apology, in a desperate attempt to ease his guilt—these are things he had almost forgotten. Being back inside the place has drawn the memory out into the light.

Eva covers his hand with his. "What happened?"

"When I got to the house, it was dark. But I looked through the window of the parlour, and I could see the coals in the grate were still hot. I knocked, but there was no answer."

Eva lets out her breath. "I wonder if it was the night we fled. Mother left everything behind that night. No doubt she left the fires in the grate burning too."

"Ward's ship was in the bay that night," Finn tells her, watching Eva trace her finger over his thumbnail. "I could see it—in the same place it is now. After I looked through the parlour window, I saw someone from his crew coming towards the house."

Eva frowns. "Was it Ward?"

"I don't know. Probably. It was too dark for me to see properly. I didn't want him to catch me, so I ran. Didn't come back to Lindisfarne for years."

Eva shifts on the bed, leaning her forehead against his. "I'm sorry you never got to tell my mother what you needed to."

Finn tucks a loose strand of hair behind her ear. "It's probably for the best," he says. "I can't imagine she would have let me just walk away unpunished, do you?"

Eva sighs. "Honestly, I don't know what she would have done. I have no sense of who she was anymore. I like to think she would have understood it was a mistake. But I know that may well be wishful thinking." She sighs. Unpins her hair and begins to unlace her shortjacket. "The bed is a little small, I'm afraid," she says, veering abruptly away from the subject of her mother. "We shall have to make do."

Finn leans over and kisses her neck, the feel of her soft skin going some way towards steading him. If he is to spend a night inside this house, he is glad he will have Eva's warm body curled up beside his own.

# CHAPTER TWENTY-THREE

Here is Lesbury Common. Dark and still, barely touched by the streetlamps of the village. Not a soul in sight. No hint of a gathering army.

Michael stops the wagon and leaps out of the box seat, the thud of his boots loud in the late-night stillness.

Inside the wagon, Harriet can hear herself breathe. Her fingers curl around the edge of the bench seat. Will he blame her? Insist the information she provided was wrong? Will he demand she return the money?

She cannot let that happen.

Tentatively, she climbs from the wagon, shoes landing on the soft grass of the common. Her legs feel weak, unsteady with the fear that has been growing with each dark mile they have covered. "I know what I heard," she tells him, with as much firmness as she can gather. "This is where the army was mustering."

Michael barely acknowledges her. He just stands with his arms folded across his chest, looking out across the dark plain of the common. His jaw is set tightly and she can see the faint tick of the muscles within. The wagon creaks. Anne climbs out and stands behind Harriet.

"We're too late," she murmurs uselessly.

The glow of a lamp appears on the edge of the common, and Michael whirls around towards it, catching sight of a young man picking his way back towards the village.

"You," he calls.

The man stops walking, lifting the lamp to help him see into the darkness.

"Where'd they go?" Michael demands. "The rebel army?"

"They left days ago," the man calls, keeping his distance. "They heard the redcoats was coming. Four whole regiments turned up here day before yesterday." He chuckles dully. "Shame they didn't catch the bastards, if you ask me."

Michael bristles. "Where'd they go?" he repeats. "The rebels?"

"They were off to Alnwick last I heard," he says. "Proclaiming James as king. That were days ago, mind. I daresay they'll not be staying in one place too long. Not with dragoons on their tail."

Michael begins to pace across the grass, boots sighing rhythmically. Harriet's hand goes instinctively to the coin pouch inside her stays. The man with the lamp disappears into the village, making the dark thicken.

Michael marches back up to the wagon and swings himself into the box seat. "Get in," he says. "We're going on to Alnwick. We can be there in less than an hour."

"Did you not hear the man?" Anne hisses. "They've four regiments on their tail. Do you really think the rebels are going to be sitting around in Alnwick waiting to be caught?"

Michael's eyes flash in the lamplight. "Get in," he says again, more firmly this time. "I've not come all this way to turn around and give up."

At the firmness in his voice, Harriet finds herself obeying. She climbs into the wagon without a word. And that woman that does not take orders, she thinks distantly, how painfully far away she is. Because she might have defied her husband by taking this foolish journey into the night, but here she is nodding along to the next man, following his instructions without complaint. Allowing him to tug on those reins and lead her towards four regiments of redcoats. She swallows down a wave of nausea.

Anne doesn't move. She glares up at Michael in the box seat. "You're a fool," she says.

"So be it," he hisses. "Just get in the wagon and do your part, like you told me you were so damn desperate to do."

Anne hesitates for a moment. Harriet clenches her hands around fistfuls of her cloak as she watches, willing her to climb into the wagon. Out here in the openness of the common, she feels intensely exposed. Feels her fear creep towards terror.

Finally, Anne turns and climbs into the wagon, a closed-off expression on her face.

The lights of Lesbury disappear, leaving long, dark ribbons of road out ahead of them. Harriet closes her eyes. This was supposed to be over by now. Michael was supposed to be gone, and she and Anne were supposed to be on their way home to Holy Island. She is suddenly, painfully aware that she is travelling with a man the British army wants to see on the scaffold. A man whose passion for his cause is preventing him from acting wisely.

Just like herself, she thinks.

Michael stops the wagon. At once, it is too still. Too silent. Lamplight pools in front of them. On either side of the road, the fields are impossibly dark.

Anne leans forward. "What is it? Why have we stopped?"

And it is not too still at all, Harriet realises. Or too silent. Or too dark. Because there are lamps moving through the darkness now, growing brighter. Horse hooves rattling the earth.

Perhaps they are just travellers. Or more Jacobites stealing towards Alnwick in an attempt to catch up with the rebel army. These, she knows, are likely possibilities.

But: *troops active*. And Harriet knows there is every chance this is the redcoats moving towards them, ready to intercept any rebels that might cross their path. Four regiments, she thinks sickly. *Shame they didn't catch the bastards if you ask me...*

She draws in a breath. Even if this is the redcoats, on the trail of the Jacobite army, it's of no matter. Is that not what she is here for? This is why her bodice is heavy with coins. They have rehearsed their story, taken their roles. The man in the box seat is a simple merchant, travelling to Lesbury to meet a client. And she is his wife. She tries to untangle her thoughts; prepare herself to adopt her role.

But before she can make sense of what is happening, Michael blows out the lamp, and the wagon is drowned in blackness.

It's a grave error. Harriet knows it at once. She and Anne are here to support Michael's cover story. The merchant, the wife, the lady's maid. But in his impulse, in his blowing out the light, he has marked them as rebels. Jacobites.

"What in hell are you doing?" Anne hisses. "Light the

lamp." She lurches forward, but Michael puts a sudden hand out into the wagon, forcing her back. Though she can see little more than his outline, Harriet can tell he is shaking. As though he knows he has made a crucial mistake. As though the bravado he has been putting on the whole time he has known her has been nothing but a cover for a deep fear of capture. Of death.

"Light the lamp," Anne says again, but her words fade out as she speaks them. Because the sound of hooves is coming closer.

The thunder of horses stops and a globe of light shines into the wagon, illuminating a bearded face. A scarlet uniform trimmed with gold braiding. The soldier lifts his lamp, shining it into Michael's eyes. "Well now," he says. "What do we have here?"

Does he recognise Michael Mitchell as the man who shot a dragoon at the protest in York? Harriet cannot tell. Michael says nothing, just stares the soldier down, though the trembling of his entire body betrays him. Betrays all of them, Harriet realises sickly. Sweat rolls down the side of his face.

"I'm on my way to Alnwick with my wife," he says. But there is no substance to his words.

The soldier pans the light past him, spearing it into Harriet's eyes. Her heart is thundering, her skin damp beneath her shift. Perhaps she ought to tell them her name. Tell them her family's house is being used by government spies, and that of course she is no Jacobite. But she knows her actions speak louder than these hollow words.

Somehow, she knows before he pulls the trigger that Michael is going to shoot. And she is leaping from the wagon seconds before the sound breaks the cold night air. She lands heavily, pain shooting through her shins as she stumbles forward, her palms planting hard against earth. And this blind instinct, it gives her the few yards' head start she needs to tear away from the soldiers and across the unseen veneer of the land. The ground seems to tilt beneath her as fear floods her body. Harriet hears Anne cry out as the dragoons seize her. And she hears a volley of gunfire.

Harriet runs, with no thought of where she is going, or where the soldiers might be. Lamplight illuminates the sorry sight of the wagon, but beyond it is inky blackness. She stumbles over uneven ground and ploughs through tangled greenery. She does not see the low-hanging tree branch until she is an inch away from it. She ducks and stumbles, feels the branch tear at her hair, scrape along her cheek. And when she lands, heavy and breathless on the cold, damp earth, it is no small part of her that is surprised she is still alive.

# CHAPTER TWENTY-FOUR

Finn lies staring at the rugged ceiling as dawn lights Eva's childhood bedroom. He shifts in the narrow bed, careful not to wake her. She is curled up on her side, her back pressed against him. He can feel her warmth through her thin nightshift, her hair tickling his bare shoulder. He has slept little, but it had felt much more reassuring to lie in bed beside his wife than to roam the house in the lightless hours of early morning, wondering at the depths of the shadows. There was something reassuring, too, about the firebasket glittering through the gap in the curtains, a reminder that he is doing all he can to make amends for Oliver's death.

In the pink dawn, the beacon is extinguished now, but Angus had kept it burning steadily throughout the night. He wonders if Michael had bothered returning to Longstone last night. When he returns, Finn will let the man know he has had enough. If Michael is willing to risk their safety by gallivanting around Lindisfarne and the mainland every two minutes, then the offer of shelter is retracted. He has enough to worry about without the threat of redcoats on his doorstep.

Eva stirs and rolls over to face him, letting her fingers run absentmindedly over his bare chest. "Are you all right?" she murmurs. Finn allows himself a smile. It must be the tenth time she has asked him that question since they set foot inside the house.

"I'm all right." And he means it. Because beyond the unease is a strangely steadying reminder that this house had let him live. This house, with its priest hole beside the fireplace and the passage within the walls, it had given him a reprieve. A chance to escape, and to try to atone for his mistakes. Somehow, that gives him the courage to believe that nothing will collapse today.

"Have you slept?" Eva asks, rubbing her eyes.

"A little." He gives her a smile he hopes looks genuine. "You know I sleep better in the daylight."

"I've not slept much either. I'm so worried about Harriet." She slides out of bed, reaching for the underskirts she had left on the floor. "Can we take the skiff out this morning? Follow the shoreline? In case there's any sign of her?"

"Aye. Of course." Finn follows her out of bed and pulls back the curtain. The tide is high, knocking roughly against the embankment. If they leave now, they will be able to circle the entire island. But if Harriet has left any hints of her whereabouts on the beaches, they will be hidden beneath the surface.

They are on the water before the sun is more than a glow on the horizon. A thin layer of mist lies over the sea, the water soupy and grey. Finn eases the skiff along the east coast of the island, past the castle and through the anchorage. Neither of them speak, unwilling to disrupt the thick silence that hangs over the sea.

As they are making their way across the ribbon of water between Lindisfarne and the mainland, Eva gets suddenly to her feet. "Over there." She points. "What is it?"

Finn squints into the rising sun, following her outstretched finger. He sees a small unidentifiable shape hanging on the tangle of greenery by the edge of Holy Island. Something woollen, perhaps. He cannot make it out.

"Clothing?" asks Eva. Finn pulls on the oars, guiding the skiff into the shallow water. Eva remains standing, hunched over and gripping the gunwale. When the water is shallow enough, she gathers her skirts in her fist and leaps out towards the edge of the island, sending a flock of gulls shooting upwards.

Finn jumps out after her and pushes the skiff up into the reeds at the water's edge. Eva grabs the piece of clothing from the bush and holds it up. It looks to be a woman's shawl, but the wool is frayed and worn to the colour of mud, with only the barest hints of its former blue still visible. It has clearly been out here for far longer than the day Harriet has been missing.

Eva drops it back onto the bush. "It's not hers. That's a good thing, I'm sure." Her voice is thin.

Finn presses a hand to the small of her back to guide her back to the skiff. And he stops at the sight of a longboat approaching. Henry Ward is watching them as his boat nears theirs, two of his crewmen manning the oars.

Finn feels Eva's muscles tense beneath his palm. "He followed us," she murmurs.

He nods. He knows there is no way Ward has come upon them by chance. No doubt he had seen them set out from

Emmanuel Head this morning.

Eva tugs Finn towards the boat. "Come on. Quickly." She thrashes through the reeds and scrambles ungracefully over the gunwale.

"There's no need to run, Eva." Ward's voice carries across the sea. "I just wish to speak with your husband."

Finn shoves the boat into the water and leaps inside. He settles the oars into the oarlocks, but does not row. The skiff drifts out towards Ward's longboat. He knows there is little point trying to avoid the confrontation. After all, Henry Ward knows exactly where to find them.

"I wondered if you have had time to consider my proposal," says Ward, when they are close enough for him to speak without raising his voice. Any last doubts Finn had had about Ward following them evaporate. He knows every piece of this is deliberate; knows Ward is speaking of his invitation to join his crew in front of Eva to put him in a difficult situation.

"I've given you my answer," Finn says tautly. "That is not going to change." He takes up the oars and pulls hard.

"Your answer to what?" Eva demands. "What is he talking about?"

"Stop, Finn," Ward orders, that forced bravado tainting his words again. "I'm speaking to you." Smoothly, he produces a pistol from within his greatcoat. He holds it in Finn's direction in a vaguely threatening manner.

Finn lets out a humourless laugh. "Really?" He lifts the oars from the water anyway. Hears Eva's sharp intake of breath.

"Your answer to what?" she repeats, voice low.

Finn presses a hand to her knee; squeezes gently. He will

pay for his secrecy later, he has no doubt. But right now, he needs her to stay quiet. He looks squarely at his former captain. "My answer is no, Ward. So if you are going to kill me, just do it. This has gone on long enough."

"Are you mad?!" Eva lurches in front of him, making the boat tilt on the swell. She stretches out her arms in an attempt to make herself as wide as possible, blocking him from the path of Ward's bullet. Ward chuckles lightly.

Finn eases her aside, doing his best to ignore the fierce glare she gives him. "It's all right," he murmurs. "Trust me." He looks back at Ward. "You can't do it, can you. Not to my face. Not when there are no crewmen willing to keel-haul me so you can keep your hands clean."

"You sound very sure of yourself," says Ward.

"That's because I know you too well. Get out of our lives, Ward. Take your crew and use that precious immunity." Somewhere at the back of his mind, Finn knows this boldness is misplaced. Knows Henry Ward has an entire crew at his disposal who will have no issue with effecting the killing that Ward is unable to execute. But he is also certain that Ward will not shoot him here, in cold blood, in front of his wife. Not the boy he had spent so many hours with in the great cabin of the *Eagle*, teaching to read nautical charts and navigate by starlight. Ward has always valued loyalty, and Finn knows he will not stoop to such a callous execution. In a strange sort of way, Henry Ward has far more decency than that.

Finn pulls on the oars to ease the skiff back around the point, then unfurls the mainsail, letting it catch the cold wind. Eva stares over her shoulder, eyes fixed to Ward's longboat. Best that way, Finn thinks. Because he is fairly certain that when she looks back at him, the anger in her eyes is going to turn him to stone.

Finally, she whirls around. And her fierce look does not leave Finn disappointed. "Your answer to what?" she hisses. "What in hell was he talking about?"

He tells her in pieces. His visit to the Lindisfarne tavern. Ward's desire to have him back in his crew. His outlandish claim of offering immunity to those who sign his pirates' articles. He says nothing of Ward's reason for wanting Finn back on his ship: to keep him away from her.

He says nothing, because there is a part of him that knows Ward is right to demand such things. Knows he had no right making Eva Blake his wife. Most of all, he says nothing, because if he speaks it out loud, it will remind him that this offer—a life for Eva without the fear of Ward in it—is exactly what is best for her.

Finn knows he's a coward. Selfish. But finding Eva had been so unlikely, so miraculous, that he does not have the strength to take what Ward is offering. How can he give her up?

Eva sits with her hands tightly clasped in her lap, spearing him with a fierce glare. "You did not think to tell me this earlier?" She flies at him suddenly, throwing her fists into his arms and chest. The boat rocks on the swell. "How could you be so foolish as to go to him in the tavern? And to goad him into shooting you? Do you truly think you know him so well? What if he's a changed man? What if I had sat there and watched him kill you?" Her voice rattles with emotion.

He takes her wrists, eases her away from him. "It's all right," he says again, running his thumbs over the backs of her hands.

She pulls away. "It is not all right," she hisses. "You are damn lucky you are still alive." She stares out across the water, avoiding his gaze. Her eyes overflow suddenly and she swipes away her tears with her palm. "It is not just you anymore," she says. "You're not alone out on that rock any longer. You do not have to keep everything to yourself." She swallows down her tears and looks at him squarely. "Henry Ward is my sister's father," she says, levelling her voice. "I am as much a part of this as you are. You ought to have told me you were going to see him. And you ought to have told me what he was offering you."

"You would have stopped me from going to see him."

"Of course I would have!" she cries.

"I'm sorry." Eva looks at him expectantly, clearly wanting more. "You are right," Finn says after a moment. "Ward *is* a changed man. His confidence, it seems forced somehow. Unnatural. As though something is troubling him. Maybe it's because he's had no choice but to turn to piracy, like he never wanted to do. Or maybe there's something more."

Eva doesn't respond at once. She stares out over the water as a gull swoops and ripples the surface. Her eyes are glassy. "Promise me," she says, "you will tell me if he comes to you again." She narrows her eyes. "Or if you go to him."

Finn says nothing. It is a promise he cannot make. Because while Henry Ward might be Eva's problem too, he longs for that not to be the case. He thinks of her standing at the window on their wedding night, looking out into the dark in fear of seeing Ward's ship. The voice in the back of his mind gnaws at him, reminds him he has a way to get Ward out of Eva's life forever. He wills it to be silent.

# CHAPTER TWENTY-FIVE

Harriet cannot make sense of how long she has been hiding in the undergrowth for. All she knows is it's eerily silent, with morning light bringing shape to the blackness that had surrounded her for what seemed an eternity. She is on the edge of a wide, flat plain, fringed with tangled gorse and low, gnarled trees. Her body is aching from a night spent huddled on the ground, and she is shivering violently. A part of her is afraid to move, her fear pulsing inside her. But stay here, and she knows it will not be long before the cold seizes her.

As she shifts slightly, trying to return feeling to her numb toes, she hears the dull shudder of the coin pouch tucked inside her bodice. The sound of it drives her to move. She crawls forward, entangling herself in mud-caked skirts. Twigs crack beneath her weight as she wriggles out from beneath the low branches. Gets shakily to her feet.

It ought to be the thought of her son driving her to self-preservation, she knows. She ought to want to live for him and him alone. But somehow, Thomas has become a symbol of the false life she is living. A life of hiding and pretending. A symbol of her loveless marriage.

Poor Thomas, she thinks. It is not his fault he was born to a woman incapable of doting on her child. Of loving him as much as she should.

The land is dizzyingly green beneath the curtain of mist. She squints into the haze, trying to catch the shape of a farmhouse or shed. She cannot be far from Lesbury. But she can see nothing around her but trees bent crooked in the wind. She cannot even tell where the road is. She stands motionless, arms wrapped around herself.

Somewhere distant, hooves echo. Harriet's heart jolts, then she realises it is just a passing wagon. In the distance, she sees its hazy shape move through the cloud. She begins to stumble towards it. She will find the road. And for better or for worse, it will lead her back to Lindisfarne.

She is following the trail before she can make sense of it; not the road, but something far worse. Dark, rusty beads, splattered against the earth. One step, then another, she follows them, not daring to look up.

And at the end of her tunnel vision, she sees it: the motionless hand, attached to the motionless arm, the motionless body. Michael Mitchell's coppery hair is plastered to his head, his beard matted with dirt. Blood has pooled beneath the bullet wound in his neck, congealing beneath a whirring black raft of insects. He lies face down beside the road, and Harriet is glad she cannot see his eyes. The horse and wagon are no longer beside him. Had the soldiers taken them and left Michael to rot?

She stands over him for several minutes, oddly transfixed

by the fly crawling up his bloodstained neck. It feels wrong to leave him here. But what choice does she have?

She begins to walk, pain shooting through her legs with each step as feeling returns to her frozen feet.

None of this feels real. Not Michael's lifeless body, or this profound emptiness, or the unnameable green vastness around her. This is not the shape of her life. Her life is neat edges: a respectable husband and son. She is *wife* and *mother* and none of this. But she knows this is a lie. Knows there are parts of her that exist far beyond those neat edges.

Because as she walks, her thoughts are pulled back into smoke-hazy rooms with her artists' circle. To lazy afternoons in Isabelle's parlour, with shoes and stockings on the floor. To glasses being filled as though the rest of the world had ceased to exist. To a wine-tainted kiss they can never speak of.

An ocean of grief surges at her. Hot and torrential and fierce. Harriet hears herself cry out in a desperate sob. Feels tears fill her eyes and spill without warning.

Beautiful, talented Isabelle. How can one person can bring her so much joy and yet so much regret? How can she be so happy in her presence, and yet simultaneously filled with such deep self-loathing and shame?

Tears pour down her cheeks, dripping unhindered from her chin. Tears she has been holding inside for longer than she can remember. Tears she learnt to push aside the moment she realised there were parts of herself that could never be spoken of. Never be brought to the light.

Because only someone with the heart of a sinner would feel such things for another woman.

She keeps following the road. Back towards her husband,

her son, towards the life she has been taught she should be living.

They are sirens, they say, the women whose wicked hearts draw them in this direction. Cursed, unnatural creatures. Witches. And isn't that how she has always felt? An unnatural being?

The broken, ill-fitting piece.

It is late morning when Eva and Finn return to the house. The sun has broken through the cloud bank in neat gold strokes, turning the water turquoise at its edges. Eva's heart is still fast after their run-in with Ward. At the knowledge that Finn had gone to him alone, and at the offer Ward had made him.

In a strange sort of way, there is something faintly settling about Ward's invitation for Finn to re-join his crew. The offer—and Ward's reluctance to pull the trigger today— suggests he is not so adamant on seeing Finn dead as she had believed. It also suggests that Ward is somewhat delusional— surely he did not imagine Finn might accept such an offer? She might have known Finn for a fraction of the time Ward has, but Eva knows with a deep certainty that no offer of pirating wealth would ever tempt her husband from her side.

Not that that knowledge does anything to lessen her anger towards him right now.

Theodora is rolling her hoop outside the house when they approach, Jenny watching from the doorway with Thomas in her arms. There's a flatness to Thea today that suggests that, while she may not know exactly what is going on, she is aware that something is amiss. Eva wonders what Nathan has told her to explain Harriet's absence.

She catches the hoop as it escapes Theodora's control and trundles over the ground towards her. She hands it back to her niece. "You're getting better," she says, forcing a smile.

"Not really," Theodora says irritably. "The ground is too bumpy here." Hunching, she attempts to twirl the hoop, but it catches on a knot of grass and falls flat. She huffs. "See?"

Eva puts a hand to her shoulder, guiding her back towards the house. "How is your story coming along?"

"Good." She looks past Eva to Finn. "The selkie made a castle on the moon for the farmer's wife to live in," she explains.

"Obviously," says Finn.

Eva smiles.

"My ma used to believe in selkies," Finn tells Theodora. Her eyes light. "She used to say that if she ever found one, she'd wish for a pot of gold and sunny skies every day."

"Mhm." Theodora nods thoughtfully. "That would be a nice wish."

Finn follows Eva up the front path towards the house, then stops walking and catches her wrist. "How angry are you?" he asks, voice low.

Eva snorts. "Do you really need to ask that?"

"Just trying to be optimistic." He squeezes her wrist gently. "You know this is what Ward wanted, aye? To unsettle us, by making sure you knew what he asked of me."

Eva narrows her eyes. "He succeeded."

Finn drops her wrist and glances up at the house. "Go on without me. I'll be in in a minute." In spite of her anger, Eva's heart lurches. She can hear the strain in his words. Can see the weariness in his eyes. Though he has not said it—would never say it—she knows he is finding it difficult to be in the house. She is finding it difficult too. Having him here reminds Eva of what she has known from the beginning: that now she has married Finn, she is condemned to keeping secrets from her family. It's a burden she had accepted when she had agreed to become Finn's wife. A burden she is willing to carry if it means spending her life with the man she loves. But it is a burden that feels twice as weighted when they are inside Highfield House.

She gives him a nod of understanding. He sinks onto the grass of the dunes, his gaze cast out to sea. A deliberate attempt, she can tell, to keep the house out of his eyeline.

Theodora tosses her hoop into the air then plants herself on the grass next to Finn. "Papa says the selkies are make believe, but Mrs Brodie doesn't think so. What do you think? Have you ever seen one?"

Eva allows herself a faint smile and makes her way inside. She had managed little more than a tiny triangle of toast this morning, and her stomach is groaning with hunger, in spite of her fear for Harriet. The smell of onion soup is drifting out from the kitchen, making her mouth water.

The house is quiet. Dust motes dance in the stream of light pouring through the narrow window above the door. It feels oddly empty without the constant barrage of hammering. No doubt Nathan and Edwin are still out looking for Harriet on the mainland. But as she makes her way towards the kitchen, Eva sees the door to the parlour open. She catches sight of her brother in an armchair, reading through a ledger with a quill in hand. A half-eaten bowl of soup sits on the tea table beside him.

She debates whether to enter. Ask if he has any news. She decides against it. Surely if he had heard word of Harriet, he would have sought her out himself to tell her. And she is far too tired to deal with any more of Nathan's saltiness.

"Is that you, Eva?" he calls, before she can leave.

She steels herself, then steps inside. "You're working?" she asks.

"Trying. I hope to have something of a business to return to once we leave this place."

The words strike her unexpectedly. Of course, she has always known her family never planned to stay here forever. But Nathan's words remind her that soon they will be so far away. She pushes the thought aside. Thinking of that future feels too difficult with Harriet missing.

"No word?" she asks.

Nathan shakes his head. "No one in Bamburgh or Beal has seen her. Edwin has gone back to the village in case anyone has heard anything since we were last there."

"Finn and I circled the island," Eva tells him. "There was no sign of her."

Nathan nods towards the armchair opposite him. "Sit down, Eva. You look exhausted."

She sits. She is exhausted, yes, but that exhaustion has come from tiptoeing around her brother, and her own secrets, for the past day. Nathan sets the ledger down beside the soup bowl.

"Where is your husband?" he asks.

"Outside. Having a pressing conversation with Thea about the potential existence of selkies." She pauses. "That is all right, isn't it?"

He chuckles. "Of course."

She dares to meet his eyes. "How are you?" she asks finally.

Nathan pinches the bridge of his nose. "That is a complicated question."

"I know."

He sighs. "I regret bringing us here. I ought to have found another way…" He fades out, but catches the faint smile on Eva's lips.

"I'm rather glad you did," she says. "Or rather, I'm glad I had no choice but to follow you up here." The moment the words are out, she regrets them, fearing they will remind Nathan of her mutilated betrothal to Matthew Walton.

To her surprise, he smiles. There's a sudden warmth in his eyes, and it makes Eva realise how much she has missed her brother's company. "You seem happy," he says after a moment.

"I am happy. Very much so." She falters. "Well. At least, I would be if it weren't for Harriet…" She decides not to mention her irritation at her husband.

Nathan toys with the cover of his ledger. "I'm glad you're happy."

"Really?"

"Yes, really. Do you truly doubt that?"

Eva hesitates for a moment. "No," she decides. "I don't."

Nathan takes a piece of bread from the plate beside the soup, but then changes his mind and puts it back on the plate without eating. "It was good of you and Finn to come," he tells her. "I suspect it was the last thing you wished to do."

Eva's heart jolts, fearful her brother has picked up on Finn's unease at being in the house. But then she realises Nathan is referring to their own strained relations. "I'm as worried for Harriet as you are," she tells him. "I could hardly stay on Longstone and just hope for the best."

Nathan looks out the window for long moments, rubbing at his jaw. "I know she has been unhappy. Even before this business with her father. Do you think it because I pushed her to marry Edwin?"

It is times like this, when Eva can see the guilt hanging on Nathan's shoulders most heavily, that she wishes he was not so averse to human contact. The touch of a hand, an embrace—she finds it hard to comprehend how these things might bring him such unease. She hates this isolation her brother has imposed on himself. Cannot imagine the loneliness that might come with it. "I don't know," she admits. "She rarely speaks to me these days. And perhaps I don't try as hard as I ought to. But none of this is your fault." She leans forward in her chair, trying to catch her brother's eye. "You have to know that."

He gives her a thin smile. But she can tell he is far from convinced.

When Theodora is herded inside by the nurse, Finn gets to his feet and follows her into the house. He knows he cannot stay outside forever.

The moment he steps through the door, the gloom of the house swallows the daylight.

His heart is hammering. He feels too unsettled to eat, too restless to sleep. He is unsure if it's the house, or concern over Ward and his cursed offer—and Eva's fresh knowledge of the situation. Either way, he needs something to occupy his thoughts.

He can hear voices coming from the parlour; Eva and Nathan. Cannot make out their words. He goes upstairs and tosses his coat across Eva's bed. A door is ajar on the other side of the hall. He steps back out into the passage and peeks inside.

The room looks like an earthquake has hit. The fireplace lies in pieces, and he can barely see the floor between the strewn bricks and fallen wood panels. A hammer and pry bar lie discarded in the corner, as though whatever attempt at restoration was being made here has been forgotten about in the stress of Harriet's disappearance. Finn steps out of the room, pulling the door closed behind him.

In a daze, he continues down the hallway to the door at the end of the passage. And he is standing outside the room in which he had killed Oliver Blake. When he had followed Eva upstairs last night; when he had glanced down this hallway at the rows of closed doors, he had been unsure of which room it was. But now it feels as though his body has led him here instinctively. As though a part of him has never forgotten.

The second storey of the house feels oddly quiet. Too empty. Hollow, somehow, with few threads of light making it into the hallway through the rows of closed doors. Finn feels the need to turn that handle and step inside. It's a strange urge; frightening. But somehow, he feels it will be easier this way, if he just confronts the reality of what lies behind that door. Like facing a predator instead of living on the run.

He steps into the room.

Oliver's bedroom does not look like he remembers. Not really. The bed is gone, leaving an empty, uninhabited space, and there has clearly been restoration work done. But he can tell the structure of the room has not been altered. The fireplace; he remembers that. Remembers searching the wooden panels around it for the priest hole behind. But the windows seem much larger, the panelling lighter, the thick beams across the ceiling not so close to the top of his head. As though his memories have distorted over time. As though he has spent so long with his thoughts in this place that the room had shrunk in on itself inside his mind, until it all it consisted of was that yard of bloodstained floor where Oliver's body had fallen.

He stands there for a long time. Can't comprehend why. Perhaps there is a sense of confronting the past, somehow. Of meeting his memories head-on, rather than letting them steep in the back of his mind. He feels rooted in place, feels old fear and desperation and guilt pushing to the front of his thoughts. He hears the footsteps distantly, but does not fully register them.

"Theodora, is that you?" Nathan appears in the doorway. Finn whirls around, jolted from his thoughts. "Oh. Forgive me. I usually keep this door locked. I forgot to close it up in all the chaos. Thea is always trying to get in here." Nathan Blake is uneasy in this room, Finn can tell. Even after all this time. Not that he blames him. Not one bit.

"Why do you lock the room?" Finn finds himself asking.

There's a moment of silence so brief he is not sure if he is imagining it.

"There's a double barrel priest hole beside the fireplace," says Nathan. "It leads to a passage within the walls. Edwin blocked the outside entrance up after we discovered the Mitchells had been using it to get into the attic. It's not a place for children to be playing."

Finn nods. He wonders distantly what the right reaction to this is. He ought to feign some surprise, surely. Something that might suggest he is hearing of this for the first time. But it feels suddenly as though Nathan is watching him too closely, and he cannot bring himself to do anything more than nod.

Nathan holds out a ring of keys. "Look as you wish. But lock the door when you're done."

"I've no need to look any further," Finn says quickly. He follows Nathan out of the room. "The fireplace," he says. "In the other room. I can help you restore it. I rebuilt the fireplace on Longstone last year."

Something flickers across Nathan's eyes. Surprise at the offer, but something else that Finn can't read.

"Thank you," he says after a moment. "But there's no need, really."

"Truly? It looks like there's a great deal of need. And I'd rather keep busy than sitting around waiting for news."

Nathan looks away for a moment, caught in hesitation. "Very well," he says finally, though his words are anything but decisive. "Do as you wish. You'll find the mortar in the shed behind the house."

# CHAPTER TWENTY-SIX

Harriet's legs and feet are aching, her head spinning with thirst. She has been walking for most of the day.

The sun is low in the sky now, much of the daylight sucked away, and the inky pall of dusk beginning to settle over the land. There's a deep ache inside her; an ache of grief, of self-loathing. Pure and utter exhaustion at this letting out of emotions she has held tightly to her chest for so many years. And yet her tears feel anything but cathartic. They have torn something open, something gaping and unfixable.

She curses this emptiness, this vast open land with its absence of life. Because it has given her the space to admit that which she cannot bear to acknowledge.

She walks slowly, crookedly. She has been following the road, keeping the ocean on her right. Has long given up attempting to stay hidden.

No redcoats have found her. But no one else has either. No rides have been offered. It is a bleak and lonely part of the country up here, especially now, with the early-autumn dusk closing in and the threat of conflict around every corner.

Now, here is Beal; beyond it, Lindisfarne. The middle of the sandy path onto the island is covered in a ribbon of sea, though the edges are still dry. How deep is the water? Harriet has no thought of it. No thought of whether the tide is rising or falling. Somehow, it had not even crossed her mind to think of such a thing as she had followed the ocean back to Lindisfarne. What a fool she is. A naïve child. How had she ever imagined she might live out from beneath the protection of her husband's shadow?

Wearily, she stands on the tiny jetty at Beal and looks out across the water. A small row boat is beached in the mud, like a forgotten children's toy. Clouds are beginning to roll in, bathing Holy Island in blue mist that seems to rise from the water. At once the island feels so close, and so far away.

Harriet sits on the edge of the jetty and pulls off her mud-caked shoes and stockings. She gathers them up in one hand, lifting her skirts above her ankles with the other. The path is cold beneath her bare feet, and sharp twigs protruding from the mud bite at her skin. She walks, attempting deliberateness, letting seawater cover her toes, her ankles, her calves. The chill of it stings, but she keeps walking. Now she has begun, she cannot stand to turn back.

How many times has she stood on the edge of Holy Island, wishing to make her escape? And now here she is, so desperate to return that she is willing to wade through the sea? The thought is so ludicrous she laughs. It's a desperate, hysterical sound; one that quickly turns into a sob of fear. Because water is gathering around her skirts now, pulling her one way, and the other, trying to yank her feet out from beneath her. The water is rushing in from the ocean, she realises sickly. The tide is rising. To trap her on Lindisfarne, or keep her out?

The water surges and her feet fly out from beneath her. She drops her shoes, unable to catch them before the tide tugs them away. She feels herself grapple with the sea floor, trying to right herself as the water rushes over her head. She kicks hard, her legs tangling in her skirts. Saltwater floods down her throat. She tries to keep her eyes open; tries to focus on those last pale threads of daylight glimmering through the surface of the water. But her eyes close instinctively, and when she next opens them, she has no thought of which way is up and which is down.

And this is right, is it not? She is the wicked siren, with her heart and her body aching after another woman. Is this not what she deserves? To drown in the sea where women of her kind come from.

She will die—the thought comes to her, violent and terrifying. But she finds herself kicking again, seeking the sea floor with her feet. She breaks through the surface, gasping and coughing. She is no closer to Lindisfarne. But she is alive. A strange thing. She had not imagined her will to live was so strong.

She drops onto her knees in the shallow water. And her hand goes instinctively to the bulge inside her bodice—to Michael Mitchell's coin pouch. To her chance at an unhemmed-in life. But that life, she realises now, it will not be unconstrained. Not really. She had tried to tell herself that being in Paris with Isabelle would bring her the greatest joy, but really, how can it do anything but cause her pain? It will only remind her of her own sin, and the things she will never have. Even if her work is to hang on gallery walls, she will still be forced to keep these darkest parts of herself hidden away.

Besides, how will she ever find the courage to step out on her own like that? She had told herself she was strong enough, but her façade of bravery had crumbled with the first hint of pressure.

"You there!" Footsteps slosh through the mud towards her, and then a man is pulling her from the shallow water, helping her stand. "What in hell are you doing out here?"

The man is wearing a long, dark greatcoat, his white beard thick and uneven. Harriet recognises him as one of the fishermen from Holy Island. Tom Cordwell. He looks her up and down, surprise in his eyes. There's recognition there too, of course—everyone from Lindisfarne knows who her family is.

"What happened to you?" he asks.

Harriet doesn't speak. Can't speak. Cordwell hauls her back towards the jetty and into the row boat, which has begun to float again on the shallow water.

He climbs in and tosses her a ream of filthy hessian from the bottom of the boat. "Warm yourself," he grunts.

Harriet wraps herself in the hessian. It is coarse and stiff, and reeks of old herrings, but it eases the violent trembling in her body.

"Water," she coughs.

Cordwell pulls on the oars without taking his eyes off the pitiful shape of her, huddled in the bottom of his rowboat. He reaches for a waterskin beside him and tosses it in her direction. Harriet gathers it from the damp floor of the boat. Fumbles with the cork and takes a long sip.

"You ought to be careful," Cordwell grunts. "Them bastards working for Cotesworth are not to be trusted." His voice is dark with threat. "Were they the ones who sent you out here? Typical, wouldn't you say?" he continues, before she can manage a word. "Sending young lasses out to do their bidding instead putting themselves in danger. Were they the ones who told you to cross back onto the island? Or was that your own wise idea?"

Harriet lets out her breath. Of course he suspects she has been working with the government spies. "No." She finds her voice. "You have it wrong. All of you." Because perhaps she has a chance here. A chance to show the villagers her family is not intertwined in the government cause. A chance, perhaps to undo a small piece of the damage this ill-fated journey has caused. "I was helping one of the rebels get to Lesbury. To re-join the Jacobite army." Even to her own ears, her words sound foolish. Like a lie. And she knows at once that this man is not going to believe her.

He snorts a laugh. "Is that so?"

"Yes. That is so." Her voice comes out sounding tiny. Weak.

Cordwell snorts. "The army moved on from Lesbury days ago, lass. You'll have to try better than that."

Harriet shoves the cork back into the mouth of waterskin. Says nothing.

"What does your husband think about this?" There is humour in Cordwell's voice now. "He know you're out here? Or are you another one of them foolish lasses gone out on their own thinking they could change the world?"

Harriet closes her eyes. "I am not trying to change the world," she mutters.

"Not sure I believe you," says Cordwell. "You see, we've heard things about your family. About all them workmen that come to your house. In and out the door, far too quick to get anything done."

Harriet's heart quickens. She opens her eyes. Tries not to react to the knowledge that the Jacobites have been watching her house. Watching her family. Watching her. She cannot be surprised at the conclusions they have drawn.

Perhaps this is the piece of knowledge that will finally get her husband to leave Lindisfarne. Get them off this cursed island. Muted hope flickers inside her for a moment, but its spark is extinguished quickly. The thought of her husband only serves to remind her of the reprimanding she is about to face.

"So you see, lass," says Cordwell, "I'm not so inclined to believe you when you tell me you're helping Jacobites get to Lesbury."

The shore is close. In mere moments, Harriet will climb from this boat and begin the long walk back to Highfield House with her clothes trailing water and her feet bare. Her soul torn open and the image of Michael Mitchell's lifeless body burning behind her eyelids.

Her family can know nothing about Cordwell's rescuing her, or the suspicions she has just confirmed. If they were to find out about the danger she has put them in, they would never forgive her. And if this journey has taught her anything, it is that she does not have the strength to face the world alone.

Rebuilding the fireplace is a simple enough task. Most of the bricks are in fine enough order to be reused, and the stone of the chimney is still entirely intact. But the chaos surrounding him has Finn on edge. It's the good condition of the bricks that tells him the fireplace has been pulled apart, rather than having fallen of its own accord. The wood panelling, too, has clearly been torn from the walls. The panelling is old, and in need of replacement. But why tear it down while the fireplace is still in pieces? Why not complete one job at a time? There is no order to this. No plan.

The room does not look like it is being restored. It looks as though it has been torn apart, as though part of a destruction mission. Or a desperate search for something. Finn presses the last brick into the row he is working on, then takes the lamp from the mantel and steps out into the passage. He hears Nathan talking to his daughter downstairs.

Finn rattles the door to Oliver's room. Locked, as he had expected. Then he nudges open the door of the room beside it. A large wooden desk is pushed up against one wall, a spying glass set up on a stand at the window. He guesses this to be Nathan's study.

The fireplace catches his eye. Like the hearth in the room he has been working on, the bricks seem to have been torn down almost haphazardly. Several of the wood panels appear loose, propped up against the wall. Had they fallen? Or have they been torn down?

Finn steps out of the room before he is caught, the floorboards creaking beneath his feet. He nudges open the door of Eva's bedroom. The floorboards creak loudly as he paces across the room. He feels them shift beneath his weight, as though they have been prised up and hastily hammered back down, in a haphazard, unplanned way.

It's an old house, he tells himself. Bound to squeak, to

groan. But he finds himself returning to the room in which he is rebuilding the fireplace. Staring at the panels torn from the walls, the half-built hearth. Is Nathan tearing the room apart to start again? It's possible, of course. But it feels like much more than that. This room, it feels like desperation. Like a frantic search has taken place. Like fear.

Finn scrubs a hand across his eyes.

He's imagining things, surely. The house has worked its way inside his head, and he is seeing drama where there is none to be found. Nathan Blake is no trained craftsman, he tells himself. The restoration has been haphazard because he has come here with no plan. Likely, Nathan was overwhelmed by the size of the task he had taken on. Any sane man would be. There is nothing more to it than that.

But the thought gnaws at him. Reminds him that this is a house full of things that hide. And as he returns to the fallen bricks of the fireplace, the thought circles through Finn's mind without pause, telling him this is not about a restoration at all.

# CHAPTER TWENTY-SEVEN

Nathan pokes his head into the dining room. Theodora is sitting at one end of the table with Jenny. Thomas lolls in the nurse's arms, mercifully quiet. Nathan watches his daughter bring a spoonful of stew to her mouth. He has been trying his best not to let her see that anything is wrong. Suspects he is doing a rather terrible job of it.

"All right, Thea?" he asks.

She nods. Dips her spoon into the bowl for another mouthful.

Nathan flashes her a smile that he knows doesn't reach his eyes, then pulls the door closed. Eating dinner with his daughter would have been wise, he supposes, but he cannot stomach the thought of food right now. Perhaps he will force something down later with Eva and her husband, at whatever ungodly hour those creatures of the night eat their supper.

He makes his way towards the parlour, and the dreary account book he had left in there. He knows he ought to have accompanied Edwin back into the village on another search for Harriet. But really, such a thing has begun to feel futile. Harriet is not in the village; of that he is certain. And wherever she has run away to, she has done her best to make sure she is not found. Besides, now Finn has set to work on the fireplace, Nathan feels a strange need to be here. To ensure he is on hand to cut off any questions that may arise.

When he steps into the parlour, he finds Julia waiting. He freezes in the doorway.

"Eva let me in." She rises from the armchair as he steps tentatively into the room.

"I did not hear the door."

"She must have seen me coming. She opened the door before I could knock." Somewhere distantly, Nathan tells himself to remind Eva of Holland's warning about having Julia in the house. But a part of him is glad she is here.

When he doesn't speak, she says, "No word on Harriet?"

"No. I'm afraid not."

"I asked around the village again this afternoon. No one has seen her."

"Thank you. I appreciate your help." Nathan tugs edgily at the hem of his waistcoat.

A faint smile flickers on the edge of her lips. "Do you?"

"Yes," he says. And somehow, he means it. He sinks onto the settle.

Julia crosses the room and sits beside him. He is too tired to protest. Too tired to pretend he does not want her here. Too tired to maintain this veneer of anger he feels he ought to put up in her presence.

She is close. Close enough for him to see the gold flecks in her eyes, the loose threads on the hem of her bodice. Close enough to smell the intricate weave of scents on her skin: ash soap and sea and something faintly floral. Her nearness makes his heart quicken. But somehow, this quickening of his heart, it is only partially in fear. Beneath the discomfort is something far warmer. Something far more alluring.

He knows that if Joseph Holland or any of the other spies were to see her at the house, they would both be in danger. But something about her makes him forget himself. And he says, "I'm afraid for Harriet. I ought to have done more to stop this from happening."

"I feel the same," Julia agrees. "I ought to have sought her out more often. Asked how she was faring."

Nathan smiles wryly. "I am sure I did not make it easy for you to come here to see her."

"Well. I know I cannot expect a welcome after all I did to your family."

Nathan doesn't respond. For several moments, they sit in a stilted silence, filled by the dull crackle of the fire in the grate.

"The other day on the beach," Nathan begins carefully, "you rushed away when you saw Joseph Holland. Why?"

Julia looks at him intently for a moment, as though trying to determine the meaning behind his question. Perhaps trying to determine how much to share. "I am not sure I trust him," she says finally. "There are rumours about him."

"What kind of rumours?"

Julia smiles crookedly. "I am no fool, Mr Blake. And neither are you. I am sure you know what rumours I am referring to."

Nathan nods faintly. He knows there is little point in pretending. If he wants Julia to be open with him, he needs to do the same for her. "They say Joseph Holland is spying for the government," he says.

"Indeed."

Nathan stares into the fire, letting his eyes grow glassy. It seems his fears about Holland's role being uncovered are not unwarranted. Does Julia have any inkling of what Highfield House is being used for? Would she tell him if she did? Would she even care?

He rubs his eyes. He cannot find space in his mind for these concerns right now. Right now, he does not want to doubt Julia, or sift through everything she says in a desperate search for the truth.

Right now, he just wants to be in her company.

"I hope you are not involving yourself in the Rising," he says gently. "I would hate to see you in danger at the hands of Holland and his kind." And his fear for her safety is real; goes far beyond his wariness over what she might be entangled in.

"It makes little difference if I am involved in the cause or not," says Julia. "My family are known Jacobites. I am aware Holland is keeping a close eye on me. And I'm sure there are others who are doing the same. I just have no thought of who they are."

"Be careful," he says. "Please."

Julia's eyes soften as they meet his. "I will. Nathan, I…" Before he can make sense of what she is doing, she reaches out and puts a hand to his wrist. Panic courses through him at the unexpected contact. He flinches violently, tossing her hand away.

She leaps to her feet and backs away. "I'm sorry," she splutters. "I'm sorry."

Regret seizes him. "Forgive me," he says hurriedly. "You

took me by surprise, is all." The half-truth stings, but it is easier than honesty. He has no thought of how he would even begin to explain his fear to another person. What sane man is so adverse to another's touch? What would Julia think of him if she knew?

Nathan hears the click of the front door and hurries out of the parlour. He had not expected Edwin back so soon, and wonders if he has news. Harriet is standing in the entrance hall, her husband's hand wrapped tightly around her upper arm, as though to prevent her from escaping again. She is barefoot and shivering, wrapped in Edwin's greatcoat, her hair wet and tangled down her back. A long, thin cut scars one cheek. Nathan is not sure if he is relieved at the sight of her or horrified by the state she is in.

"Where have you been, Harriet?" he demands. "What on earth has happened?"

At the sound of the door, Eva hurries down the stairs, Finn at her shoulder. Harriet's gaze shifts between them. "I…"

"The truth," Edwin hisses, shaking her arm forcefully. "Tell them everything you told me." His gaze snaps to Mrs Brodie as she hurries in from the kitchen. "Prepare hot water for a bath."

"Yes sir." The housekeeper disappears back down the passage.

Harriet's eyes linger on Julia, who is hovering behind Nathan, careful to keep her distance. "Your brother. Michael." Her voice is cold and expressionless. "He wanted to re-join the rebels. At Lesbury Common… I said I would help him…"

"You were with Michael?" Julia's eyes widen. "He left?

He's re-joined the army?"

Harriet looks down. "We were caught by dragoons. He...
Michael was killed."

Julia makes a sound from her throat, presses a hand to her
mouth.

Nathan feels something twist in his belly. But he has no
thought of whether it is empathy for Julia, or the knowledge
that once again her family has put his in danger. This news is
a reminder of what he has allowed himself to forget all too
easily: that the Mitchells cannot be trusted. And this, he
thinks, this is why he cannot allow himself to get close to
Julia. This is just another in a long line of reasons why he
cannot allow these feelings he has for her to turn into
anything at all.

"What happened?" Julia coughs. "Where is he?"

"I hardly think that's of consequence right now," Edwin
snaps, a firm hand on Harriet's arm guiding her towards the
staircase.

Julia grabs Harriet's wrist before Edwin can whisk her
away. "What happened, Harriet?" she asks, her voice rattling.
"Please tell me. How did he die? Are you hurt? What did—"

"Leave," Edwin tells her firmly. He pushes past Eva and
Finn as he marches Harriet up the staircase.

For a second, Julia looks at questioningly at Nathan. He
swallows. "Edwin is right," he says after a moment. "It's best
that you leave. I'm sorry."

Her eyes flash. And she charges out of the house, as
though her hatred for his family is suddenly far more potent
than his loathing of hers.

# CHAPTER TWENTY-EIGHT

Edwin banks up the fire in the bedroom and guides Harriet towards it, his grip on her arm unyielding. Mrs Brodie elbows open the door and carries in a pot of boiling water. She tips it carefully into the tin bathtub she has set up in the corner of the room. She tops it up with cold water from the washbin. "I've some more water on the range now, Mr Whitley. Shouldn't be too long."

Edwin nods brusquely.

Once the door has clicked closed behind her, he pulls his coat from Harriet's shoulders and tosses it on the bed. "Get in the bath." His voice is low.

Harriet shivers. "I wish to see Thomas." She keeps her eyes down, unable to look at him.

"He's with Jenny." Edwin folds his arms. "Get in the bath," he says again.

"I wish to hold him. I missed him." It's true, she realises. She wants her son. Needs him. At least, she needs the comfort of his warm body pressed against her own. Her infant child feels like the only person in the world not yet capable of judging her.

Edwin snorts. "Curious that you only feel such things now."

She does not press the issue. She knows he is right. Wordlessly, she reaches down to open her shortjacket, but her cold, stiff fingers fumble with the laces. Edwin pushes her hand aside and steps close to her, working at the lacing down her chest.

"I can do it myself," Harriet coughs, suddenly remembering the coin pouch inside her bodice. She turns away, fumbling with the last of the eyelets. She pushes her shortjacket and dress from her shoulders, hiding the pouch in the pile of her clothing as she lowers it to the floor. She unlaces her stays and wrestles off her shift, the damp fabric clinging to her skin. Instinctively, she wraps her arms around herself, hiding her naked body from her husband. But when she glances Edwin's way, his eyes are fixed to the floor.

She steps into the bathtub and draws her knees to her chest, shivering in the thin puddle of water. Edwin takes the jug from the washbin and comes to kneel beside her. He scoops up the bathwater and pours it over her bare back. The feel of it is faintly soothing, but her husband's wordlessness chills her. He pours another jug of water over her shoulders, lifting her damp hair from her neck. For a moment, he leans close, his lips at her ear. But then he seems to decide against speaking. He puts the jug down and gets to his feet, moving across the room to stand by the window.

When a knock comes, he opens the door and takes the fresh pan of hot water from Mrs Brodie. He pours it into the bathtub, then lets it clatter to the floor. The sound echoes, making the muscles in Harriet's neck tighten. Hot water swells around her legs, but she can find no comfort in it. Everything feels so colourless and cold. Michael, dead. Anne in the hands of the redcoats. The Jacobites in the village spying on the house, their suspicions heightened by her own foolish behaviour.

"That's enough," Edwin says after a few more minutes. "Get out."

Harriet stands slowly and climbs out of the bathtub, refusing his hand. She trails water across the floorboards as she reaches hurriedly for her robe. She slides it on over her wet shoulders, barely bothering to dry herself. The need to cover herself feels far more pressing.

For long moments, Edwin stares at her, as though trying to see behind her eyes. "Why?" he says finally. "Is this whole sorry escapade because I did not agree to you travelling to Paris?"

Harriet says nothing.

"This family is under enough suspicion," he hisses. "Did you stop for a moment to think how your actions might affect me? Your brother and sister? Your son?" He shakes his head. "Lord only knows who saw you creeping across the island barefoot and soaking wet. I hardly dare imagine how suspicious the villagers will be if they hear about it."

"No one saw—"

"Quiet!" Edwin's palm flies to her cheek, silencing her lie. She reels backwards with the shock of it. Tears well behind her eyes at the sudden sting, but she refuses to let them fall. She stares him down with hard eyes.

At the sight of her unshed tears, Edwin's lips part. Harriet knows he has never seen anything close to such emotion from her.

But there is no reaction from him. No vague sense of regret, or even satisfaction, at his raising his hand to his wife. He is as emotionless and wooden as he always is.

She has made the right decision, she thinks, in not telling him all that Tom Cordwell had said to her. If this is what happens when she opens her mouth, she will keep to herself the fact that somehow, Cordwell already knew what the house was being used for. His finding her in the water this evening may have confirmed the suspicions the Jacobites have about this family, but it was not what had sparked them. Clearly, there are people in the village who have been watching Highfield House since long before she involved herself in Michael Mitchell's plans.

Harriet turns and walks towards the door.

"Where do you think you're going?" Edwin demands, suddenly sparking to life.

"I'm going to my workroom." Harriet doesn't look at him. The need to escape the bedchamber is suddenly overwhelming. A physical ache.

"No. I'll not have you leave my sight. And you are not to go anywhere near that workroom." Edwin paces across the room, blocking her path to the door. "I gave you your liberties, Harriet. I allowed you to keep painting. Allowed you meet with your artist friends. And this is how you repay me?"

Harriet closes her eyes, forcing her tears away. This is to be expected, she supposes. But Edwin will sleep. He will work. He cannot keep watch over her every hour of every day. And she will sneak back into her workroom then. Bring those moonlit scenes to life.

But he watches her, and for a horrible, fleeting second, it

as though he can read her thoughts. Perhaps it is not surprising. What other thoughts would she have other than ones of rebellion, railing against this harshest of punishments?

Edwin throws open the door and strides down the stairs.

"Where are you going?" Harriet dares to ask.

He does not respond. She races down the staircase after him, her robe clinging to her damp legs.

Edwin charges into her workroom, the door thumping loudly against the wall. He grabs at the cloth she has wrapped her brushes in and they clatter to the floor. He reaches down to gather them. With his spare hand, he snatches her half-finished painting from the easel. Harriet makes a desperate grab at her canvas, but Edwin charges past her into the passage.

"Where are you going?" she cries. "Edwin. Please. *Please.*"

She chases him into the parlour, where a fire is roaring in the grate. He flings her brushes into the flames. Harriet flies at him, trying to grab the painting, but he shoves her back.

The canvas is large. Too large to be swallowed by the fireplace in one mouthful. But Harriet watches in horror as Edwin feeds the painting into the fire, and lets the flames burn away the moon. Her stomach dives, but she has gone far beyond tears now. Hatred burns inside her. And for a fleeting, foolish second, she wishes she was back on the road to Alnwick, hiding in the undergrowth, with nothing and no one around. For right now, the thought of sleeping, waking, breathing, next to this man feels like a trial she would rather not survive.

Edwin stares glassy-eyed into the flames. "I thought to allow you to take the trip," he says distantly. "Before you ran away. I decided it might do you some good. I thought once the restoration was done, you and I could go to Paris together and you could meet with these sponsors." His words strike her. He is lying, surely. After all, he had sent Eva to try and talk her out of meeting with the Baillieus. "Your brother and sister," he continues, "they both convinced me this was a fine opportunity for you. I did not want you to miss out on such a chance on account of me."

Harriet swallows hard. She cannot look at her husband in case she sees something in his eyes that tells her he is speaking the truth.

Edwin watches the corner of the frame splinter into the fire. The canvas curls like a slow-moving wave. He looks back at her with a faintly bewildered look. "What was I to have done, Harriet? Tell me."

She doesn't reply. Just stares into the fireplace until the last of her painting is gone.

Nathan closes the door of the study and leans his back against it. He closes his eyes, a sick feeling in the pit of his stomach. He is not sure if it comes from the thought of whatever punishment Edwin is inflicting on his wayward wife, or the look in Julia's eyes when she had run from Highfield House. He can feel the ghost of her touch on his arm, as though her fingers are still pressed to his skin.

He goes to the desk chair and opens his account book. He stares down at it blankly, numbers swimming in front of his eyes. His unease ought to have settled now Harriet has returned. But the sight of his sister appearing at the house in such a state had done little to calm his anxiousness. Of all the things he had imagined her doing, running off to assist the Jacobite cause had not been one of them. He cannot imagine what could have driven her to do such a thing. Was it merely an act of rebellion? Or has Harriet become even more of a stranger to them than he had imagined?

There is a knock at the door of the study. "Come in." He looks up, surprised to see Finn. He wears rolled-up shirtsleeves, with the grime of the broken fireplace clinging to the linen. Light-brown hair is coming loose from his queue, his shirt open at the neck.

"I'm sorry you had to witness all that business with Harriet," says Nathan, before Finn can speak. "I'm sure you and Eva are in quite some hurry to get home. Are you finished with the fireplace?"

For a second, Finn does not reply. He hesitates for a moment, and his eyes shift, as though seeming to change his mind about whatever it is he has come here to say. Then he closes the door behind him. Folds his arms across his chest.

"Nathan," he says, "what are you really doing in this house?"

# CHAPTER TWENTY-NINE

"What do you mean? Edwin and I are restoring it." Nathan forces a laugh. "As you can see, I'm not much of a handyman."

"This is not about a restoration." His guess is not wrong; Finn can tell by the look in Nathan's eyes. It's a look of defeat; fear, perhaps. It is mere seconds before his shoulders slump forward. He rubs his eyes and plants his elbows against the pages of the ledger opened in front of him.

"I'm searching for something. A document. Apparently my mother hid it somewhere in the house. And now its owner wants it back."

Finn leans his back against the door. Keeps his voice low. "Its owner. And who is that?"

"Henry Ward."

Finn nods slightly. He had expected the name before Nathan had spoken it. It feels like a piece falling into place. He takes a chair from the corner of the room and plants it in front of Nathan's desk. Sits. "What's the document?" he asks.

Nathan sighs. "A letter, I'm told. Kept safe in a brass box. Revealing the Jacobite leanings of someone high up in the Whig government."

"A dissenter," says Finn. "That's not so uncommon, surely."

"Ward says this letter has blackmailing power—particularly now the Whigs are in such a position of strength. Far more so than they were twenty years ago when Ward would first have received the letter." Nathan drums his fingers edgily against the arm of his desk chair. "I don't know who the letter speaks of. Or how Ward got it. But he seems certain that the government would go to great lengths to keep this a secret."

Finn nods slowly. So this is how Ward plans to offer his crew immunity: by blackmailing the authorities and threatening to reveal this damaging information.

None of this is a surprise to him—he knows how shrewd and calculating Henry Ward is. But fearing Ward had his eye on the Blakes was one thing. Knowing it for certain makes him distinctly afraid.

"Apparently he gave the letter to my mother to keep safe," says Nathan. "And now he wants it back." He rubs his eyes. "I do not know if Ward truly ever owned such a letter, or if these are just fanciful stories."

"There's every chance he's telling the truth," Finn says. "Ward was a respected privateer. He was active in the war at the end of last century, so someone may well have shared information with him about the French and their Jacobite allies."

"You sailed with him."

"Aye. For a short time." Finn hopes he does not ask any

more questions. Nathan's assumption, surely, is that he sailed with Ward as a young man—not as the boy he was when he had fought with and killed Oliver Blake. "Ward's a dangerous man," he says. "But he's not one to lie."

"I see."

Finn can tell this was not news he wished to hear. For long moments, Nathan turns to look through the undrawn curtains. The night is black and starlit, the sea invisible behind the glass.

"Ward was adamant that I return to Lindisfarne and recover this letter," says Nathan. "He's made threats. Against me. And my daughter."

Little wonder Nathan Blake looks so haunted. Finn thinks of the way Ward had spoken so brassily about offering his crew immunity; spoken as though he already had the letter in his hand. No doubt he has made promises to his crew; promises he will struggle to keep if the letter is not found. Finn knows how much such a thing will gall a man who prides himself on honour as Ward does. But are these empty threats he has made against Nathan and Theodora? Finn can't be sure. Would Ward's affection for Abigail prevent him from harming her son and granddaughter? Or has that been overridden by his need for this letter? His need to keep his word to his crew, and prove himself a man of honour?

"Who knows about this?" Finn asks. "Who knows the real reason you're here?"

"Edwin knows I'm here looking for the box containing the letter," says Nathan. "But I've told him nothing about Ward. I told him the box contains my mother's jewellery. He doesn't appreciate the seriousness of the situation. He thinks I ought to put an end to the search and concentrate on restoring the house. Eva and Harriet know nothing about it. And I would appreciate it if you did not tell them."

Finn bristles. "You're asking me to keep this a secret from my wife?"

Nathan looks at him squarely. "I'm not asking you. I'm telling you."

The sharp look in Nathan's eye catches Finn off guard. It's a look of hardness he has not seen from Eva's brother before. And for a horrifying second, Finn is afraid he has been recognised. It's an irrational thought, of course—the night of Oliver's death, he and Nathan had been boys. This is just the house playing tricks.

"Eva could handle the truth," Finn says.

Nathan passes a quill between his fingers. "Perhaps. But not Harriet. Certainly not after…all this." He waves a hand in the vague direction of Harriet and Edwin's bedchamber.

Nathan reaches down and pulls open the cabinet beneath his desk. He produces a bottle of brandy and two glasses. The bottle is ornate, old-looking, and Finn wonders if it has been here since Abigail had lived in the house. Perhaps a bottle Henry Ward had brought her. Nathan fills the cups and hands one to Finn.

He gulps it down. It's rich and fragrant, smooth on his tongue. Far better than the moonshine he usually tosses back on Longstone.

Nathan leans back in his chair as he drinks. And that look in his eyes, it is not a threat, or recognition, Finn realises. It is complete and utter exhaustion. Finn knows all too well what it's like to be pursued by Henry Ward. Knows the stress of trying to protect those he loves.

The stress of trying to keep a secret.

It's almost a relief to share this after so many harrowing months. And while Finn Murray is not the man he had imagined unloading all this on, Nathan can't deny that speaking of it makes the weight upon his shoulders a scrap more manageable.

"It was not supposed to be like this, with the whole family here," he says. "I thought it would just be Edwin and me. I thought we'd come up here and I'd find the damn letter, and that would be the end of it. Then I could sell the house and be done with it. I did not expect Edwin to bring Harriet and Thomas with him. And I certainly did not expect Eva and my daughter…" He scrubs a hand over his eyes. "I told my sisters I was coming up here to restore and sell the house. Once they were here, I had to carry on with the charade."

Nathan knows he ought to have told them the truth. But how could he have admitted to the trouble he was in? He is supposed to be the head of this family—and all he has done is drive them into financial ruin. Secure Harriet into an unhappy marriage and turn Eva wild. He feels like an utter failure.

The first letter from Ward had arrived at Nathan's office several months ago. Ward had introduced himself as an acquaintance of Nathan's mother. Had expressed his sadness at Abigail's passing. Nathan had vaguely recognised Henry Ward's name. A distant figure from a forgotten childhood on Holy Island. He wondered how Ward had come to hear of his mother's death, but did not dwell on it. No doubt she and Ward had shared acquaintances who had passed on the news.

Ward had explained, in polite and reasonable terms, of the valuable letter he had given Abigail for safekeeping more than twenty years earlier, sealed in a brass box to protect it.

And then: *Some months before your mother's death, I managed to contact her through my London solicitors, after searching for her for many years. She assured me the letter was securely deposited in the safe I had opened under my name at the Bank of England.*

*I returned to London last week after several years abroad. Imagine my surprise when I discovered the letter was not in the safe.*

The tone of Ward's letter had grown increasingly threatening. *I struggle to believe Abigail would have lied to me on such an issue. Therefore, Mr Blake, I must ask you if you know of the whereabouts of this most valuable of my possessions.*

Nathan scrawled back a short reply. He knew of no such letter, and had certainly not taken it from a safe at the Bank of England. Ward's correspondence was bewildering. Nathan had never known his mother to own anything valuable enough to be stored in a bank safe—and surely something as insubstantial as a letter could not have the immense value Henry Ward attributed to it. He wondered at the truth of the issue. Surely there had to be more in this locked box than a mere piece of paper. Jewels, perhaps. The pirating treasures he had imagined Henry Ward collecting back when he was a child. In any case, he told Ward, everything his mother had owned in those years she had left behind at Highfield House the night they had made their hurried escape. Of this, he was certain. The night they had fled, Abigail had taken nothing but the clothes on her back. Her hands had been far too full of her screaming children to have taken Ward's precious box with her, no matter how valuable it might have been.

The next letter came quickly, Ward's accusation thinly

veiled. *Once again, I am certain Abigail would have had no cause to lie to me. If, however, the letter remains at Highfield House, as you so adamantly believe, I humbly request you return to Lindisfarne at your earliest convenience and retrieve it...*

It was a request Nathan had no time for. He was struggling to rebuild his business, struggling with a daughter plagued by nightmares. Traipsing up to Lindisfarne at the whim of this man from his mother's past was not something he was willing to entertain.

But when Ward turned up on the doorstep of his Islington townhouse, Nathan knew he did not have the luxury of ignorance. He had recently sold the family home, and knew it was no easy thing for a stranger to hunt down the address of his rented house on the outskirts of the city. No doubt Henry Ward had put the same effort into finding him that he had put into hunting down Abigail in those months before her death.

"I need that letter," said Ward. "Urgently. It is non-negotiable"—his words highlighted by the pistol tied to his belt, deliberately positioned, Nathan felt sure, to provide him with nothing more than glimpse of the threat at hand.

"I do not have this letter," he hissed. "If Mother had deposited it in a safe in your name, how would I even have got to it?"

Something passed across Ward's eyes. "The safe was in your name too, as her eldest surviving son. As I suspect you well know."

Nathan blinked. "What?"

Ward hesitated. "Abigail insisted on it. She wanted a little security for you and your sister. She could not bear the thought of you returning to the same financial trouble she was in after your father died. Of course, I respected her wishes. She and I…" He cleared his throat. "Well. Suffice to say the future I had planned with her did not come to fruition."

Nathan frowned. He had had no idea his mother had ever planned a future with a man other than his father, or that she had ever suffered financially. The knowledge was unsettling. After they had left Lindisfarne, Abigail had never shown the slightest interest in taking another husband. Nathan had assumed their finances secure enough for her not to need to. What else had he been wrong about?

"Why would I even think to steal a letter, of all things?" he demanded, rattled at Ward's upturning of his version of the past.

"You seem an intelligent man, Mr Blake. I am sure you can see the value in such a piece of correspondence. If the nation was to find out a covert Jacobite had made it into the upper echelons of the Whig party, their support would weaken considerably. I imagine they would be willing to pay a substantial fee to make sure the knowledge of such a betrayal was not made public."

The back of Nathan's neck prickled. "I am not the kind for extortion."

"I suspect that's the truth," said Ward. "But I also know your business has suffered something of a setback. And an intelligent man like you would know he could fetch a hefty price for a letter of such value. Enough to cover the losses you have incurred of late."

Nathan pressed his shoulders back, trying not to let Ward see his unease. He felt like a child under the thrall of an angry guardian; far from the head of a respectable family he was supposed to be. "If you truly believe I've sold the letter, why are you here demanding I give it back to you?"

Ward smiled thinly. "Because I am hoping you will have the sense to buy it back from whoever you sold it to. And return it to me."

Nathan closed her eyes. "I told you, I know nothing of this letter. If it is not in your safe, it must still be in Highfield House. Or else Mother rid herself of it."

"She would not have done that," Ward said firmly, as if that was the end of the matter. "I'm certain of it. But if you truly believe the letter to still be in the house, then you will go up to Lindisfarne and find it for me." Ward produced a key from his pocket and held it up for Nathan to see. "A small brass box. The lock fits this key. The last I saw of it, Abigail was keeping it in a drawer in her nightstand." He slid the key back into his pocket.

"I'm sorry, Mr Ward," said Nathan, trying hard not to think of how in hell this man knew anything of his mother's nightstand. "But I am afraid this is not my problem."

Ward was silent for a moment. "You have a young daughter, I believe?" The words were spoken warmly enough, but Nathan could see through to the threat beneath. He had been painfully deliberate in keeping Theodora out of sight. And yet somehow, Ward had known of her anyway, just as he had known of the collapse of the business. And just as he had known where to find them.

Nathan felt hot and sick with dread. He wanted to tell Henry Ward he was not the kind of man he could coerce with hollow threats. But he knew that was a lie. He could see the distrust in Ward's eyes. Could tell the man did not believe him when he promised he knew nothing of this precious letter in a box.

Nathan was wracked with fear over what Ward could do to his daughter, to his sisters, to him. And so, with no other choice, he promised he would return to Lindisfarne for the first time in twenty years. Find the box his mother had left behind in her hurry to escape the island.

He told his family he was going north to meet with a new manufacturer. Told them he would be home in a matter of weeks. Surely this damn box would be tucked away in a drawer or cupboard, forgotten about by their mother when she had torn out into the night.

Once on the island, Nathan had done his best to hurry out to the house without any of the villagers seeing him. He had known, even then, before they had branded his family as spies, that his being there would raise questions. And they were questions he had no thought of how to answer.

It was dusk when the hulk of Highfield House loomed between the dunes, a deep shadow, a shape from half-remembered dreams. The sight of it drew him back into all the worst pieces of the past: to burying his father, to being trapped in the priest hole, to his brother's lifeless eyes staring up at the beams of the ceiling. His mother tugging at his hand as they ran across the Pilgrims' Way towards the mainland, water licking at his ankles, knees, thighs.

He had wondered then, as he had trudged grimly towards the house, what bearing Henry Ward had had on his mother's leaving. What had his mother gotten herself involved in all those years ago? Why would she have promised to keep this letter safe for a man like Ward? What was between them? Ward had spoken of them planning a future together—if this was the case, why had Abigail fled Holy Island so impulsively?

As a boy, Nathan had known of the man from the sea who would come to the house. He had met Henry Ward on a few occasions, but most of his memories of him were hazy, formed by overhearing conversations on the edge of sleep. Now, with Highfield House looming ahead of him, those nights spent listening to Ward's deep laughter felt far more present. Felt like they belonged to something other than the distant past.

Nathan had always assumed their leaving Lindisfarne had come from his mother's grief. Her need to escape the house where her husband and son had died in quick succession. But now he began to wonder if there was more to the story. Was Henry Ward somehow tied into their reason for escape?

He slid the rusty house key from his pocket, dimly aware that he had spent most of the journey, and certainly the entire walk up from the village, with his fingers tight around its cold metal. He would get inside, find the damn box, and suffer through one night in this lonely old place. When he returned to London, he would give the letter to Ward and get him out of their lives. And then start the process of getting the house out of their lives too.

Nathan wondered why he had been so reluctant to sell the place. Until last year, when his business had collapsed, he had not needed the money, and he had always been certain the house was in a state. Selling it had all felt too hard. But at the back of his mind, he could not help but wonder if there was more to it. If it was some misplaced loyalty to his brother that kept him holding on to the place where Oliver had lost his life.

Nathan shook the thought away. Oliver had been a callous

bully, and his body had long turned to dust. He deserved no loyalty.

Inexplicably, his heart quickened as he followed the faint path through the long grass leading up to the house. Strange that a track might still be worn into the earth, given two decades had passed since anyone had lived here. He supposed the house was something of a curiosity to the people of Holy Island, lonely and windblown out on Emmanuel Head. No doubt it had had its share of curious eyes pressed to the grimy windows.

Nathan slid the key into the lock, half surprised when the front door opened with little more protest than a loud groan. Ahead of him, the house was dark and cavernous, the air stale and thick as water. As he stepped across the flagstones in the entrance hall, he heard the faint scrabble of unseen mice. In the last light of dusk, he could feel the painted eyes of an ancestor boring into him, the sight of the familiar portrait making the years unwind. Another painting lay on the floor at his feet, its frame in pieces and its hook fallen from the crumbling mortar of the wall.

Nathan pulled a tinderbox and candle from his bag and lit the wick with mildly trembling hands.

It was too dark to search the house properly. Long shadows lay over everything, and the dark was seeping in like liquid. But he felt restless, impatient. He did not want to look too closely at the house they had left behind. He wanted to find that box by lamplight and be saved from having to delve too deep.

With the lamp in one hand, he went first to his mother's old bedchamber and opened the drawer of the nightstand. In spite of his need to find the letter, he was mildly relieved to find Henry Ward had not been correct about her having stored it there. He made his way through the house, opening the cupboards and drawers, and peering under the beds, every glimpse a piece of his old life. Old clothes still hung in the wardrobes; his own boyish trimmed coats and Eva's tiny smock dresses. The sugar loaf hat his mother had worn to church. Plates and bowls with chips in the same places, books that were familiar before he was even old enough to read them. So many years had turned over while this house had lain entombed in the past. In the morning, he would pack up all these old clothes and memories and take them to the church for the charity collection. Start the process of setting time moving again in Highfield House. Because what good was it doing to keep the past locked up in here, poisonous and unbreathable? But among all those old clothes, those old memories, he found no box. No letter.

Finally, exhausted, his instinct drew him back down the passage to his old childhood bedroom. He lay beneath the blankets and their decades-long veneer of dust, his mind refusing to still. He thought of the night Oliver had died. The memory was vivid and bitter, though he had no thought of how much time had distorted it. He remembered the laughter of the men in the parlour floating up the staircase. Somehow, he knew one of the men was Henry Ward; the boy who had fought with Oliver, a member of his crew. Whether a long-buried childhood memory, or a piecing together of this puzzle he had now become entangled in, Nathan was not sure.

The next morning, with bronze light pouring through the windows, he searched and searched. Every cupboard, every drawer, every shelf. If this letter truly was as valuable as Ward claimed, there was every chance his mother had hidden it somewhere more secretive. Beneath a floorboard. Behind a wall panel. Inside an unused chimney, perhaps. And in a place as sprawling as Highfield House, the list of places to hide— or be hidden—was near endless. Impossible to search alone, and with his bare hands.

He went back to London. *A box*, he told Edwin, *containing some of my mother's jewellery. I need to sell it to rebuild the business.* Somewhere in the back of his mind, Nathan knew lying to his brother-in-law was not the wisest course of action. But he knew Edwin considered him weak. Knew that if he told him about Ward, Edwin would insist they fight. Whether in the courtroom, or with pistols on Tothill Fields, Nathan had no thought. And it didn't matter. He had seen the pistol in Ward's belt. *You have a young daughter, I believe?* No. There would be no fighting. With Edwin's carpentry expertise, they would tear the house apart as quickly as possible. Find the box containing the letter. Get Henry Ward out of their lives.

Edwin had jumped at the chance. "About time you did something with that old place, Nate. You'll thank yourself when you sell it." He chuckled. "It will do far more for your business than a measly old box of jewellery."

Nathan tried to hold him back, tell him he had no desire to restore the house, or sell it, or do anything other than burn it to the ground. But Edwin was already running with the idea. Besides, Nathan knew Edwin was right: if he was to have any chance of rebuilding his business, he needed the money that would come from the sale of the house. He would let Edwin do as he wished to the place, as long as he also did all he could to find the letter. Soon Henry Ward would be nothing but a memory and Nathan could begin to rebuild his life.

By this point, his finances were dire, and continuing to

rent the house in London while he was unable to work was not an option. But nor was taking his daughter with him to Holy Island with a man like Henry Ward breathing down his neck.

Nathan had not expected Edwin to rent out his home and cart his entire family up to Northumberland.

"Lindisfarne is no place for Harriet," he had tried to argue. "You know how much she loves the city. Why not let her stay in London with Eva and Theodora? Matthew Walton has offered them his empty townhouse."

"Getting away from London will be good for her. She's far too absorbed in that dreadful clique of painters. She could use some time away from the city. Might remind her she's also a wife and mother."

With Harriet present, Nathan had had no choice but to play up the lie that he was in the house to restore it. His cover story had become a reluctant truth.

With a bowed head, he tells Finn everything. His new brother-in-law knows Henry Ward, of course. Knows what he is capable of. And Nathan is sure that, unlike Edwin, Finn appreciates the gravity of the situation. Finn nods along slowly to the story, bringing his glass to his lips with almost rhythmic regularity. He is quiet for several moments after Nathan finishes speaking. Turns his glass around in his hand.

"I saw Ward's ship passing Longstone not long after Eva first came to stay with me," he says finally. "Was that when he first returned to Northumberland?"

"I believe so," says Nathan. "I told him I would need longer than I initially thought to find the letter. He turned up at the house a few weeks after we arrived, hounding me to produce it. I asked him not to come here again. I told him I would leave word at the village tavern the moment I found the letter."

Finn taps his fingers against the side of his glass, his brow creased in thought. "And he agreed to that?"

"He did. But his ship has been moored in front of the house for the past few weeks. A means of threatening me, I presume."

Finn nods slowly. Nathan appreciates his calmness. It goes some way to settling the deep panic that had taken root inside him when Ward had first appeared at his door. When he had first decided to keep this a secret.

"Your family has never been suspicious?" Finn asks.

"Eva has been out at Longstone with you, and Harriet is far too absorbed in her own world to take note of what's going on around her. I told Edwin that Henry Ward was just a potential buyer interested in seeing the house." He leans back in his chair and rubs his eyes. "As you can see, I've torn the place apart. There is no letter. I'm sure Ward knows that by now. I think he is just doing all this to punish me for that."

"Are you sure your mother didn't take it with her when she left the house?" asks Finn.

"I'm certain. I remember that night like it was yesterday. Mother had nothing with her."

"She could have carried the letter in her pocket. Or inside her stays."

"Ward gave it to her in a locked brass box," says Nathan. "I suppose it's possible that she might have smashed the box open and taken the letter with her in her pocket. But I suspect she got rid of it before we left. Perhaps she did not want something so inflammatory in her possession." He sips his brandy. "I told all this to Ward. He did not seem to want to hear it."

Finn smiles wryly. "I can imagine. He's lured an entire crew of men into his pirating crew with the promise of the immunity that letter will give them."

Nathan curses under his breath. Having Henry Ward in his shadow is bad enough; he had not stopped to consider he might have an entire crew at his disposal.

Finn looks out the window, scratching his bristled chin. "Ward said nothing of this to Eva when he met her aboard his ship."

"I told him I wished to keep it from the rest of the family," says Nathan. "It seems he has respected my wishes."

Finn nods, clearly unsurprised. "He has a strange sense of honour. Some decency about him. But he'll not hesitate to punish people he thinks have deceived him."

Nathan stares into the bronze halo at the bottom of his glass. "I've not deceived him. But perhaps my mother did."

"Aye. And I suspect that's the last thing Ward wishes to hear."

"Yes," says Nathan. He opens his mouth to speak, then wavers. "Harriet..." he begins. "I suspect she is..." He catches Finn's faint nod. "You knew."

"Eva came to suspect it, aye."

Nathan shifts uncomfortably in his chair. A part of him had been hoping Finn would argue; tell him he is mistaken about Ward being Harriet's father. Not that Nathan had really had any doubts. The resemblance between father and daughter is far too strong to be a coincidence. The knowledge is uncomfortable, but Nathan knows trying to ignore it will do him no good.

He has little doubt now that Henry Ward had had

something to do with why they had left Holy Island. Had Abigail been shamed by the villagers for her relations with him? Or had she fled to prevent him from finding out about his child? Perhaps both.

"I've not told Harriet," Nathan says. "I do not want her to know anything about the man. How can it do her any good to know she's that scoundrel's daughter?"

Finn nods. "Let me tell all this to Eva," he says. "She can help. You know she can."

Nathan sighs. "I did not want her involved in this. She was not even supposed to be here. She was supposed to be—"

"In London marrying that toff Walton," Finn finishes tautly. "Aye, I know. But things have not worked out the way you planned. And it sounds as though you could use a little help."

Nathan draws in a long breath. Involving his sister in this was the last thing he had ever wanted to do. But he knows it is too late for that. Eva has already entangled herself with Henry Ward. Besides, perhaps it would do him good to have her input. Eva is intelligent, level-headed. Perhaps she really can be of some assistance.

"All right," he says finally, tossing back the last of his brandy in an attempt to steel himself. "But let me be the one to tell her." He needs the chance to explain. A chance to apologise for his failures. "If she must hear it, I would like her to hear it from me."

Harriet stands motionless outside Nathan's study. *Listen. Observe. Gather the pieces.*

The raw anger she had felt after watching her painting burn has been sloughed away by her brother's words: *How can it do her any good to know she's that scoundrel's daughter?*

Harriet closes her eyes, pressing her back against the wall to keep her balance. Once again, she has just fragments of the story. But those fragments are enough.

How many people have sought to keep this a secret from her? How many people know the truth of who her father is? Nathan and Finn. Eva too?

She has no idea who this Henry Ward is. The scoundrel. Faceless—but she has a name. Precious pieces of the story.

The floor creaks in Nathan's study and Harriet darts across the hallway into her bedroom. The tin bath still sits in front of the dying fire, the pile of her wet clothes beside it. Michael's coin pouch she has tucked beneath her mattress.

She goes to the desk in the corner of the room and pulls paper and an ink pot from the top drawer. Dips her quill into the ink and begins to write words that at once mean nothing and everything to her:

*Come at once to Highfield House. Letter has been found.*

What this letter is, she has no thought of. She has caught just pieces of Nathan and Finn's conversation. But those pieces are of infinite value.

She signs the letter with her brother's name. Throws a dress on over her nightshift and hunts around the room for her cloak.

# CHAPTER THIRTY

Eva knocks on the side door of the curiosity shop. It's late—far too late to be traipsing alone across the island. But Finn has finally dropped into an exhausted sleep, and Eva knows Nathan's stubbornness would never allow him to visit Julia. In spite of all Julia has done, Eva is more than a little ashamed at the way her family sent her on her way after hearing of her brother's death. When had they become so heartless?

For a long time, there is silence. Eva steps around the corner to peer through the dark windows, the globe of light from her lantern reflected back at her. She squints. Is that movement in the darkness of the shop? Or is it just her imagination? She darts a glance over her shoulder, wary of eyes upon her.

Just as she is about to begin the unnerving walk back to the house, she hears the door creak open. Julia's eyes are red rimmed and swollen, a tatty green shawl draped around her shoulders. Her curls hang messily around her face. At the sight of Eva, she wraps her arms about herself tightly, an almost protective gesture.

"Have you come here to criticise me?" she snaps. "Blame my family for the trouble Harriet got into?"

Eva absorbs her sharpness. "I've come to see if you are all right."

Julia lets out a breath, shaking her head incredulously.

"I'm sorry," says Eva. "I'm sure that's a foolish question." Julia stays planted in the doorway, making it clear an invitation to enter will not be forthcoming. Eva shifts the lamp to her other hand. "I am sorry about your brother. And I'm sorry for the way Edwin and Nathan treated you this evening."

Julia snorts. "I thought you despised me as much as they do."

"Nathan does not despise you," says Eva. "Believe me."

Julia lowers her eyes. A ginger cat appears from behind her and she bends down to scoop it into her arms. She smooths the cat's fur for a moment, lost in her own thoughts. "In the morning, I need to go to Longstone and tell Angus what happened to Michael," she says distantly. "I'd appreciate it if you didn't say anything to him. I would like to be the one to tell him."

Eva nods. "Of course. And I'm sorry. I ought to have told you how often Michael was leaving the island."

Julia shakes her head, her eyes softening a little. "It was not your fault, Eva. It was not your job to keep watch over him."

"Angus will go to London?"

"I suspect so. It's clear by now that Hugh is not coming back." Julia speaks in a thin, guarded voice that Eva suspects is only just keeping her grief at bay. She can only imagine how Julia must feel: one brother dead, one missing, one about to flee into the city.

"I'm sorry," she says again. Her apology feels hollow, empty. "If there is anything you need..." She trails off, Julia's closed expression letting her know she is the last person she will come to with her needs. "I'll leave you be," Eva says finally. "But you know where to find us."

Julia nods.

As she is about to close the door, Eva turns back suddenly. "Julia," she says hesitantly. "Do not give up on Nathan."

Julia raises her eyebrows, clearly caught off guard. "I would have thought I was the last person you wanted around your brother."

Eva hesitates. "Well. The way he is around you... it's a rare thing. What I think has little to do with it."

Julia frowns. But she nods slightly. Doesn't speak. Just closes the door, making it clear the conversation is over.

Harriet presses herself against the stone wall of the apothecary, holding her breath as her sister passes on her way back to the house. When she is sure Eva has not seen her, she hurries towards the tavern.

Lamplight spills out onto the cobbles, along with the soft murmur of voices, punctuated by a loud laugh. Harriet pulls up the hood of her cloak and steps inside. Her heart is quick, but somehow, this piece of knowledge about her father, and his unexpected nearness, has allowed her to find some hidden reserve of courage.

The place is sparsely lit, with the hearth smouldering orange. A few men cluster in corners, chatting in low voices beneath curls of pipe smoke, but Harriet is relieved to find the tavern largely empty. Surely if she is seen in such a place, it will raise far more questions than her rescue at the hands of Tom Cordwell. She approaches the bar with her head down. Hands the folded page to the barkeep. "A message," she says. "For Mr Ward."

She holds her breath, hoping the man will not ask for more information. A look in his eyes tells her he recognises her, but he does little more than nod. Perhaps the mention of this Mr Ward's name has encouraged him into silence.

Perhaps he has learnt well enough not to ask questions.

Nathan takes the telescope outside. He needs to escape the house and the poisonous air the last few hours have filled the place with. Needs the calmness of the night sky to ease the shame of his unearthed secrets, the stress of his predicament. The memory of the anger in Julia's eyes as she had charged away from the house.

He finds a flat patch of earth behind the manor, away from the lights of the mainland. He sets the telescope up on its stand, angling it towards the sky. Mars is at its brightest from now until Christmas, and he hopes to examine it through the glass. Let the enormity of the universe, the mystique of distant planets, quieten his racing thoughts.

Footsteps in the dark make him turn. On edge, he whirls around. Somehow, he is not surprised to see Julia emerging from the dunes.

"You," she hisses, jabbing a finger in his direction. Her curls are untamed, whipping around her face like bracken blown wild in a storm. In the glow of her lantern and the sparse light spilling from the house, he sees the clutter of emotions on her face. "You act so damn self-righteous. But you're no better than I am. In fact," she snaps, "you're worse. I might have deceived you to save Angus and Michael's lives, but at least I have some damn compassion in me. My brother has just been murdered, and all you can do is let Harriet's husband order me from the house?" Her eyes are wide and tearful. "Do you not think I have a right to know how my own brother died?" Her voice wavers. "I have no thought of what has even happened to his body. I cannot even bury him. Give him a proper farewell."

For several moments, Nathan doesn't speak. Everything she has said is right, and he can think of nothing to say but a meagre, watery apology. He can imagine how little good that will do. Julia lets out a frustrated breath and turns on her heel. And all Nathan can think about is how much he does not want her to leave.

Impulsively, his hand shoots out and snatches hers. The gesture surprises himself as much as it does her—that searing jolt up his arm, hot and cold at once, a flood of goosebumps over his skin. And the feel of her, it is not unpleasant, he realises. It is not unpleasant at all. But it is almost painfully overwhelming, and he lets his hand fall.

"Please don't go," he hears himself say.

For a moment, Julia is frozen, lips parted, eyes wide. Nathan takes a step towards her. "I am sorry about your brother," he says. "I truly am. And I am sorry for letting Edwin send you away like that." Shame churns inside him.

She swallows. Nods.

Nathan's heart is thundering with the remnants of the contact, and with the knowledge that he has only just allowed himself to admit to: that he wants to be around her. That he wants her close to him.

Julia scrubs away a stray tear, wind off the sea blowing hair across her eyes. "I'm glad you are using the telescope," she says finally. Her lips tilt upwards slightly. "I thought you planned to return it."

Nathan gives her a sheepish smile. "Well. It's a fine piece. It would be a shame to let it go to waste." He bends, training the barrel across the sky until he captures the faint red eye of Mars. "Here." He nudges her towards the telescope. "Look."

Julia bends. Looks through the eyepiece for a moment. He can see her back and shoulders rising and falling with slightly quickened breath.

"Mars is at its brightest for the next two months," Nathan tells her. "If you look carefully, you can just make out the dark spots on its surface. Huygens spoke of them when he first depicted the planet last century."

"You know a lot about this," says Julia.

"A little. My father taught me when I was a lad."

She stands and turns back to Nathan. There is a ghost of smile on her lips at his use of the Northumbrian vernacular. It disappears so quickly he is not sure if he imagined it. "I'm sure it was Michael's fault that Harriet got involved in his business," she says. "But I just want you to know that I knew nothing of it." She looks down. "For whatever that's worth."

Nathan nods shortly. He believes her, he realises. "Well. For whatever it's worth, I do not imagine Harriet would have taken much convincing." He clears his throat. "Mars will get brighter as it gets closer to dawn," he says. "I am sure it's of no interest to you. But… I do find looking at the sky makes one's problems a little easier to carry. If you would like to stay…" He shakes his head. "I'm sorry. It was a foolish suggestion. I'm sure you've too much on your mind to—"

"I'd like that a lot," Julia cuts in. Her smile is pale, but this time he knows he is not imagining it. "Thank you."

She cannot be here—at the back of his mind, Nathan knows that. Knows it is only a matter of time before Holland and the other government spies are back at Highfield House. And he has no thought of how deeply Julia is entrenched in the Jacobite cause. Her reaction the day she had seen Holland on the Heugh suggests she has much to hide.

Nathan pushes those thoughts away. He will revisit them again when the sun rises and the stars disappear into the daylight. Because surely, surely, he and Julia will not be spotted together now, so late at night. Surely, just for these few hours, they are safe in this moonless darkness, with their eyes turned to the sky.

# CHAPTER THIRTY-ONE

Nathan is surprised when pale dawn begins to push against the bottom of the sky. He had not intended to stay out here all night, but the stars are disappearing into the light now, after moving in their wide arcs towards the horizon.

He and Julia sit side by side on the dunes. So close that from time to time, her shoulder brushes his. He finds himself welcoming the soft jolt it sends through him. Finds himself almost craving it.

Julia lifts the telescope from her lap and brings it to her eye, looking out over the lightening water towards the firebasket her youngest brother is keeping alive. Throughout the night, their discussion had shifted from the stars and planets to the safe ground of their children, to finally touching on their own parallel childhoods on Holy Island. Julia had wanted to speak of her lost brother, Nathan had realised, her stories peppered with brash and headstrong Michael, who could swim across to the mainland and liked to play in the rain. From time to time, she would bring the telescope to her eye to pull in some more of the universe, and its power to make trouble seem distant.

"I ought to get back," she says finally. "I need to collect Bobby from Alice's. The poor lad'll think I've forgotten him."

Nathan can't take his eyes from her. With each minute, the sky grows lighter, and her profile becomes sharper, clearer. He can see the freckles on her cheeks and nose, the stray piece of grass caught in one of her curls.

He gets to his feet, offering her his hand. She takes it as she climbs to her feet, then releases her grip quickly. He has not said a word to her about his difficulty with physical contact. But he can sense she is aware of it, at least on some level.

She hands him the telescope. "Thank you, Nathan. For all of this." Her eyes meet his and he feels a warmth in his chest.

He nods. "Of course. I hope it helped a little."

Julia smiles faintly. "More than you could know." Her look is pointed and meaningful. And where do they go from here, Nathan wonders? The safest thing, he knows all too well, is to turn his back. Put as much distance between himself and Julia as he can. But right now, that does not feel possible.

"Shall I see you back to the village?" he asks.

"No. It's all right." She takes a step closer, and Nathan can feel her breath against his chin, mingling with the cool breeze of morning. A shiver goes through him. "But will you call on me?" She sounds tentative, more uncertain than he has ever heard her before.

He swallows hard. "I will, yes."

Julia flashes him a short smile. Then she turns towards the path that leads back to the village.

At the sound of footsteps, she stops, frozen on top of the

shallow dune. There are men coming towards them, Nathan realises sickly, their figures emerging from the early-morning dimness. Men charging towards the house with hunting muskets in their hands.

Nathan recognises Tom Cordwell. Martin Macauley. Two other men from the fishing fleet. All four of them known Jacobites. His heart begins to thunder.

Julia whirls around to face him, panic in her eyes, but something else beneath. Something questioning. "Why are they here?" she demands. "What do they want?"

Nathan shakes his head. "I don't know." It's only a half-truth, of course. But how can he manage otherwise, with four armed men charging towards his house and this look of bewilderment in Julia's eyes?

She rushes down the side of the dune and blocks the men's path. "What do you want with them?"

"Get out the way, Miss Mitchell," Cordwell snorts.

Julia grabs Martin Macauley's arm as he charges past. "What do you want with them?" she repeats.

"What do you think we want?" he says tautly. "Bloody spies, aren't they. Keeping government intelligence at their house. Spies coming and going at all hours. And Tom caught one of them out running messages for Cotesworth."

Nathan's stomach dives. "No. You're wrong. You're—"

Macauley swings the butt of his musket, pounding Nathan in the stomach. He hunches over, gasping for breath, the telescope falling from his hand and thudding dully to the grass. A cry of shock from Julia, but when he looks up, there is no hint of sympathy in her eyes.

"Government intelligence?" she repeats. "Is this true?"

"I…" His moment of hesitation is enough. Because that

look of betrayal he sees, Nathan knows it well. He had given her that very same look when he had found her brothers hiding in his attic.

"I trusted you," she hisses. "Even after everything people said about you. I told them they were wrong."

Nathan reaches for her, but she pulls away. "Julia," he manages. "Please. I…"

She shakes her head. Backs away. And she is charging down the path away from the house, without a single look in his direction.

Harriet hears them come to the door. Hears them thunder inside, searching, breaking. Edwin flies out of bed, snatching his pistol from the nightstand and rushing downstairs. Harriet hears more footsteps on the stairs; guesses they belong to Eva and Finn.

She slides out of bed and steps out into the hallway. At the bottom of the stairs, she sees Tom Cordwell, and three—four?—other men with muskets in their hands, shoving their way past Finn in an attempt to get to the parlour. Harriet knows what they want. Last night, as Cordwell had scooped her from the rising water, she had confirmed his suspicions that there are government missives hiding in Highfield House. No doubt they have come here to find them.

It is her doing that has brought these men here, Harriet thinks distantly. She knows she ought to feel shame. Regret. But she cannot quite make herself do so. Because her family had kept the truth of her father from her. And for that, it feels as though they need to be punished. If that punishment comes at the hands of the Jacobites, so be it.

She goes back to the bedroom and dresses slowly, lacing herself back into the bodice and skirts she had only stepped out of a few hours earlier. She feels oddly calm. Oddly detached. Downstairs, she hears the crash of breaking glass, shouts of men.

"You will find nothing," she hears Nathan say. And, "You are mistaken."

"Get out of our house this instant," Edwin demands, his hollow threat punctuated by the dull thud of what she assumes are books being torn from the shelf. There is something oddly enjoyable about this cursed house being ravaged like this, as though the men are only hastening the ruin it has already started to descend into. She wonders if they will find what they are looking for. Nathan can claim they are mistaken all he wants, but Harriet knows that, more often than not these days, there really are government missives tucked away in this house somewhere.

She pulls on her shoes. As she steps out into the passage, she sees the men charging up the staircase, muskets held out into front of them. Her calmness evaporates, and her heart jumps into her throat.

She thinks suddenly of her son. Is afraid for him—a belated reaction, but at least it has come at all. She flies towards the nursery, waiting to be hit, the thunder of the men's footsteps on the staircase rattling around inside her.

Before she can reach the nursery door, a shot breaks through the chaos. The bullet careens into the stone wall of the stairwell, inches above Cordwell's head. Stone sprays out across the steps.

"Stop." It's a voice Harriet doesn't recognise. A voice with far more gravity than Nathan or Edwin's. Cordwell and the other men halt their charge up the staircase and turn back to face him.

Harriet looks past them to the man who had pulled the trigger. He is a stranger. And yet, she feels instinctively that he is anything but. Because somewhere deep inside herself, she knows this is the man she had summoned with the message she had left at the tavern.

She knows this man is her father.

She wraps longs fingers around the banister, feeling strangely unsteady.

The four men hold their muskets out in front of them. Undaunted, her father meets their weapons with his own single pistol. Despite the early hour, he is dressed in a neat maroon justacorps with a row of brass buttons, a fine lace cravat tied at his throat. "Get out," he says. And there is something in his voice that makes the men obey him. Something cold, even, authoritative. Perhaps, with his firing into the wall above Cordwell's head, he has proven himself the only man willing to pull the trigger.

Footsteps thump down the staircase, and in moments, Cordwell and the other men are gone, leaving a weighted silence in their place. One of the paintings in the entrance hall has fallen, another hangs crookedly. Someone shifts their feet, and Harriet hears the crunch of broken glass. In the open doorway of the parlour, she can see books strewn across the floor.

Nathan stands opposite her father at the bottom of the stairs. The look of fear on his face is blatant. Finn has a tight grip on Eva's wrist, and she takes a step backwards, putting as much space between herself and this man as possible. This

Henry Ward, he feels like an impossibly imposing presence.

Harriet watches from halfway down the stairs. No one looks at her, acknowledges her. They are all far too entranced by her father. This man is not a stranger to any of them, she realises. Not Nathan, or Eva, or Finn. They all know him, and they all fear him. And not one of them had seen fit to tell her who he was.

Ward looks at Nathan. "Where is the letter?" His words are sharp and measured. Impatient, but not angry. "Give it to me."

"You know I've not found it, Ward," says Nathan. "And I have asked you before to please stay away from this house." There's a thinness to his words, belying his pathetic attempt at forcefulness.

Eva's eyes dart between Finn and her brother, then back to Ward. "What are you talking about?" she demands. "What letter?"

"A very valuable letter your mother took care of for me," Ward tells her, "that your brother seems unwilling to part with."

"There is no letter, Ward," Nathan hisses. "I've torn the whole damn house apart."

"This is why you came to Holy Island?" Eva demands. "At Henry Ward's bidding?"

Harriet lets out her breath. This man is not only known to her brother; he had been the reason they had come to Lindisfarne in the first place. Little wonder Nathan's restoration has been so chaotic—it is all an utter lie.

Before Nathan can manage a word, Ward says, "Is this why you sent for me? To tell me this same sorry story all over again?"

"Sent for you?" Nathan repeats. "I did not send for you."

Ward shoves a crumpled note into his hand. Nathan unfolds it and reads. His face turns blank, pale, and it brings Harriet more than a little satisfaction. Almost absentmindedly, he passes the page to Eva.

As she registers her sister's handwriting, Eva's gaze drifts upward, finding Harriet on the staircase. The horror in her eyes is blatant, but there is confusion there too.

Ward lurches forward suddenly, shoving Nathan back against the wall. "I have had enough of these games, Blake. Just give me what I came for."

"I have nothing to give you," Nathan hisses. "If I did, do you truly think I would have let this go on so long?" Nathan lets out a feverish laugh. "The damn letter does not exist. It is not here. I think it's time you accept that." His voice wavers with forced bravado. "Whatever my mother did with it, she did not keep it safe like she told you she did. Whatever was between the two of you was not what you think it was."

Harriet watches something almost imperceptible pass across her father's eyes. "You know nothing of what was between your mother and me, Mr Blake." She can hear the strain in his voice. Harriet's hand tightens around the banister. She feels oddly invisible, excluded from this conversation between people who, she sees now, are already entangled in each other's lives. And yet somehow, she is at the centre of all this. No longer the ill-fitting piece, but rather, the connecting one.

Ward takes a step closer to Nathan, but Finn steps in front of him, holding a palm flat to his chest, pushing him away. "The letter is not in the house, Ward. Threatening them is not going to change that. Just take your crew back to Nassau and get the hell away from here."

A wry smile appears on Ward's face at Finn's outburst, but it disappears quickly when Edwin whips his pistol out from inside his coat. It's an almost theatrical gesture, and Harriet has to bite her lip to keep a burst of hysterical laughter from escaping.

"He's right," says Edwin, almost managing to sound threatening. "Get out of our house."

Ward looks at the pistol, then back at Edwin. "I rid your home of those thugs, and this is how you seek to repay me?" Edwin falters. "I was sent for," Ward hisses. "I only came here because I believed the letter had been found." He turns to look at Nathan. "What else was I to think when the note was signed with your name?"

"Nathan didn't send for you," Harriet says suddenly. "I did."

At the sound of her voice, her father turns, noticing her for the first time. He frowns in confusion, pins her with his gaze. It's an intense look, one full of questions. She finds herself returning it.

"Please, Harriet," she hears Eva murmur. "Don't."

Harriet ignores her. She makes her way down the staircase, gripping tightly to the banister.

"Who are you?" Ward asks. "Why did you send for me?"

Harriet swallows. "I need to speak with you."

An odd look comes over Ward's face. Harriet can tell that, somehow, he senses the gravity of this situation. Does he see himself in her, as she does in him? He glances briefly at Nathan, then at Finn. And then he turns back to Harriet and nods without speaking. Makes his way out the open front door.

"Please, Harriet," Eva says desperately. "Please don't go with him." The look on her face is one of blatant dread.

"Why?" Harriet hisses. "What are you so afraid of?"

Eva's lips part. "I..." She falls silent. Take a step closer to her husband. He murmurs something to her that Harriet cannot make out.

She shakes her head. "You knew," she hisses, "didn't you? You knew and you did not think to tell me." She glares at Nathan. "You all knew."

Her brother says nothing.

"Harriet." Edwin takes a step towards her. "Don't." He wraps a hand around her upper arm, but there's a forced gentleness to it, as though he does not want the rest of the family to see the harshness with which he had treated her last night. She pulls easily from his grip.

"Do you not think I have the right to speak to my own father?"

She does not wait for a response. Just turns and walks out the door. And despite the looks of horror and despair that Henry Ward has the power to elicit from her family, not one of them attempts to stop her.

# CHAPTER THIRTY-TWO

Henry Ward stands on the edge of the embankment with his back to the sea, passing his tricorn hat between his hands. Wind ruffles his powdered hair, lifting a single stray strand from his cheek. For a long time, he looks at Harriet without speaking.

She stares back at him. A part of her had not truly believed it until now. But when she looks at Henry Ward, she sees her own straw-coloured curls, her own hooded blue eyes. That darkness at her edges. And she feels a greater sense of belonging than she ever has with her husband, or with her half-brother and -sister.

She glances back towards the house. No one has come after her. Still, she can practically feel the eyes at the windows. She has no doubt every one of her family is watching her.

Beneath Ward's open justacorps, she can see the glimpse of the pistol tucked back into his belt. It feels right that she might be the daughter of a man with a pistol in his belt. A curious thing though, that he had not sought to reload it after firing at Cordwell and the other men. Not even as he had looked down the barrel of Edwin's weapon.

He knows who she is, Harriet can feel that instinctively. But she also senses that he does not wish to put his suspicions—his knowledge—into words. In case he is wrong. Or perhaps, in case he is right.

"You are Abigail's daughter," he says finally.

Is he asking or stating a fact? Harriet cannot tell. But she says, "Yes."

"Why did you send for me?" His voice is husky, uneasy, devoid of the commanding tone he had spoken with inside the house.

She swallows, her mouth suddenly dry. Away from her family, she feels suddenly vulnerable. Raw and exposed. "I suspect you know the answer to that."

Ward nods, so faint it is almost imperceptible. He looks wide-eyed and haunted. And what is it that has rattled him so, Harriet wonders? Is it the knowledge of her, or the knowledge that her mother had hidden her away; perhaps fled Holy Island so the two of them might never meet?

"What's your name?" asks her father.

"Harriet. Harriet Whitley."

"Harriet." He speaks her name slowly, tentatively, as though testing himself. He stays planted in the shingle at the top of the beach, barely noticing when the fringe of a wave reaches his boots.

"Did you know about me?" she asks. Her heart quickens in anticipation of his answer.

"No."

"Then she betrayed you as well as me."

"Yes." She hears regret in his voice. "I suppose she did."

"The letter that you and Nathan were speaking of," she says. "What is it all about? What do you want with my family? You have made threats against them?"

Ward rubs his eyes. There is a heaviness to him, Harriet realises. An almost visible weight on his shoulders, as though he is carrying a perpetual strain. A burden he cannot lift. "I know the way it looks," he says. "But these threats. They do not come from me."

She eyes him. "Who do they come from?"

He exhales slowly. "A man I ought never have allowed to remain in my life."

Harriet lets out a short, humourless laugh. "So it is going to be like this, is it? We are to speak in riddles?"

A look of curiosity passes across Ward's eyes, as though he is taken aback by her boldness. He tilts his head, taking her in, contemplating. "You are my daughter," he says, as though finding the courage to speak the words.

Harriet nods, his own frankness stealing her own.

Ward begins to walk along the top of the beach. Wind flutters his open justacorps, making him appear broader, and even more imposing than before. Harriet's eyes are drawn to the sailing vessel sitting at anchor in the sea beyond Emmanuel Head. His ship, she realises now. All these weeks, her father's ship has been visible from the window of her workroom. She finds herself walking beside him.

"Your mother used to have a saying," Ward says, watching his boots as he walks, "that come midnight, all truths would be revealed. She believed we could not hide things forever. That sooner or later, we all grow tired of keeping secrets." He glances sideways at her. "I suspect she thought you were the exception. No doubt she thought she had succeeded in keeping you hidden away." He nods at the longboat beached on the embankment. "I would like to speak with you further," he says carefully. "If you will permit me?"

Harriet glances at her father, then back at the house. Climbing into his longboat, she feels instinctively, will untether her from her family even further. But such a thing no longer feels so frightening. Because just like her mother, her siblings have shown themselves adept at hiding things. And she has had quite enough of being shielded from the truth.

She accepts her father's hand. Allows him to help her over the gunwale. And she feels herself become weightless as the boat rises. Pulls her out to sea.

# ABOUT THE AUTHOR

A lover of old stuff, folk music, and ghost stories, Johanna Craven bases her books around little-known true events from the past. She divides her time between the UK and Australia, and can be very easily persuaded to tell you about the time she accidently swam with seals on Holy Island.

Find out more at www.johannacraven.com.

Printed in the USA
CPSIA information can be obtained
at www.ICGtesting.com
CBHW020652260924
14901CB00027B/275

9 780645 106961